CW01433715

VENGEANCE

FREES

HER

ALEXIS C. MANESS

Copyright © 2023 Alexis C. Maness

Cover design by Adriatica Creation
Character art on cover, interior illustrations by Amberlee Tryon
Interior map created by Saumya Singh (Map by @Saumyasvision/Inkarnate)
Developmental editing provided by Lunar Rose Editing Services
Line editing, copy editing, and proofreading provided by Miss Eloquent
Edits
Interior formatting by Miss Eloquent Edits
Sensitivity and beta reading provided by Alexia at BookishEnds
Author photo by Katie Orchard (katieomedia)
Character Guide Art (Rhiannon, Tristain, Silas) by Emilia Mildner;
(Kyra, Samara, Delphine) by Alyonivn Art

All rights reserved.
All rights reserved. No part of this book may be reproduced or used in any
manner without the prior
written permission of the copyright owner.

This is a work of fiction. Names, places, characters, events, and incidents
are the product or depiction of the author's imagination and are completely
fictitious. Any resemblance to actual persons, living or dead, events or
establishments is purely coincidental.

To the survivors,

It's worth the fight to find your way back to yourself.
May you find happiness again.

With love, Alexis

you don't belong to anyone but yourself

Before Reading

This is an adult dark fantasy that contains graphic and explicit content as well as dark themes. The content of this book is only intended for adults of legal age. See a full list of warnings below.

Please note, *Vengeance Frees Her* includes sexual activities that are inspired by kinks but they are not accurate representations of BDSM and are not meant to act as a guide for engaging in such activities.

- Abduction (mentioned/referenced)
- Beheading/Decapitation
- Blood
- Blood play
- Blood magic/manifestations
- Chasing
- Conversations about loss
- Cussing
- Choking (kinky and life-threatening)
- Dark magic
- Graphic sexual content
- Heavy themes of death
- Hematolognia
- Insinuation of imprisonment
- Insinuation of sexual assault occurring
- Knife play
- Murder
- Misogyny

- Possession
- PTSD
- Public sexual acts
- Restraints during sexual acts
- Sexism
- Self-injury
- Suicidal ideation
- Threats of sexual assault
- Toxic relationship dynamics
- Violence - general
- Violence against women
- Vomiting and nausea (non-pregnancy related—don't worry, babes)
- Wax play
- Witchcraft

Your mental health and safety matters to me. Please make note of the resources below if this list or any content in this book is triggering for you:

- Dial 988 for the Suicide & Crisis Helpline or visit their website for more resources
- Call 800.656.HOPE (4673) for the National Sexual Assault Telephone Hotline or visit the RAINN website for more resources
- Call 1-800-662-HELP (4357) for SAMHSA'S national helpline or visit the Substance Abuse and Mental Health Services Administration) website for more resources
- Call 800-799-7233 (SAFE) or visit the National Domestic Violence website for more resources

KYRA

One of Silas's victims

From Wispombra

SAMARA

One of Silas's victims

From Norhavalta

DELPHINE

Silas's ex, the witch who originally summoned the Volskruga

From Norhavalta originally

IVISALLA

MONERTI

OCEAN

MARIDROVA

SALDOVA

NORMANIA
RIVER

SANGRAVIAN
WOODS

WISPOMERA

VRUGIAN WOODS

HORVALA RIVER

VRUGIAN WOODS

TOVIGIAN
RIVER

NORHAVALTA

LAKE
LYRA

OAKHAVEN

TARGARTEN

LARINDIA

LEGEND

TOWN

SMALL
TOWN

VILLAGE

ROUTES

Book I Recap

Where we left off:

- Rhiannon killed Silas.
- The Volskruga tried to force Rhiannon to host it during their final face off in the woods, but failed.
- Rhiannon is revealed to have power that the Volskruga claims is because she is the foretold Daughter of Desire Born of Death and Blood.
- With this magic Rhiannon is able to trap the Volskruga in her dagger.
- Not knowing what she's capable of, Rhiannon banishes Kyra, Samara, and Tristain from the woods.
- In the final chapter of the book, her friends are angry at her for sneaking away without them to face off with the Volskruga and Silas on her own and her decision to sacrifice herself. When she sends them away against their will, this further compounds their hurt and anger, which is left unresolved.
- To keep people away, Rhiannon has cloaked the woods in a foreboding red mist.
- As part of the manifestation of magic that she absorbed from the Volskruga, she now has a magic-bound wolf, Morana, which serves her.
- Delphine's consciousness was transferred into Morana, the next fitting vessel, when Silas died.
- Morana and Delphine can both communicate telepathically with Rhiannon.

- When book 1 ends, they are in Wispombra (where Kyra is from) and Rhiannon is in the Sagravian Woods that lie on the outskirts of Wispombra.
- At the end of the book, they do not have an understanding of the prophecy or Rhiannon's magic.

Minor Characters Reminders:

- Jade is Rhiannon's sister, who is back home in Oakhaven.
- Leylah is Tristain's dead ex-fiancé who was killed by Silas.
- Idris is Rhiannon's best friend/friend with benefits from Oak Haven.

Part I

Prologue

When the father of greed and desire is awakened, he will spread a poison through our soil.

Darkness is coming to sweep across the land.

And with it, the clash of good and evil will come to a boil.

*In death and rebirth, they will be bonded
spirit to soul.*

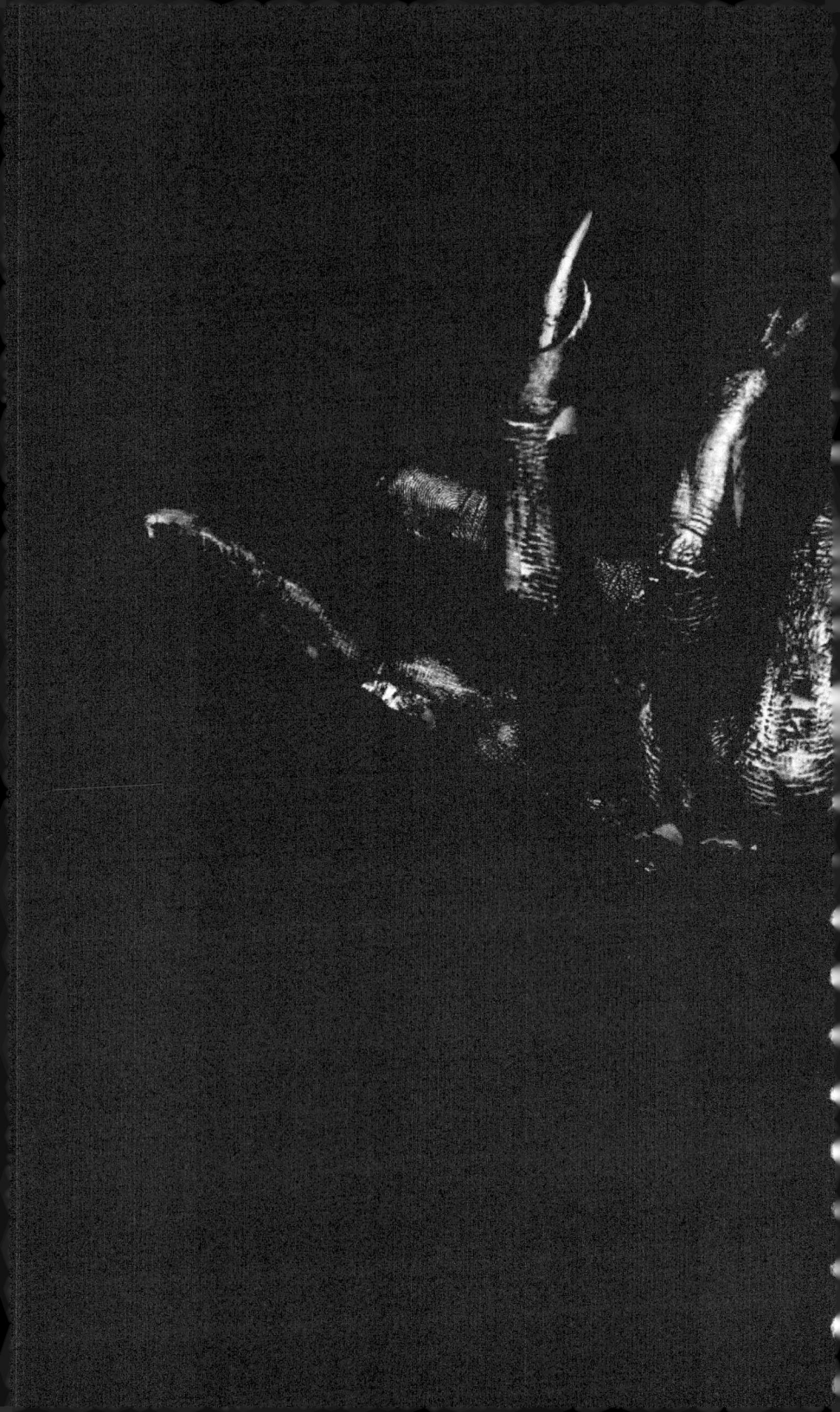

CHAPTER ONE

H er vengeance had become her.
        Trapped her.
        Ruined her.
Devastated her.
Changed her.
And it was all her fault.

When Rhiannon closed her eyes, streams of blood, shrouds of blackness, and clawed, mangled fingers flicked through her mind in blurry repetition. Visions of destruction flooded her head, while echoes of her friends' screams piercing her eardrums accompanied horrifying imagery. Tristain's pleading joined the symphony of her suffering, followed by the haunting, guttural voice of the Volskruga's whispered threats. Melancholy melodies picked away at her failing sanity.

She couldn't escape the wrongness remaining in her body after the Volskruga had filled her with its overwhelming presence and tried to force her limbs to act at its will. A sting of torturous pain lingered as she'd slashed the blade across her skin in a last attempt to go out on her own terms. A shiver skated across her skin as she recalled the shards of her armor burrowing deep within her arms.

Everything had gone awry.

There was no peace to be found within herself. Her mind and body had been taken from her despite how hard she'd fought. Despite everything she'd sacrificed. She was forced to face her reality.

She wasn't sure how many hours she'd been standing motionless since her entire world imploded, but her stiff body made it difficult to shake herself free.

One eye, then the other peeled open. Tiny icy crystals splintered away. The sudden coldness pricked at her burning eyes, pulling tears over the rims in quick succession.

She wasn't crying. She didn't have the energy for that— besides, it wouldn't do her any good.

Wind whistled through the trees, and those horrifying memories whispered in the surrounding emptiness, threatening to come back, but she wouldn't let them. She couldn't, wouldn't survive it.

Once again, she found herself disappointed to be alive.

That disappointment whipped into a fury, flooding her system from her numb fingertips to her toes. The urge to let it out was too much to contain as she saw red. Anger rolled through her veins, hotter than her own blood. Hatred for herself, for Silas, for the Volskruga, violently shook her, her bones and teeth clattering with it.

Rhiannon was fucking furious that she was still trapped on the path Silas and the Volskruga had shoved her down. When she'd fought with the Volskruga for control over her form, she'd thought she'd come out victorious.

Then this foreign power had clung to her the moment she was most vulnerable. While she was grateful for the strength it had lent her at the time, she soon realized it wasn't a savior but another force invading her. It hadn't given her a choice. Rhiannon had never set out to become like them. The only power she'd sought was that of a blade to take the life of those who harmed her and others.

Rhiannon had earned that.

In the end, all she'd wanted was to find her own peace. Peace wasn't sharing ownership of herself. It's why she'd turned away the destructive reign that the Volskruga had offered her. It had taken her desires for justice and retribution, sullying them with its need to control her.

Driven here by her own bloodthirsty relentlessness. She could place only part of the blame on them. More than that, she was enraged with herself for not letting it go, for *needing* her revenge.

And fuck if she had needed it. It had become the sustenance she required to keep going.

Memories of when Silas left her lying there on the brink of death plagued her, the night she held Silas's dagger to her thudding chest, and the day she stormed away from the council. Those events had crumbled the pillars that kept her standing and brought her to her knees.

Bruised and bleeding, she'd had nothing to live for. But then she found a new purpose . . . revenge.

Then Tristain came along. She slashed at the treacherous, unwelcome thoughts. Stabbing pain of loss riddled her heart and stomach. Everything fucking hurt. No emotion, no movement was safe.

Did she survive? Was this living? Had she truly liberated herself?

It didn't feel like it. Not when her regret clutched its formidable grip around her throat. Not when the hollow loneliness within her left her concave and breathless.

The cost was so much higher than she'd ever expected. She'd gone from being trapped in her grief to being tied down by something so much bigger than her, and it threatened to crush her. Death, she could have accepted. She'd walked into it willingly. But this? No. She hadn't chosen this. She'd been forced into it.

Like the most malevolent of wraiths, the truth of her choices would haunt her. Rhiannon had no doubt she'd face the bloodcurdling reminder of her mistakes every time she looked in her reflection's catatonic stare.

Everything she'd cared about had been ripped away from her with a sentence Rhiannon had been unwillingly bound to serve. The embrace of her mother, days spent under the trees with her sister, Tristain's touch, and the joy and challenging nature of her newfound friends.

All of it—gone.

She'd fallen into a trap and had run right toward it. Her single-mindedness was to blame. That truth hurt her more than anything. It infuriated her to her very core. Grief's merciless claws dug into her and dragged out her insides until she was an empty, lifeless vessel.

Heat prickled at her fingertips like scorching fire; she shoved them into the snow, hoping to stop it. Upon contact, streaks of red shot forward, darkening the snow and traveling up the trunk of the nearest tree. Bloody tendrils wrapped around bark, clinging to it in a sticky mess. Its jagged crevices seeped blood, and straggling brown leaves turned scarlet upon impact.

Shocked by the jolt of violent magic, Rhiannon scrambled backward, a gasp tearing reluctantly from her throat. Fear rattled her bones and torched her skin. She blinked once, then twice, waiting for her mind to catch up with the scene in front of her. Her eyes traced over the webs of blood coating the tree. It pulsed with a threatening energy, the crimson defiant and sinister against the serene white landscape.

Its eager violence matched her own, but it was far more intimidating, even to her. Rhiannon observed, frozen, wondering if it was waiting to attack her, too. When she let out a bated breath, it responded with a warning. A shudder of power ran through the tree, resulting in a resounding crack that made Rhiannon flinch.

The involuntary show of fear ignited her confrontational spirit, sending her pulse pounding and her spine straightening.

She rose to her feet from where she'd crouched in awe. Her knees shifted stiffly from the aching cold.

All was silent but for her rasping breath as she stared at the eerie manifestation of magic, as if it were a normal opponent. More constriction and the tree groaned, begging for mercy.

While that tree was malleable in its state of slumber, she wasn't willing to bend to the magic's will. She may not understand it, but she wouldn't submit so easily.

"You belong to me." She grunted through gritted teeth. Rhiannon's muscles tensed, her tendons straining underneath the resistance she was facing. "I control you, not the other way around." Sweat had broken out along her hairline and coated her brow.

Strain turned to discomfort, leaving her panting for relief.

Harsh cracking branches and crinkling leaves pierced the air as the bloody tendrils clung adamantly, fighting against her will. When her back curved and her lungs fluttered helplessly under the exertion, the strands unwound and slithered back to her.

Moments of stretched silence passed by as she replayed the battle she'd just won. Narrowly, by the skin of her teeth.

It couldn't be trusted.

She couldn't be trusted.

It wasn't safe.

She wasn't safe.

She'd known that, which is why she'd sent everyone away. Why she'd refused their help and betrayed their trust by using her magic against them. But this was the moment the horrific truth was so starkly clear.

Without understanding what her newly endowed power could do, she was a danger to herself and others. That, she'd known, but the undeniable proof further cemented her necessary isolation.

The admission punched her in the gut, knocked the wind out of her, and left her gasping. Her head pounded as the dam of tears broke and coated her face in shame and want.

Her existence was so bleak. She wanted to destroy everything, including what was left of herself. A guttural cry tore from her throat, along with a burst of red mist that shot out in all directions. Distorted, disturbing growls, snarls, howls, and the sharp twisting of wood followed, a symphony of destruction calling to the force nestled within her.

Rhiannon was determined to see the damage she'd done, and her steps propelled her forward. Trees leaning away from the clearing warped, their trunks and limbs twisting unnaturally. But that was all she could see from where she stood; she wanted to investigate further.

As she passed tangled, naked trees, she saw the extent of her vengeful magic. Animals' eyes became red, replacing amber hues. Soft coats that once camouflaged against the snowy landscape shifted into stiffened black fur. They scurried frantically, the disturbing metamorphosis leaving them confused and uneasy. Foxes sprang from beneath blankets of snow, their screeching vibrating in Rhiannon's ears. Rabbits bared their teeth and stood menacingly on hind legs.

Guilt gripped her, but she dared not violate them further by attempting to touch them. Everywhere her eyes touched, scarlet eyes flared back at her as if to say "look at what you've done."

Her breaths were shallow as sobs racked her chest painfully.

"I'm sorry," she confessed. "I'm sorry. I'm sorry. I'm sorry."

The chant echoed in the unfamiliar scenery.

Gone were the soft brown-and-gray hues. Crimson droplets beaded on leaves and flowers, sticky garnet sap leaking out of trees, and the sleepy gray bark had turned to an utterly lifeless ash-white.

The Volskruga had long since poisoned these woods before she had ever stepped foot here, but she'd taken it past the point of no return. Like everything else she touched, she'd darkened and bled it out until it became unrecognizable.

She desperately hoped she hadn't doomed the land to such a bleak future. She wanted to believe life could bloom here again.

Even without knowing the full prophecy, the insinuation that she was the product of blood and death rang true as she looked around at the destruction she'd wrought upon the innocent life here.

Everything she'd become was rooted in the ruthless path she'd carved for herself to get to this point.

Self-loathing, heavy as a great ship's anchor, weighed her soul down. Her bones ached beneath her skin. She'd seen enough of what she'd done, and it broke her heart—whatever was left of it. Rhiannon would look upon the full extent of the carnage and apologize to every creature she'd condemned but not that day. She yearned for rest she did not deserve.

But what was one more selfish act?

Eerie silence blanketed the woods. The quiet of death after destruction echoed as she ventured to the cottage. However, she didn't make it back to its wooden warmth. When she entered the clearing, she collapsed from the exhaustion of her outburst.

After a few hours, the anxious voices of Delphine and Morana warring in her mind disrupted her short-lived, peaceful slumber. She was exhausted by this new existence already. When she didn't answer them, Morana rushed to her, then licked her face with a phantom tongue that made her shudder. When the wolf pulled away, thick blood coated her tongue and dripped down her muzzle.

Fear tore away the lingering drowsiness of slumber at the sight of all that red. Rhiannon raised her elbows and looked sticky scarlet dress but lying in her old clothes. What should have comforted her only frustrated her more. She had no understanding of how it all worked. However, she was grateful to find that it hadn't left her naked and exposed.

Delphine urged her to move, to go inside before she fell ill, but she knew in her bones that she was no longer susceptible to the elements, that she was no longer quite human, not really. The cold couldn't hurt her, and she suspected that neither could the average blade. She was something else entirely. The surety of that beat through her, echoed by the steady thrum of her heart.

That didn't excite her, though. It only confirmed the deep loneliness of her present state—and, likely, her future.

That was always how it should have been.

Fear.

Despair.

Misery.

They should have all been coursing through her, but she felt . . . nothing. Everything inside her was numb, how her limbs should have been from the elements. She only yearned for deep sleep, so she lay back into the snow and closed her eyes once more, unconcerned whether she'd wake up again. Nothing mattered anyway.

lurries fell around her, but Rhiannon paid them no mind. Woodland creatures growled and scurried in her peripherals, investigating who had disturbed their home. Nothing penetrated the numb shell she'd burrowed herself into.

Rhiannon sat, frozen in the snow, as the self-hatred and pity ruthlessly fighting for her heart battered her, threatening to tear her at the seams. Small puffs of white air contrasted against the endless red mist hanging menacingly above them. Morana sat next to her, letting out periodic howls as she and Delphine had waited for Rhiannon to snap out of her vacant state. The wolf's black shadows flickered restlessly, but she didn't interact with her.

Meanwhile, Delphine tried to press against her mental walls, but Rhiannon was far more powerful. She was able to resist, so she did, reinforcing the invisible barricades.

She was too busy grappling with the storm of emotions, laying a path of destruction to avoid letting anyone else in. She needed to remain isolated but didn't want to be alone.

Part of her yearned for the comfort of her friends. Even though she'd disregarded their pleading and sent them away, she wanted them to come back for her. But that wasn't right. For their safety, they'd find their way back to their lives. To let her go. To forget. To move on.

That was what was best.

It was easier said than done.

Memories of Tristain's screams breaking through the endless silence were nearly enough to shred her resolve. She had become aware of the exact moment he'd woken up to find himself separated from her, listening to how inconsolable he was. His pain, a tether tugging at her heart in the most excruciating way. His voice had been raw and hoarse by the end of it.

They must have journeyed into the village because he had grown quieter and quieter, her name a torturously faint whisper on the wind before disappearing.

She hoped that would be true for his memory of her as well. In their final moments together, before she'd used her magic to force him unconscious, she'd pleaded with him to move on and forget her.

But she wasn't naive enough to believe it would be so easy for either of them. It was why she'd been standing here instead of sleeping inside, staring off into the distance, where she imagined she could hear his heart beating and breaking for her. A mourning song.

This yearning was pointless. She wouldn't cave. There were no options. Isolation was critical. She'd remind herself of that as much as she needed to.

Finally tiring of the masochism, Rhiannon forced herself to take to the shelter of the cottage. She took a deep breath upon entering and left the door open behind her.

The space wasn't as unsettling in the soft morning light, but it was still in disarray. Overturned chairs lay by the dining table that was sitting diagonally. Broken glassware was scattered on the floor in the far corner. Grime rimmed the windowsills, and cobwebs hung from the modest chandeliers. Muted tones of the furniture, bedding, and limited decor made it feel even more dull and desolate.

Her steps faltered when she caught a glimpse of herself in the cracked mirror. She leaned close and held her breath, expecting to see fangs and wild eyes glazed with untamed magic. Instead, she only saw heavy brown eyes with dark bags around them, chapped lips, and the telling lines of grief drawing her features downward.

The image of her misery haunted her, like the dust dancing in the air with each step she took across the creaking, uneven floorboards. Morana padded along silently behind her. They paused at the cracked wood where her body had been battered by the Volskruga. She kneeled, pressing her fingers to the indentation. It seemed like a lifetime ago.

Everything had changed.

She had changed.

The fact hit her again, like a punch to the gut. She was no longer the woman she'd been when she came here and fallen into Silas's trap.

Part of her wished she'd never left Oakhaven, that she could console herself in the comfort of home. But wishes were for children. The reality was she could never go back. Not like this. Her mind turned to her mother and sister.

Morana whimpered, an echo of Rhiannon's pain.

She crouched, stroking wisps of cool, smooth smoke that tickled her fingertips as they billowed off the black wolf's massive form.

Morana wasn't quite solid, comprising rolling shadows ascending into the air, but it was the touch of another being she craved, and this was enough.

"They'll be devastated when the days and months continue to pass and they realize I'm not coming back." Her voice croaked with sorrow. "I've made their worst fears come true."

Guilt was strangling her. Broken promises lodged in her throat, where they should have stayed.

She'd done her best to keep them out of her thoughts after she'd left Oakhaven. But now, they were all she could think about. She craved the days of ease when she and Jade would read and paint in amicable silence, enjoying each other's company. Or the way she and her mother would spend their mornings on the porch, talking and laughing after a hearty breakfast. But those beautiful moments she'd forgotten to cherish were pushed out by the reminder of how her need for revenge would leave them grieving after all they'd done to help her come back to herself.

She didn't regret making Silas pay but judged herself for not considering the gravity of her consequences on those around her. She should have said genuine goodbyes instead of leaving them with hope.

That choice sat like a rock in her stomach. There was no way to digest it; she'd have to live with the pain.

Rhiannon couldn't help but hate herself. Her refusal to see what she had to lose. Her inability to see the bigger picture. That's what collapsed her world around her.

Rhiannon folded in on herself as the air left her lungs like the snuffed flame of a candle. Clouds of dust plumed around her when her body collided with the floor.

How was she supposed to live like this? She was lost and didn't know how to find her way back to herself.

She didn't know if she could.

She didn't know if she wanted to.

Hot tears poured down her face, blurring the disheveled details of her surroundings.

Morana lay beside her, head somberly on her paws, as Rhiannon's aching cries echoed in the solitude.

"What have I done?" She gasped between sobs. "It wasn't supposed to end like this."

Rhiannon wanted to take it all back. To go back in time. To erase Silas's touch on her life. To have her family back. To have her long-gone sanity back.

But it was all ripped away from her. All she had was herself and the clinging misery, the sticky web of a spider. And she allowed it to entangle her until she was stuck with no other choice but to struggle in it all alone.

Days blurred together as Rhiannon disappeared into her grief. She'd hoped it would swallow her whole and relieve her of the burden of what came next. But there would be no such mercy.

With a muzzle pressed to her back, Morana had forced her into the old bed, brought her food, and stood watch over her during what felt like endless nights of despair. When she'd finally exhausted herself, she'd fallen into a deep sleep, which lowered her guard, and Delphine entered her mind once again.

"Rhiannon, you cannot give up. Allowing your own misery to consume you is pathetic. You're wasting away for no reason. Why even fight the Volskruga if you were just going to let yourself wither away?"

"I thought I would die and finally be free. Not this. Not alone. Not this warped version of myself. Not a tool that could be used to destroy. I would rather be dead than something I did not choose."

"Must you always be so melodramatic?" Rhiannon didn't answer the rhetorical question, so Delphine continued. *"Sorry to disappoint you, but you're very much alive, and you have the power to create the world you want to live in. If anything, you are more capable now than ever."*

"This is not what I meant when I said I wanted to get justice for myself and the other women of Larindia. I'm nothing more than a monster of my own making."

"I know it feels like that now. You're grieving. But think of all you could do with this new power. With us by your side," Delphine insisted.

"I don't even know what I'm capable of. Without a true understanding of the prophecy, how can I ever feel safe enough to control what I've become?"

"I will help you. We will help you. But, Rhiannon, do not give up. Think of all that you accomplished with your blade. Now

imagine what you can do with real power. You can be a protector. You can be equal parts terror and savior. You can be the reckoning this unfair world needs."

Delphine's voice picked up in excitement.

"I won't risk harming innocent people," Rhiannon argued.

"So, learn to wield it on the guilty."

This brought Rhiannon to wakefulness. Her head whipped toward Morana, who stood at the end of her bed, her eyes boring into Rhiannon as Delphine's voice played in her mind. Shadows expanded and contracted around the wolf in a slow rhythm.

"And how am I supposed to do that?" she asked Delphine and Morana. Her voice echoed off the old wooden walls and slanted roof.

"Practice. Find out what you are capable of by practicing on those who will not be missed," Delphine answered.

"I can't just . . ."

She realized it wasn't an unreasonable idea but couldn't ignore the fact that she could hurt someone else by accident if she lost control.

"You know you can."

Rhiannon sighed, a lifetime of ache weighing down her tired limbs.

"I'm not ready. I need time. I need to think. I need to heal." She looked down, noticing she was still in her dirty clothes. *"How did these even come back?"*

Morana's voice entered her mind. *"It's the magic. It's intuitive. It comes and goes as you need it."*

"But how did it go from blood to fabric? It doesn't make sense."

"The magic manipulates the substances it comes into contact with. While it may absorb them into itself, it can also release them when it's done. So, if it consumes your clothing to cover you in its essence, it can relinquish it once it's finished. Everything in this world comes from this land, so the magic that originates from the same can manipulate it at its will," Delphine explained.

"*Sure.*" Rhiannon huffed.

Overwhelmed by the changes, Rhiannon ran a hand through her hair. The strands felt foreign as it tickled her fingertips. With the magic buzzing beneath her skin, she felt like a stranger in her own body, knowing she didn't have full autonomy anymore. But she couldn't do anything about it for now. She'd need to wait until she had answers about the magic she'd inherited.

Rhiannon needed to find the full prophecy.

It seemed impossible, that she was part of some foretold reckoning. That she was supposed to be someone who could change the world.

She didn't sign up for that. All she'd wanted was to get her own life back. The burden was heavy and discomforting, as it took up too much space in her mind.

"*How will you find answers if you make no effort to look for them?*"

Delphine's invasion tugged her attention to Morana's eyes, which were locked on Rhiannon, her large black head resting on her paws.

"*How can I make any real progress if I don't know where to start?*" she retorted.

"*I can assure you the answers you need aren't buried in this mess of a cottage. If anything, your best bet is speaking to others in the village,*" Delphine pushed. "*If Kyra had heard of the prophecy, surely, others have. Hopefully, one of them will know more than any of us do.*"

"*I can't go there, where all those people are. I won't risk hurting someone. It's best for everyone if I stay here, where I'm isolated.*"

"*Possibly. Or you could be doing more good out there. You simply cannot know that without seeking more information.*"

Annoyance flared within her. While grateful for what the witch had done for her, she'd be a liar if she didn't admit she held Delphine somewhat responsible for everything. Delphine meddling in magic she didn't understand is what started the chain of events leading to this. If Delphine had never accidentally awoken the Volskruga all those years ago, Rhiannon wouldn't be here, at the end of everything she knew.

She turned her frustration on Morana.

"Shouldn't you know something?" Rhiannon pointed at the wolf.

"I am a manifestation of your own power, Rhiannon. I don't know how to guide you in this. I am not here to be your moral compass. However, I am here to stand by your side, and I'll do that with whatever you choose to do." Morana watched her thoughtfully.

Everything was so far out of her control. She had no idea what she wanted, no idea what to do. No answers were within reach.

With the name told of in the prophecy—the Daughter of Desire, born of Death and Blood—she knew some ways the magic could manifest but didn't know enough for something this massive, this life-changing. She felt trapped and feral as the frustration between her and her new force fought for dominance to determine who she was to be now.

Rhiannon didn't see this playing out well for her, but she wouldn't give in so easily.

CHAPTER THREE

W ith Delphine's bold insistence, Morana's looming
presence, and Rhiannon's mounting restlessness,
the cottage quickly became suffocating as days
blended into weeks. The three of them existed peacefully
enough—especially with Delphine and Morana sharing the
wolf's form with ease—but she couldn't think or wallow in
her misery privately. The deteriorating walnut walls closing
in on her retreated when she took her first breath of crisp air.
But she wasn't alone.

Rhiannon turned to Silas's body, taking tentative steps,
careful not to crunch too deeply into the snow, as if he might
reanimate. Freezing temperatures had spared his corpse
from the ravages of full decomposition. But his gaping throat
slashed by her blade and the deteriorated flesh of his once-
handsome face was a comforting sight. He'd gotten what was
coming to him. She was content to leave him in the snow as
food for the animals, but even they didn't want his rotted
remains. It would have been satisfying to watch his corpse
disintegrate unceremoniously as the weather warmed, but
having him here was also a painful reminder of her failure.

Rhiannon let out a scream of frustration that cut the air
like the slash of her blade. Everything stilled around her. Not
even the wind dared to breathe a gust of air.

The dark power within her thrummed, almost purring. It thrived in her rage, just like she did. She directed that anger toward the final remains of Silas. A flurry of bloodred mist descended upon him, swallowing him whole, just like he'd once done to her. When it cleared, he was gone. No trace left except for the invisible cracks he'd hollowed out within her.

Her chest expanded fully for the first time in far too long. The weight of his hatred, which he brought out in her, finally lightened.

Was this what it felt like not to have a demon breathing down your neck? Rhiannon took deep pulls of air.

That bit of restored control made her hungry for more. Maybe she could bear what another long meaningless day had in store for her. Perhaps she'd use this sliver of energy to do something purposeful.

She spent the afternoon manifesting the mist and dispelling it, willing it to take shape and shift at her command. It unfurled smoothly in the air, winding through the empty space, caressing the trees it brushed past. If this was all there was to it, she'd welcome it with open arms. This was something she could manage, something that could reside within her peacefully.

It was curious to her how Silas's magic had been all-black shadow, while hers resembled the blood that had coated her hands so many times over the last few months.

She suspected it must mean something. A reflection of their nature, perhaps, but that didn't seem quite right. It could be related to the source of their magic. But she didn't understand where her power had come from, so she couldn't be sure. Rhiannon tried not to dwell on it too long. It was another mystery.

Instead, she focused on what consumed her day and night—how she'd lost everything. The way she hadn't even realized how much she'd had to lose until it was too late.

How she'd found herself in a circumstance she didn't choose. Again.

But Delphine thought she did still have a choice. But what would embracing this magic really get her? It would end in isolation anyway. Anyone could see she had become a monster, even if the magic sleeps beneath her skin at her will. There was no hiding her nature. Even before this, it had ruled her.

She could admit Delphine wasn't the only one who'd made mistakes. Fitting that they'd end up here. Survivors, but at what cost?

Rhiannon didn't regret the lives she'd taken or the blood that had stained her hands the most glorious shade of crimson. No. She regretted letting her hunger for vengeance steal what was truly sustaining her—her family, Tristain, her friends, herself.

That craving had been sated but hadn't filled her.

Rhiannon's mind was fuzzy, but the world burst into clarity when she came to with a bloody heart in her hands and ragged strips of flesh hanging from her sharp nails.

She gripped it, watching the scarlet liquid drip over her fingers and blend with the substance coating her skin.

Warm.

Comforting.

Grounding.

She hummed at the satisfying familiarity.

The peace was short-lived as she took in the scene around her. Her eyes darted from the trees to the vast emptiness of white, searching for answers as to why she was no longer under the worn covers. The star-filled sky hung above her. The landscape was serene, but her heart was sprinting. The heavy metallic scent of spilled blood mixed with the rich, earthy notes carrying on the wind.

Snow clung to her hair and peppered the congealed film that was her new second skin. When she turned to the left, she found who the heart belonged to. A pale man with dark hair lay with unseeing green eyes that were frozen open, and his arms spread wide. A discarded knife glinted in the moonlight a few inches away from his rigid, gloved hand.

A deep throb picked up pace in her skull as she forced her memories to surface. With some insistence, she recalled the last hour.

She'd been lurking on the outskirts of town, watching between the trees. The tension in her shoulders had been almost painful. Her hand rubbed into the muscle as she sat up. She'd been waiting for . . . something.

Then he'd crossed her path.

Shocked by her unnatural appearance, he'd pulled his knife, unleashing the latent predator within Rhiannon. Without hesitation, she'd snapped his wrist in a sharp crack to disarm him and ripped his erratically beating heart out before his quivering, chapped lips could even form a scream for help.

Her body had felt light with satisfaction. That was no longer the case. That rock formed in her stomach again. Heavier this time. It wasn't that she regretted it. After all, she'd protected herself. But not being in control when she did it terrified her. More than that, it pissed her off.

All of this, everything she'd done, was because her independence had been taken from her. And here she was again. Forces larger than her were making decisions about her life, stealing her choice, doing as they pleased with her.

She wasn't fucking having that. Not after everything she'd given up.

Before, she'd thought the magic simply possessed a willful energy, but it was proving to be more than that. It had its own intentions, and she wasn't sure what that meant for her. Rhiannon didn't care how ancient or powerful the magic was. This was her body, and she wasn't going to let it push her to the background.

Rejecting the choice the mysterious force within her had made, she threw the heart. After ripping her dagger from its holster, Rhiannon pierced the dripping scarlet organ and sent it thudding against the nearest tree.

That was new. Rhiannon admired the precision and ease with which the movement came to her. It would come in useful. She smirked, seeing the silver lining of her situation.

She was lethal. Unlike before, she was unstoppable. Well, at least for the average person. The average *man*. Speaking of which . . .

Rhiannon returned her attention to the lifeless man who'd been claimed by her blade. It was just one more life, one more threat she'd cut down. Yet, it was different.

The shock etched into the man's tight, frozen features told her it was a quick and painful death. Rhiannon didn't know anything about him but couldn't be sorry he was dead. Without ceremony, she willed the mist to crawl forward from her fingertips. It descended upon the body, swallowing him whole. When it retreated, not even a scrap of clothing was left, just an indent in the snow.

After taking a deep breath and centering herself, she called upon the magic cautiously and extended long bloody webs to retrieve her knife. It returned with ease, the still heart encasing the glinting metal. In her other hand, she slowly released a controlled wisp of mist that vaporized the organ within seconds. In moments like this, when the magic bent to her will, it was easy to see why others would pursue it. But as Rhiannon wiped the stranger's scarlet essence from her blade, she caught her reflection in the gleaming metal and was reminded of her circumstances. A terrifying edge crept onto her features as feral power danced in her eyes and blood covered her up to her neck. She turned the dagger and caught the glow of moonlight twinkling off the shards of armor that had lodged in her shoulders and arms. This unfamiliar version of herself sent a chill across her skin, and she hastily returned her dagger to its holster.

With a heavy sigh and all evidence of her presence eliminated, she started her short journey to the clearing she'd made her own.

The walk back went quickly as she reflected on this new state of being. It was reassuring she could trust the magic to protect her. But she wasn't sure just how far she should extend that trust. What would it have influenced her to do next? Would there have been more bodies? Would she have gone back without covering her tracks? She wasn't sure. And until she was, this was a very dangerous way to exist.

It would have to be dealt with—and soon.

When the familiar, dilapidated, wooden structure came into view, Morana was sitting out front, waiting for her.

"I'd gone to eat, and when I came back, you were gone." The wolf worried.

"I'm okay."

A sense of pride mixed with pleasure radiated within her, but the emotions didn't feel quite like her own. Rhiannon shuddered and willed the increasingly powerful magic to calm, forcing it back into a temporary state of dormancy. As she did, her all-black garb returned effortlessly. She wasn't sure she could ever accept that as normal.

Delphine's voice broke her from her thoughts. *"What happened?"*

"I don't know. I woke up, and a man was dead. We might have a slight issue. It would appear the magic is able to exercise its will over me. I don't have full control of myself anymore."

"But control can be learned. The forces of magic in this world are old and strong. If you continue to nurture what's inside you,

you can find harmony. You could mold it to your will with practice. I know you can," Delphine soothed.

"And if I don't? Do I lose my freedom? Am I just supposed to be okay with murdering people without discretion? Killing abusers is one thing, but I don't want the blood of innocent people on my hands." Rhiannon took a deep breath, trying to keep the panic at bay. *"If I try to tame it, will it turn on me and take over?"*

"You're acting as if you've done anything under its influence that you wouldn't do otherwise. Is this not the kind of power you've wanted? Because your desires seem aligned to me."

"The point is that it has taken away my choice to act on those desires." Rhiannon stomped toward the cottage. *"And I never asked for this. I was in control when I exacted my vengeance. I was able to make the call on who I cut down to get what I wanted. Now, I am at the whim of this burden that has been forced upon me."* Tiredness was creeping up on Rhiannon and chasing away her patience. *"I will chain myself to this damned bed if that's what it takes."*

That wasn't a terrible idea, she decided. It was better than losing control. Without another word, she stepped into the cottage to try to sleep until the shops opened.

First thing in the morning, she left to find shackles for herself.

What had her life come to? Tying herself up to keep herself at bay. It wasn't even the fun kind of submission.

Stormy skies matched her mood as she trudged from shop to shop until she found what she needed.

Strapping herself in was a bit difficult without anyone else to help her, but she made it work. Once she was secured to the headboard, she willed thick ropes of blood to wind around her wrists, through the cuffs, and wrap around the wood slats of the headboard to anchor her in place. Rhiannon pulled against them and thrashed, but her movements were so restrained they had no effect on the bindings. She settled, reassured they would hold should the magic take control again.

As she lay there, she felt anything but peace of mind. Every muscle twitched and throbbed to move, to break free. She'd felt like a prisoner in her own body before, but it felt more real than ever. There was no use in lingering on it, though. It had to be this way. At least for now.

"You can fight me all you want, but we both know your true nature. You will submit. We will be one."

An unfamiliar growl came from the darkest corner of her mind. One she hadn't dared touch.

Rhiannon flinched at the threat. The unfamiliar intrusion in her mind was rough and more animal-sounding than woman.

"What are you?" she dared to ask.

"There is no you and me anymore. It's we. Us. And we are going to make them pay. Just wait and see."

Rhiannon had thought that struggling to tame the magic had been bad enough, that accidentally unleashing it was the worst possible outcome. She'd been wrong. It intended to be unleashed. There was a monster within her wanting to break free. And it was ready to wreak havoc.

CHAPTER FOUR

A bloodcurdling cry woke Rhiannon from a fitful sleep. The terror in it made the hair on the back of her neck spring to life and turned her stomach. With little effort, she shattered the reinforced shackles from her wrists. Her breath stuttered at the ease with which she tore through them. It was disheartening, seeing the hope that she could subdue this beastly magic within her splinter so quickly.

However, the need in her gut that had awakened her outweighed that disappointment as she rose from bed. She slipped on a black turtleneck and leggings that stretched snugly over her full figure. Once her boots were laced and her cloak was secured, she exited on silent feet. When screams rang out again, she abandoned caution and called her magic forward. If she wanted to intervene, she needed to act fast. She traveled at an inhuman pace through the dense snow, heading for the outskirts of the woods. An innate sense of need thrummed through her, something she didn't understand but couldn't deny. Emaciated creatures watched her through red eyes as she darted past them. Their bared teeth and crooked spines would have been intimidating if she wasn't their creator.

As Rhiannon drew closer to the source, the screams had dulled to whimpers and cries. A young blonde woman with disheveled hair lay, sobbing in the snow. She subdued her magic before exiting the trees and then crouched to the woman, cautiously reaching out and placing a hand on her side. Upon closer inspection, Rhiannon noted her corset had been cut open and the front of her dress torn. Her monster wrestled for control, gnashing in fury at the sight, but Rhiannon resisted the growing urge to slip into a feral state. For now.

"What happened?" Her eyes honed in on the marks around the woman's throat and then flicked to the large fresh boot prints leading into the village. "Let me help you up." Rhiannon pulled her to a standing position.

The woman was shaking violently in her arms, and it wasn't just because of the sharp wind lashing at her exposed skin. Shock and fear danced in her wide gaze as she watched Rhiannon carefully through wet lashes.

"Is there somewhere safe I can take you?"

Rhiannon tried to keep her voice soft as the entity's rage clawed to be unleashed. She doubled over with the discomfort of trying to keep her magic at bay. She didn't want to scare the woman more, so she endured it. With a few deep, steadying breaths, she regained her composure.

When Rhiannon returned her attention to the woman, her eyes were wide with concern, but then she nodded and pointed to a building ahead.

Rhiannon wouldn't pry. It wasn't her business, so she took the woman where she'd indicated.

She was a lady of the night, by the looks of her revealing attire. Someone thought it would be easy to silence her. Too bad for them; they were wrong. The monster's need for violence built within her, matching her own.

A moment of synchronicity that was a onetime occurrence, she rationalized as she plotted. She would find the person who did this and make them scream even louder than their victim had.

Once she'd ensured the woman was safe with the people she'd been left with, Rhiannon returned to where she'd found her beaten and in shock, then followed the uneven footprints sunken into the powder-covered ground.

Such arrogance. Whoever did this didn't even try to hide their actions.

The sloppy path led her to a gambling room. Rhiannon lifted her black hood as she entered, looking around for the culprit. She took a turn around the room, her eyes roaming over the men holding cards as they gathered around packed tables. In many of their laps were women dressed similarly to the one she'd just encountered. It confirmed her suspicions. Rhiannon only hoped they met better fates and left safely with their pockets lined. As she neared the bar lining the back wall, she noticed a muscular, bald man with soaked knees and wind-reddened cheeks. It had to be him.

She ordered two fire ales and drank deeply from the first glass. She had missed the warmth of alcohol—and the way it quieted that rational part of her mind. She took a few minutes to observe and blend in. When her presence faded into the scene around her, Rhiannon was ready to take action. Tossing back her hood, she tousled her hair and softened her expression. The man looked up at her as she approached, his eager green eyes wandering over her ample body greedily. If she didn't know what kind of man he was, she might be fooled by his fine features.

"Would you like a drink?" Rhiannon extended it to him with a flirtatious smile. The muscles in her cheeks spasmed in objection.

Her unsuspecting prey took it without question, patting his lap for her to perch on.

She did. Internally, Rhiannon was writhing with revulsion, but she would play her part. It was even amusing to her how easy it was to gain his trust.

She leaned back into him, arching, as she whispered in his ear, "For a few coins, I can make you the luckiest man of the night."

He chuckled as his left arm banded across her stomach. She fought the urge to hold her breath as he spoke over the music. "How can I be sure you're worth it?"

"You're a gambling man, aren't you?" Rhiannon looked up at him from beneath her lashes in a seductive challenge.

As she expected, he was a man with something to prove. He finished his beer and urged her off his lap, then nearly dragged her through the room and outside into the alley.

Rhiannon's lips curled into a wicked smile as they stepped deeper into the darkness. With so many people nearby, she didn't want to risk drawing attention with her still-unfamiliar magic. Instead, she took advantage of her newfound physical strength. Recalling the bruises around the woman's neck, Rhiannon waited for him to turn, then wrapped one hand around his throat, pressing tightly.

"What the hell do you think you're doing?" The man's eyes widened wildly.

"Giving you what you deserve."

Her fingers tightened.

"I. Can't. Breathe."

"I know." She laughed. "I would love nothing more than to hear you uselessly beg for your life." Rhiannon leaned in, whispering in his ear. "But we have to be quiet." She steadily crushed his throat, holding him in the air until crunching and cracking vibrated beneath her fingers.

Finally, the man's gasping and flailing stopped.

When the light left his eyes, she dropped him to the ground unceremoniously. His limbs folded unnaturally beneath him. She smiled. They'd find him the next day, and the woman could take comfort in the fact that he would never harm her again.

Without looking back, she disappeared into the woods. There was a spring in her step as she went back the way she came. She returned to the cottage, feeling more like herself than she had in a while, her monster purring with satisfaction.

Darkness parted with the first tendrils of morning light as Rhiannon approached the clearing. Her steps faltered as movement caught her eye. Kyra was standing in the clearing, staring at the cottage. She was clad in all black, and her cloak rippled in the wind.

Her partially pinned-back onyx braids swayed delicately across her back, free of the weight of her dual swords.

Rhiannon's chest tightened as she approached. She couldn't blame Kyra for being cautious, but she doubted her swords would do much. With silent footfalls, Rhiannon stepped out from behind the trees.

Kyra felt her. She turned to face Rhiannon, swords raised. Soft blues of morning light were cool against her warm brown skin and gleamed off the silver in warning. She halted and dropped her glamor. The magic slipped to the surface with ease, coating her in scarlet. Menacing bits of metal stuck out of her arms. Disgust, then terror, flicked in her friend's gaze. It hurt, but it was better to get this over with sooner.

Tension weighted the air as she waited for Kyra to say something, giving her a moment to take in her appearance. The first time she'd seen Rhiannon like this, a lot had happened. After watching Rhiannon take her own life, face off with the Volskruga, and wield magic in a final fight for their lives, she wasn't sure Kyra had processed what she'd become.

When Kyra stayed silent, Rhiannon spoke.

"What are you doing here? I told you to stay away."

She chased off the guilt rising within her as those final moments in the woods crept up on her.

Kyra had offered her support, had wanted to get her help, and Rhiannon had pushed her away. No, worse than that. Using her magic, she'd slammed the door of their friendship in Kyra's face. She'd done the thing she hated most and made the choice to separate them without their permission.

"I needed to know."

Kyra's steady gaze gave away nothing. Her anger was warranted, but her forced calm told Rhiannon it was more complex.

"Know what?"

"What had become of you. If my mind had played a trick on me." Her expression softened when their eyes met. She hesitated to step closer but put her guard back up. "I couldn't let you stay out here when I don't know what you're capable of. I have people to protect. My family lives just outside these woods. This is my community, my entire world."

Rhiannon nodded, understanding washing over her. "You've come to kill me?"

"Not just yet. But if I feel I need to, I will. My priorities remain the same." Kyra's voice cracked beneath her facade. "I appreciate the sacrifices you were willing to make, but I barely know you. These people are my entire life."

"That's what I respect most about you. You know what matters most." Rhiannon turned her back and continued toward the cottage. "Well, in the meantime, do you want to come in?"

Kyra entered cautiously and kept her distance from Morana, who sat at the foot of the bed, her gaze locked on them. "Do you remember when we were traveling through the Vrugian Woods?"

Rhiannon stopped walking, turned to her, and nodded. "Well, after the Volskruga claimed that you were supposedly some bringer of darkness, I couldn't help but think there was some kind of connection. I'd never heard the actual prophecy myself, just whispered warnings around it. I never intended to disturb any lying entities, so it never seemed important."

"And now?" Rhiannon asked.

"And now it seems important." Kyra cleared her throat. "According to my father, the prophecy states, 'When the father of greed and desire is awakened, he will spread a poison through our soil. Darkness is coming to sweep across the land. And with it, the clash of good and evil will come to a boil.'"

"Well, fuck. That definitely sounds similar to what it claimed." They stood in silence. Rhiannon dissected each word, trying to pull clues from the short verse. "I mean, it's confirmation, but that's not much to go on. It's not really telling us anything new. There's no context for how to stop it. So, what? We're just fucked?"

Kyra shrugged. "Like you said, it's a start. We're going to need to dig for more information. Stories, prophecies, all these things are passed down verbally from generation to generation. It's possible there is more to it. We just have to find someone who knows more than my father."

"Thanks for telling me. I can't say I feel much better, but at least we have something more substantial to go by as we search."

The scent of herbs and cinnamon floated between them as Rhiannon lit candles around the room. The warm glow revealed the concern weighing down Kyra's features. Indecisiveness darkened her amber eyes.

"Say whatever else it is you want to say. You've never been one to hold back your words. Don't start now."

Kyra sheathed her swords and pushed her intricate obsidian braids over her shoulder. "Where did you just come from?"

"I was helping someone," Rhiannon retorted.

"You helping people means leaving a trail of blood. Did you kill someone?"

"Possibly . . ." Rhiannon smirked, recalling how easily she'd crushed his windpipe with her grip. "But there was no blood." She arched a brow.

Kyra scoffed and crossed her arms. "Do I even want to know?"

"He put his hands on someone he had no right to. One of those people in your community you care for so much. Don't you want to rid Wispombra of those who are a danger to others?"

"What do you think gives you the right to be the one who gets to carry out sentences unchecked?" Kyra stepped forward. "You can't just be judge, jury, and executioner without consequence. This is my home. I won't let you bring blood and destruction to my people."

Rhiannon could feel power pulse within her as she bristled at Kyra's words. Her monster didn't like threats.

"I don't need your permission to protect others as I see fit. I won't sit by and listen to screams in the night when I can stop their pain."

"At what point do you become no better than them? When will it end, Rhiannon?"

"When men stop using the lack of accountability in this world as a free pass to prey on those they think are weaker. They might be used to being the predators here, but they'll quickly learn that I'm the rogue wolf in the night, tracing their steps, waiting for the perfect moment to rip out their throats."

"Just because you have power doesn't mean you should wield it."

"In case you've forgotten, I am the one who was chosen to carry this magic. I didn't go seeking it out. Now that I have it, I will use it at my discretion."

"We know almost nothing about how or why it was bestowed upon you. You, of all people, with your reckless temper and your unbelievably stubborn attitude." She shook her head. "You act as if it's some kind of gift and not a curse."

"You have no idea what it's been like the past month. You couldn't possibly understand the loss and agony that I've endured." The flash of hurt in Kyra's gaze challenged that claim. "I have no fucking choice to accept what has become of me if I don't want to completely fall apart." Rhiannon turned from Kyra. "I don't know what the monster within me is capable of, but I'm doing my best to be a responsible gatekeeper."

"Even more of a reason to avoid anything that might get a rise out of you. Whatever facade of control you think you have, you're mistaken. I don't know much about this prophecy. Obviously, it is so much more than I expected. But I do know this. Whatever force now resides within you is dangerous. For once in your life, do the mature thing. Use some damned restraint."

"Why am I the one who's out of line for retaliating? If they didn't want consequences, they should keep their hands to them-fucking-selves."

Kyra slammed her fist on the table. "Dammit, Rhiannon, this isn't the way the world works. There are systems in place."

Her tone solicited a growl from Morana, who crept forward, hackles raised.

Rhiannon put her hand up to Morana. "What good do those systems do when they turn their back on people who would need them most?"

"Wispombra isn't Oakhaven. Things are different here."

"Even if that's true, no one else was there to help that woman. What are the odds she would've told anyone what happened to her when she would, surely, be met with shame? I did the right thing by helping her, and you can't convince me otherwise." She looked down at Morana. "I won't harm innocents, but I won't hesitate to spill the blood of those who would."

"And what if I can no longer trust your word?" Kyra gripped the pommel of one of her swords over her shoulder.

"Then, I suppose we both must do what we feel is right." Rhiannon stepped closer to her friend. "If I break my promise, I hope you will run that blade through me without hesitation. At that point, I will be too far gone anyway."

Kyra's fingers tightened before she finally released the sword and let her arm fall to her side. "I hope it won't come to that, but I've never been much of an optimist."

A dark chuckle left Rhiannon as she rounded the table and poured them a glass of wine. She held out one cup to her. Kyra took it hesitantly, avoiding making contact with her.

"To doing what we must." Rhiannon raised her glass before bringing it to her lips.

Kyra brought it to her lips silently.

"So, are you going to stay here and watch over me, make sure I don't get up to anything too nefarious?" Rhiannon arched a brow.

The other woman shook her head as she looked around the cottage in disgust. "No, and you shouldn't be staying here, either."

"But I will." Rhiannon shrugged.

"At least tidy the place up a bit. I know you think you're doing everyone a favor by punishing yourself, but what we really want is for you to find a way to end this for good."

"Who's we?" Rhiannon gritted her teeth in anticipation.

"Samara, Tristain, and I."

Kyra avoided eye contact.

"What do you mean? Why is he still here?"

Distress flared within her, disrupting the control she'd had of her powers. The wine glass shattered in her grip.

Kyra's hand flew to the pommel of her sword once again. She studied her, waiting for impending danger. When nothing else happened, she continued. "He refused to leave, but we got him the help he needs. He's being cared for. It'll be a process for his leg to fully recover, but he's doing much better."

"Where is he staying?"

"You should stay away from him. It's what's best." Kyra made her way to the door, but Morana appeared in front of it first.

"You don't think I know that? You don't think that's why I've done everything I've done?"

Rhiannon's voice dropped an octave as her anger built.

"You tried to do right by him, but you two aren't good for each other. You'll bleed one another dry if you're not careful. I won't be part of that."

Morana growled at Kyra.

"Too bad that isn't a decision that's within your power to make. Tell me where he is and then you can leave."

"It's a small enough village, Rhiannon. If you want to see him so badly, find him yourself. I wouldn't get your hopes up for a happy reunion, though. We've all seen the monster you've become."

Kyra knew exactly what she was saying. Her words pierced Rhiannon's anger, exposing her biggest vulnerability.

As Rhiannon's rage weakened to sorrow, she spewed, "Get out."

Morana stepped aside, and Kyra left without another word.

CHAPTER FIVE

The idea of Tristain being so close created an insatiable itch Rhiannon couldn't ignore. Every distraction she busied herself with failed at preventing her thoughts from straying. When she slept, she dreamed of him. When she cleaned, she worried over him. When she practiced with her magic, she wondered what he would think of her power. Would he shrink away in fear, or would he embrace her?

Rhiannon wasn't quite ready to find out, but she didn't think she'd be able to resist the pull in her gut much longer. She *needed* to know how he was.

Had there been more distance between them, she'd like to believe the temptation would've been less. But he was less than a mile away from her. So close she could imagine the scent of rain and eucalyptus drifting through the air. What she would give to press her nose to his neck and breathe it in straight from the source, perfectly balanced by the warmth of his skin. Rhiannon closed her eyes as she lost herself to the fantasy.

Kyra's admonishment rang in her ears, disrupting it as soon as she started. She knew Kyra was just looking out for him—for them, really. But it still hurt. That she thought Rhiannon was bad for him and vice versa. She wasn't wrong, but she wasn't completely right, either.

Morana yelped her dismay from behind Rhiannon, who rolled her eyes. "Can I never have a single private thought?" Her frustrated voice echoed around the space. "I just want to see that he's okay. I wouldn't even talk to him. I wouldn't even touch him. I wouldn't even—"

Morana growled.

"Kyra said they wanted to help. If they're going to be involved, I'm probably going to see him eventually anyway. But this waiting is *killing* me."

Rhiannon whined to the wolf.

"And by 'help you,' they mean tame you," Delphine interjected. *"They are going to find a way to drain this power from you the first chance they get."*

"Would that be such a bad thing?"

"Yes. It would be a waste of such potential." Delphine sighed wistfully. *"What I would have given to have a fraction of the magic you so easily wield now."*

"It's dangerous. I don't understand it. Who knows how out of hand things could get. Not to mention, we need to get rid of the Volskruga once and for all. There's no telling how long that blade will hold it."

Rhiannon was trying to be responsible.

"You'd be willing to trade your magic for that?" Delphine questioned skeptically.

Rhiannon could picture an arched, fiery brow above gleaming green eyes. For a moment, it made her miss the days when Delphine could appear as herself instead of just a detached voice.

Finally, she resumed. *"Maybe there are more important things than what I want."*

She wanted to mean it, but her heart clenched at the thought of having to say goodbye to this new part of herself. It terrified her. She hated that it was trying to control her. Yet, what she was able to do to that man in the alley was the strength she'd been looking for all along. And she had it. It was better than a blade. More efficient, less messy, less risky. With it, Rhiannon could save so many more people. One village at a time, she could wipe away the predators lurking in Larindia and beyond. She could take the darkness infesting her life and rotting away her will to live and turn it into something good. Just because she was made up of darkness and death and blood didn't mean she had to be a plight on the people of her country.

Perhaps what she'd gleaned of the prophecy through her visions and the Volskruga's insinuations wasn't set in stone. Maybe Rhiannon could usher in a new era, but it wouldn't be one soaked in the blood of the innocent. It would be a purge of darkness infecting the land. She could topple the system built on the greed and perversion of men and free herself and others from its abuses.

"Set me free. Together, we can unleash true terror. How fun would it be to bask in their screams. To relish in their uncontainable fear," the monster encouraged.

Fighting against her nature was exhausting. A war brewed within her, and as strong as she believed she was, she didn't know how long she could keep it at bay on her own. Her dilemma reminded her of just how alone she was.

The visit from Kyra, even if it had come out of suspicion, had been a nice reprieve from the loneliness and despair of her reality.

Rhiannon had been so lost since that day Silas destroyed her peace and shattered her sense of self. She'd crawled on bloodied knees to put those pieces back together, but she'd never gotten them to fit just right. Since, jagged edges and cracks left cavernous flaws in her foundation, easily invaded by wicked intentions seeking to take root within her.

A monster lived there, and she couldn't escape it. Its claws prodded and poked at those holes, looking for a way out, so it could consume her completely. She was trying to appease it as best she could, but it was exhausting. Keeping the fear, pain, and anger it fed off at bay was no easy feat, and it was one of those times when she had no strength to do it.

Seeing Kyra had reminded her of the companionship she'd lost. Even if they were offering to help her, she wasn't delusional enough to believe things would go back to the way they were. Not after how she'd betrayed them.

Then there was Tristain. Her heart quaked and splintered at the thought of him. Her mind was plagued by him. Remembering all the times he'd been there for her, cared for her, fulfilled her, only intensified the fierce yearning to know how he was doing. Was his leg going to heal? Did he begrudge her for what she'd done? Did he hate her?

She flinched as that possibility crossed her mind.

Morana whined with concern. Rhiannon stroked her cool, smoky fur. She was grateful for the wolf that had found her and stayed by her side at her lowest.

Then there was Delphine's presence. The witch tried her best to bump up against Rhiannon's consciousness and ran her nails along the mental barrier she'd put up, but Rhiannon wasn't interested in her judgment or her calls for her to lean into her circumstances. She just wanted to wallow in the despair that racked through her from head to toe. Pain humbled her and weakened her, but just for this moment. She'd pull herself together again, but for now, she needed this. She couldn't go on without acknowledging it, or it would tear her apart until those pieces she'd painstakingly put back together shattered once again, and they couldn't afford that.

It wasn't just her fate hanging in the balance; she needed to be strong for all of them. And she would be, even if it destroyed her. She would not fail.

The sharp crack of a stick sounded in the distance, accompanied by the tread of heavy boots. The steps were uneven, not unsteady. Whoever it was, they were injured. The restless huntress within her awakened.

"Their heart pumps so sweetly for us. The rhythm of their fear is a most pleasing song," her monster mused.

Rhiannon tried to drown that malevolent voice in her head, deciding to investigate. She quietly opened the door to the cottage, peering out into the darkness. Between the tangle of trees, she spotted a man in the distance. Even with her heightened senses, they were still too far off to pick up a clear scent. She could, however, hear their labored breathing, their stride uncoordinated with exhaustion.

Someone had dared to come into her woods despite the clear warning of the foreboding mist, and they'd pay for their mistake.

This was an opportunity to put her magic to the test. Her demon hummed at the idea. The raw satisfaction was contagious, pulling her lips into a feral smile.

Rhiannon didn't bother to put on shoes as she stepped into the blanket of snow. The white powder was soft and cool on her feet, but it wasn't painful. The elements were no longer a distraction or weakness for her. Every fiber of her being had changed.

Once, she had been prey.

She then became a hunter.

Now, she was a predator.

Determination to prove that pulled her toward the intruder as she shifted through the air at a lethal pace.

When she made it to another small clearing, she stopped and listened closely for any clues of where they might be. Their footsteps had stopped, and everything had fallen silent but for the animals who remained despite her fury. Had the unwanted visitor been wise enough to turn back? Rhiannon hadn't bothered to be quiet as she tore through the snow.

Faint breathing grabbed her attention. For a split second, the fear of being hunted sparked within her, heat running up her spine—but then she remembered what she was. Rhiannon called her magic forward as she waited.

For some reason, they weren't afraid. Did they know of the prophecy? Perhaps they'd sought her out on purpose.

Crunching behind her disrupted her wayward thoughts. She swiveled, prepared to take a life, but she froze when their eyes met. Confusion scattered her mind, creating distance between her and the monster momentarily. She blinked once, twice, three times, refusing to believe what she was seeing. When her lashes fluttered open one last time, he was still there.

Moonlight bathed Tristain as he stood in front of her, panting. The icy swirl of his breath unfurled in her direction, like it was reaching for her, inviting her into his embrace. She wanted to step closer, but the fear of rejection kept her frozen.

The woodland held its breath as they took each other in. It had been just over a month since they'd parted, but so much had changed. She'd changed, yes. But something fundamental had shifted within him, too. Rhiannon didn't see the soft warmth she was used to when those brown eyes rested upon her. There was an edge to his gaze. The surety had left them, replaced by questions and heartache that were so heavy on her soul that they nearly brought her to her knees. She couldn't let that happen.

Rhiannon steeled her spine, shifting her shoulders back. Her resolve stalled, her words fighting quicksand to make it to her tongue.

"What are you doing back here? I told you to leave, to move on. You're a fool for coming here. I could kill you."

He shook his head. "You won't."

His voice wavered, betraying his confident words.

A mistake on his part. The shock had loosened the reins Rhiannon had on her monster. Her hand snapped around his throat, raising him in the air so his toes hovered inches above the ground. "There's that arrogance." She laughed, gritty and guttural, her voice low and even. Swallowing thickly, she pushed it down, down, down. "I'm a danger to you." She gasped, exuding effort. "Something wicked lives and breathes within me, and I don't know how to keep it at bay." She held his gaze. "I'm not even sure that I want to."

Tristain's neck muscles flexed as he tried to shake his restrained head. He settled for a bitter laugh. "We both know you'll never set it free, not really. You're too stubborn, too proud. You'd never allow it to overshadow you, to take away what makes you *you*." He rested his hands on her shoulders.

Rhiannon intensified her grip, a threat not to push her. "Whatever you think you know. Whoever you thought I was, she's dead now. She died when that dagger slid through my veins. What came back when the Volskruga forced my return is not the one who'd tried to spare your life. She's the one who'd take it if it meant saving herself."

"Ever one from the dramatics. I was there. I know you've changed. But you're still you. No matter what lies you tell yourself, I see you. Always have." His eyes narrowed to slits, an expression she'd never seen from him.

On the surface, it looked like hatred. But if she dared to look a little closer, which she most definitely wouldn't, it might be closer to love.

"Tristain . . ." Her voice cracked like a tree struck by lightning, starting out steady and strong, but her vocal cords were on fire with the pain lancing through them as she tried to get the damning words out. "What you saw that day is not even half of it. You don't understand what you're dealing with. I will poison you, and there will be no turning back. Can't you see it? Look around you. It's undeniable. I won't have your destruction on my hands, too. Stay away from me."

His eyes didn't sway from her, ignoring the carnage around them. Like always, he only had eyes for her. And how that gaze pleaded with her. For what, she didn't want to know. His pulse sprinted beneath her fingers, but she couldn't help but wonder if it was in fear or desire. Being in his presence scattered her hardened resolve into fragmented uncertainty that slipped through her hands, like the sand of an hourglass. She hated how she wavered as his words wormed their way through her mind, the truth of them taking root.

Rhiannon slammed Tristain against the nearest tree, ripping the dangerous weeds from their fresh soil. The thump of his head turned her stomach, and she looked away to hide her grimace. "Why are you here? Why didn't you leave?" Rhiannon hadn't realized she was lowering him back down to the ground until she heard the weight of his boots sink into the snow. "You're a glutton for punishment. Do you know that?"

"Yes." Tristain's hands rested on the one she had locked around his throat. The warmth of his fingers seeped into her as his thumb caressed her tense knuckles. "I don't care. I would allow myself to be torn to shreds a hundred times over by these new claws of yours if it meant getting you back."

His words were like a teasing flame licking her skin, a bright light chasing away the darkness she'd started to accept was going to consume her. She couldn't bask in that warmth, or she'd burn them both down with it.

Regaining composure, she ripped her hand away, stepping back from the spark he'd ignited between them. Tristain's relentless desire was dangerous for her; it made her unpredictable and unsteady. She wasn't disciplined enough for this. He made her want things she knew she couldn't have.

It fucking hurt so good. But she was always great at withstanding pain. Him, not so much. She just had to hurt him worse and then it would end. Then he'd go away. Then maybe he'd show some self-preservation.

"You're wasting your time. I told you before—there can be no more us. You may think you're willing to step into the darkness with me, but you clearly don't understand its depth. When you step off that ledge, there is no soft landing. It's rocky, and it's bloody. You won't get back up." She struggled to keep her voice even. "Look at this. Do you see the death and decay that I leave in my wake?" She jerked his chin to the trees' wretched, twisted limbs and the emaciated creatures watching their every move.

Tristain's gaze slowly traveled across the warped landscape around them. His brow furrowed for a fraction of a second before he smoothed it out. He closed the last bit of distance between them, his hands splaying across her cheeks, wiping away her involuntary tears.

"I don't care. There will always be an *us*, as long as this heart beats and air flows through my lungs." Tristain pressed her palm to his chest.

Their pulses throbbing in harmony was the sweetest melody she'd ever heard, and it was almost enough to soften her resolve. But nothing had changed. She was a threat to him, and she wasn't really Rhiannon, not the one he'd fallen in love with. She'd told him, and he hadn't listened. She needed to show him.

Both hands met his chest as she shoved him with all of her strength. Its force sent him back at least twenty feet.

Tristain rose to one knee, breathing hard, and his brown eyes widened.

"Stay away from me, or I will show you just how little you know of what I've become." Morana appeared beside her, called to her by the storm of pain, anger whipping through her.

Tristain's jaw tightened. "What if I love you still, despite what this magic is doing to you? What if I'm okay with loving this version of you?"

"It's not about what it's doing to me. It's about what it can do to you."

Rhiannon's voice was shrill with frustration.

"Why don't you show me and let me decide for myself?"

She would be a liar if she said she wasn't tempted. It would be so easy to have Tristain by her side. To not be alone. To let his love break the cage of fate holding her captive.

"You don't know what you're asking for. I've already hurt you enough."

Tristain rose. Resolve hardened his expression as he looked at her. "Do your worst, Rhiannon."

He was infuriating, but his devotion was breathtaking. She was at war with herself over what to do. Her monster didn't give her a choice.

"It would be so easy for us to break him. To end him. Just like you did the others," the monster inside her urged.

The moment the thought pulsed through her, her flimsy control slipped from her grasp. In a quick strike, stringy red webs grew from her fingers and burrowed into his chest.

Tristain's grunting and furrowed brow were evidence of his pain, but she couldn't stop herself.

She didn't have the upper hand on it yet. She was horrified, yet feeling the beating of his heart in her fingertips proved blissful. The demon within her filled with glee. Yet, it was gut-wrenching watching him suffer, knowing she was the cause of it. As his grimace grew and breathing stuttered, she fought for dominance. Only she decided what their fate was. She used her willpower to still the coursing magic exuding from her.

"Leave. Now." Rhiannon turned to the statuesque wolf. "Make sure he doesn't stop until he's out of the woods. Make sure he is afraid enough not to try to come back."

Smoke furled upward off Morana's back as she ducked and pulled her lips back. The growl ripping from the wolf's throat had Tristain scurrying backward. His eyes flicked to Rhiannon's for a moment. What he saw must have frozen any words in his throat because he pursed his lips and made the wolf his sole focus as he backed up to the tree line.

Even from where she stood, she could still read the threat in his gaze as he watched her from outside the woods. Tristain wouldn't be giving up on her, not yet.

Rhiannon forced herself to turn her back on him, but his hope sank like claws in her back, slowly bleeding out her willpower. The agony that night's encounter caused her had chased away sleep.

CHAPTER SIX

With calming breaths, Rhiannon dropped her shoulders and let her guard down, encouraging her monster to the surface. Her skin tingled as the magic rushed through her, making her heart race. The slick blood coating her was still jarring, but she was growing accustomed to the weight of it on her skin. Now that she'd seen the capabilities of the magic to a larger extent, she was ready to practice more. If Rhiannon couldn't get rid of it, she was determined to mold it to her.

For the time being, it belonged to *her*. Not the other way around.

Rhiannon concentrated, visualizing something that resembled her preferred clothing. Within seconds, the substance slid along her limbs, shifting to take her desired shape. A draping river of crimson split and wrapped around each leg, hugging her generous thighs. It then closed seamlessly across her chest and up to the middle of her neck, covering her in a warmth that ran bone-deep.

Gone was the gratuitous gown of blood, and in its place was something that felt much more like her. She ran her fingers over the smooth second skin, careful to avoid the sharp pieces sticking out of her arms. The fluidity of it rippled beneath her hands. When she pulled away her fingers, bright scarlet smudges followed.

Rhiannon tried something more challenging. She visualized herself on the other side of the clearing where the trees huddled. When she opened her eyes, she was there. A huff of disbelief left her. She'd seen Silas do it, but experiencing it was something completely different. Lightness spread through her. It was incredible to be able to move with such ease, such speed.

Wielding the magic like this was invigorating, as it felt like an extension of herself. More intuitive than something she needed to react to. Next, she willed the blood to extend from her body and latch onto a nearby branch. With more concentration, she ripped it free from the tree. There was little — if any — resistance.

With newfound confidence, she practiced repeatedly, well into the evening, until manipulating the blood-borne magic became second nature.

When Rhiannon called it quits for the day, she was exhausted. Her back and arm muscles throbbed from exertion. Her thoughts were sluggish. Despite feeling like she could barely bat an eyelash, within minutes of laying her head against the cool pillow, the image of Tristain's warm body wrapped around hers wormed its way into her mind. If she closed her eyes, she could feel his heart pumping steadily against her own and feel his breath against her hair. The need to see Tristain viscously possessed her. The incessant desire prodded her, tugged at her, bit and scratched at her until she couldn't stand it anymore.

She would just peek in on him. A quick look, just to see for herself he was okay, and she'd come back.

"Let's go get him. Let's touch him, taste him, devour him. I can still taste the desperation that wafts off him in rich plumes. It's decadent," her monster hummed in appreciation.

Rhiannon's stomach knotted. She didn't like her interest in Tristain, but she couldn't resist the temptation any longer. As the sun set, she moseyed through the clustered trees. She needed time to calm the hungry, gnashing demon within her. Rhiannon didn't know where she was going, but once again, intuition drew her forward. Breaking through the trees, she breached the outskirts of town and ended up standing outside a tavern.

A laugh of surprise broke her anxious silence. She couldn't be sure whether it was her subconscious seeking the numbing relief of a drink or Tristain's presence that had drawn her here. She'd only get her answer if she went in. Rhiannon took a deep, steadying breath, pulled her black hood up to conceal her face, and gently pushed the heavy mahogany door open.

A glance around had disappointment hovering over her shoulders, but there were still many spots Rhiannon couldn't see from where she stood. To blend in, she ordered an ale. It wasn't one of the dark ones Tristain preferred, but the smell of it shook free the memory of him leaning over a candle, lids heavy and eyes aglow, as he listened to her speak like he always had when they'd have a drink together. A kindling of warmth lit within her as she sat in the corner, observing the citizens of Wispombra and spare travelers trickling in with the approach of spring.

While the weather was harsh and the winters were cold, the people were warm and friendly. Most of them seemed to know each other, and many were engaged in deep conversation that had them shaking with hearty laughter.

Rhiannon was quickly enraptured by her observations and the pull of energy she found here. However, after a few minutes, there was a tug in her gut, calling her attention to the left. When she finally looked over, she flushed with surprise.

There was no mistaking the short crop of brown waves crowning his head or those large strong hands that had held her together for so long. Watching him from where she sat, she felt the warmth emanating from those around her disappear, with an anxious chill setting in. Longing that had been waiting in the wings chased away contentedness.

Looking at him now, she was desperate. Her ribs fractured, and her skin split as her broken heart tried to crawl out of her and back to him. The simple act of looking upon his profile was bitter and painful, but every atom of her awakened.

She'd been sleepwalking these last few days, and his presence ripped her violently into wakefulness. A flutter of happiness worked its way through her. But it was too much, too abrasive, all these feelings rushing back at once.

Rhiannon stood abruptly and walked outside to catch her breath. Shakily, she focused her energy on slowly inhaling and exhaling. Snow flurries caught in her throat, and the harsh winter air coated her lungs. She concentrated, slowing her mind and all the memories rushing through it, squashing the seed of hope sprouting within the hollowness of her gut at his nearness.

Rhiannon meant what she said about her being dangerous for him. About needing him to stay away. But she'd always struggled with self-control. What she wanted, she got. She'd thought she'd grown, but apparently, not. Being near him again was as hard as Rhiannon expected, but it was nothing compared to the ache that had driven her mad when they were apart.

Her fingers were restless with the need to run through his hair, to drag along the warmth of his torso, to brush his lips before they crashed into hers. She knew she shouldn't, but Rhiannon couldn't run from this desire, so she went back inside to watch over him. After she'd finish her drink, she'd leave. A few more minutes wouldn't do any harm. She was in control.

When Rhiannon returned to her seat, nothing had changed. Conversation buzzed, and the drinks flowed. Tristain remained in his seat, staring into the glass in his hand.

Time stilled, and everything else fell away when his gaze traveled to hers. Tristain's plump lips tilted upward. They shouldn't have. He should fear her—or at least hate her.

She'd tried her hardest to make sure that was the case. Pain glossed over his eyes. The melancholy made them somehow darker, deeper than they'd ever been. The embers of easy joy had been doused. She'd done that.

Seeing him again, like this, was too much. Rhiannon followed the signs for the washroom. She needed a minute. She needed to catch the breath that had been punched out of her. Rhiannon slipped into the darkness of the hallway, hidden away from prying eyes. She paced as her emotions splintered and overwhelmed her.

Rhiannon was so lost in the chaos she didn't notice anyone had approached until a hand grasped her waist and another clamped her mouth shut, pulling her against the wall. A large body pressed against her backside. She could feel a rapid, pounding heartbeat against her shoulder blades, accompanied by hot, panting breaths on her neck, but it was the scent of a rain-drenched forest that melted away her defenses. Her limbs loosened, and she relaxed into him. Rhiannon was tired of resisting her instincts.

Tristain pulled his hand away from her mouth but kept her tucked against him. His grip was firm, as if any give would allow her to disappear into the night.

"Just stay a minute, please."

"I told you to stay away." Rhiannon breathed harshly as she wrestled temptation to keep her composure.

"Tell me you didn't come here looking for me," he whispered into her hair as he pinned her against him.

"I shouldn't have." Her throat constricted as the longing she'd buried crept up. "It was a moment of weakness. I don't want to hurt you again."

"What if I'm giving you permission to?"

They were both silent.

Rhiannon rubbed her thighs together as her inner walls clenched at the words she'd desperately wanted to hear, even though it was wrong.

Her hesitation had Tristain shifting behind her. His free hand slowly ascended the slit on her thigh.

"Tell me you don't want me to touch you like this."

Her body arched toward him. It felt so good to be touched so tenderly after their time apart, a heaven she'd been chasing since grieving the possibility of never seeing him again. A whimper of desperation left her lips as his fingers traced the roll of her lower stomach and wandered closer to her throbbing pussy.

"Tristain, we can't."

He stilled. "Are you telling me you don't want this?"

"I didn't say that. But . . . we shouldn't."

She was at war with herself. Her restraint was rapidly slipping from her grasp.

Rhiannon let out a ragged breath and exhaled her inhibitions. "Don't stop."

As if those two words broke his restraint, Tristain slid two fingers into her wet cunt. He dipped into her several times before pulling them out and spreading it across her lips. "You can deny it all you want, but you need me, Rhiannon. Taste your desperation."

She licked her lips clean as he returned his fingers to where she needed them. His forearm was still bound under her heaving breasts, holding her to him as he fucked her with his thick fingers in the dim hallway of the tavern.

A moan escaped her lips as she bucked against the expert digits that knew her body so well.

Tristain nipped at her earlobe. "Quiet, Rhi. You don't want anyone to catch us, do you?"

Her voice was rough with frustration when she answered. "If they bother us, I'll kill them." She thrust her hips once again as he rolled his thumb over her clit.

"Fuck, why does it go straight to my cock when you say things like that?" He increased his speed, pushing her closer to the edge by the second.

Rhiannon gasped as her orgasm rocked her. Tristain pressed his hand over her lips, which she promptly bit into. His blood invaded her mouth, the flavor of his essence bursting across her eager tongue.

His hardened cock pressed against her ass, straining for release. And she wanted to give it to him. Rhiannon made to move, but Tristain glided his hands under the two slits in the front of her dress and gripped her shaking thighs.

"Where are you going?"

"Nowhere yet." She tilted her head to gaze into his eyes. "I promise."

His clutch loosened hesitantly before he allowed his hands to fall away.

Rhiannon turned to look at him, taking him in. She noted how he leaned against the wall and favored his left leg. Guilt racked through her.

"Don't look at me like that."

She looked at Tristain's face. His jaw was tense, his eyes hardening.

"Like what?" she whispered.

"With regret." He swallowed hard. "I'll be fully healed soon. I'm more or less fine already."

"Tristain, this is literal evidence of how bad I am for you. You deserve better."

"Don't do that," he bit out. "I deserve what I want. And that's you."

Rhiannon couldn't argue. She would say the same thing. Instead, she dropped to her knees to show him just how sorry she was.

Her fingers worked to undo his trousers quickly. The weight of his throbbing cock in her hand was grounding as she licked the smooth underside. Tristain hissed as she took the tip in her mouth. Rhiannon welcomed the stretch of her lips and jaw as she took him deeper. It was a comforting reminder that, despite everything, he was still hers. She gave his ass a possessive squeeze, digging her nails into the thick flesh.

"Fucking hell. Yes, just like that."

Rhiannon worked his delicious length with her lips and tongue, pulling shuddering breaths from him as he praised her. And when he came, she continued to suck and swallow every last drop. It tasted like salvation. She looked up at him from beneath fluttering lashes, praying he'd forgive her, even though she didn't deserve it. Everything else fell away as he looked down at her like she was his entire world. He pulled Rhiannon to her feet and crushed her lips to his. It made her knees weak as she clung to his strong shoulders.

Tristain squeezed the soft fullness of her thighs once again as he deepened their kiss. His tongue ravished her own, like it would if it were between her legs. Instead of giving into the desire, she pressed her palms to his chest and slid them lower to close his trousers before stepping away.

"Not here. Not now."

"Don't leave."

Tristain's voice was laced with desperation that matched hers.

"I have to." Rhiannon avoided his gaze.

"Why do you insist on making things more complicated than they need to be?" He fisted his hair in that frustrated way of his, tugging the grown-out curls away from his face.

His words picked at the scab of shame and guilt she felt for what she'd done to him.

"You're right. I am difficult. Your life would be so much easier, so much better if I were no longer part of it. So, why won't you let me go? I betrayed you. You should hate me."

"I am angry with you, but I could never hate you. You know that, though. It would be easier for you if I did. Then you wouldn't have to face this. But I won't let you get off that easy. Not when you hurt me the way you did. But even still, I love you. I'm frustrated with you, but I can forgive you. I've already started to, obviously."

"I can handle this myself. It's my burden to carry, no one else's."

Rhiannon was determined to stand firm, but she would be a liar to deny the warring desires within her. She was miserable and hollow without him, but she wouldn't voice that need at the expense of his life.

Tristain grasping her by the shoulders and switching their positions broke her train of thought. His large arms caged her in, trying to force her to stay and listen to him.

"You're not doing this alone."

His tone was firm as he pressed her into the wall.

Frustration mounted within her.

"I won't be alone. I have Morana and Delphine. And, likely, Kyra."

"And me." He held up a hand between them, halting the argument on her lips. "I set out to find a way to stop the death of women at my brother's hand, and I won't stop until I complete that mission. I know you handled Silas for yourself, but this is so much bigger than either of us anticipated. I will not leave you to deal with that fallout on your own, especially because it could cost you your life. Hell, it already has—too many times over. I will be with you until the end, until we lay this evil to rest once and for all. Don't try to dissuade me again. I'm a grown man, and I've made my decision, just like you made yours back in those woods."

The memories of that day were still too painful to face head on, so she pushed them away.

"I did what I had to do. I wanted to spare you from this darkness. I wanted to save your life."

"And you did. But you never asked me if I would have chosen a life without you. Now it's my turn to make that choice for myself."

"You don't even know what you're becoming a part of. You can't even begin to imagine the true horror of what I've become."

Her voice wavered, despite her best efforts, as his sincere devotion slipped past her defenses and lit a torch in her heart.

Tristain cupped her face, caressing her round cheeks, as he stared deeply into her eyes. "Show me what you have become, and I promise I will still love you."

Rhiannon couldn't speak; she was so overcome with emotion. She shook her head, trying to dispel the hope growing inside her.

"Listen to me when I say this. You could rip this entire world apart with your bare hands, and I would gladly follow you into the destruction. Whatever must be done to end this, I won't lose you again. Not in this life and not in death. You are mine, and I am yours."

She nodded and pressed her lips to his.

The sincerity of his words rang true, but how much weight could they hold when he hadn't seen the ugliness within her yet? She didn't know if anyone could truly love that.

CHAPTER SEVEN

D espite the heated words they'd shared, Rhiannon was still apprehensive about Tristain being in her life. She'd conceded to him. She'd been weak in the moment. But she would keep her distance as much as possible. However, Rhiannon couldn't deny how valuable he could be to their efforts as they tried to uncover the secrets of the prophecy. He could speak with the locals. He had the temperament for it, and people always seemed to like him. He had that easy way about him. Her heart clenched.

Next time she saw him or Kyra, she would make the request and then she'd back off. While Rhiannon had full intentions of being responsible, she knew Tristain would not be easy to deter. He wasn't listening to reason. Clearly, he needed to see the horrific truth of her for himself. Once she'd shown what she was capable of, then maybe some sense would come to him, and he'd see how unrealistic it was of him to think they could be together.

Pain lanced through Rhiannon. That thought was a dagger to the heart. The sudden mood shift awoke her magic without her permission. Warmth spread over her as blood coated her skin in the film that felt more comfortable than her own clothing. Scarlet mist swelled around her, mirroring her unsettled emotional state. She tried to restrain it. It pushed back, ebbing and flowing in an overwhelming mass looming over her. The violently red sky was a reminder of what she was capable of.

Rhiannon shook with exertion as she tried to force it to dissipate. It didn't go anywhere. If anything, her boiling frustration expanded it. It beat down upon her, engulfing her in the blood staining her hands. She grunted as she redoubled her efforts. It only barely receded. Quickly tiring, she sank to her knees, but she didn't give up. If Rhiannon was one thing, it was persistent, and she would force it to succumb to her will.

What was once a rumbling mass had become the silhouettes of three women. Feminine figures wafted smoky crimson tendrils that vibrated the air around them as they waited for her command.

Silas had sought power in beasts, but she knew there was nothing more powerful than a determined woman who wanted revenge. She'd proven that to herself. And now, she'd manifested that power in a form that best suited her. Rhiannon was pleased with how fitting it was. It was everything Silas and the Volskruga would hate.

What she would do with them, what they were capable of doing, she didn't know. Part of her hoped she'd never have to find out. Danger and violence emanated from them in waves. Chills skated across her skin as she stood in their reverence.

They were glorious.

The figures smiled back, razor-sharp teeth gleaming white and feral within their crimson jaws. They were just like her.

A pounding fist caused the door to rattle on its rusty hinges, interrupting a fleeting moment of peace Rhiannon had found in the old book that had been under the bed. While its pages were brown, and it smelled rotten, it'd keep her mind quiet. But a hornet's nest of stress had been kicked into action. Irritation drove her feet to smack the worn floorboards as she walked, but the hope stirring within her stilled her hand on the cold knob. She couldn't afford to hope. Even if it were one of her friends, it would be all business. They needed each other to uncover the prophecy. They weren't here because they wanted to see her.

Rhiannon opened the door hesitantly, a high-pitched creaking cutting through the silence.

To her surprise, it was Samara. Her gaze was flat with annoyance, and her thin arms were crossed over her chest. It was definitely not a friendly visit.

"What are you doing here?"

"Came to see for myself. Tristain said you're the same." Her icy glare raked over Rhiannon with distaste. "I don't believe it."

Jealousy sparked within Rhiannon at the thought of them talking about her. It was unwarranted; she should be happy they've found friendship in all this. After all, someone needed to look after his well-being if he wouldn't. But still, Rhiannon envied that closeness she couldn't have with him.

"I think we all know that's not the truth." She rolled her eyes at his hopeless optimism. "I told him that I was dangerous, and he needed to stay away. I don't want him to get hurt any more than you do."

"And yet, you still sought him out?" Samara arched a knowing brow as she pulled her long blond hair into a high ponytail. "Doesn't seem like you're trying very hard to keep him safe."

"I had a moment of weakness. You have no idea what it's been like." Rhiannon shifted her gaze away to hide the vulnerability threatening to spill. "I've tried warning him. Hell, I've tried scaring him. There's not much else I can do other than put myself on a leash." She leaned into the doorframe, assessing Samara. "But at the end of the day, he's the one who has to make his own decisions. I've made every sacrifice I can, and he keeps coming back."

"Not every sacrifice." Samara winced. "I didn't mean it like that. It's just—it's a lot to try to rationalize. You becoming"— she waved up and down—"whatever this is."

"You're telling me." Rhiannon let out a long sigh. "So, did you just come here to lecture me about things I already know?"

It was Samara's turn to roll her eyes. "I told myself that's why I came. But in truth, I've missed you. I needed to see you. It's been difficult to stay away, knowing you're suffering out here alone."

"I thought you'd never want to see me again." Rhiannon gulped. "The way you looked at me that day"—she cleared her throat—"I wasn't sure you'd ever be able to forgive me."

She didn't know if she needed them to. She could understand if that'd planted a seed of mistrust and hurt that had grown too much in their time apart to be uprooted. However, for all they'd seen of her that day in the woods, none of them seemed as afraid of her as they should be. It was a comforting thought, even if it shouldn't be.

Samara's airy voice recaptured her attention. "I've tried to understand why you did what you did. Why you didn't let us help you in the end. Am I still angry about how you went behind our backs? Yes. Can I forgive you? I'm trying. But this new Rhiannon, I don't know her. Not really." Her brow furrowed with concern.

Rhiannon studied her friend for a moment, then opened the door wider and turned back inside. After a few seconds, Samara followed her.

Samara's gaze traveled around the cottage, taking inventory of the sagging roof, broken floorboards, and discolored walls. When she looked back at Rhiannon, her face was set in a grimace.

"How are you living here? It looks like it's going to crumble at any minute. It's so dirty in here. Have you not cleaned in all this time?"

"Does a monster deserve nice things?" Rhiannon said as her eyes lingered on the dusty bedside table holding her few personal items.

"Rhiannon . . ."

The pity in Samara's voice made Rhiannon nauseous. She needed that to stop.

"Besides, I've been a bit busy dying, coming back to life, losing everything I love, turning into whatever the fuck this is, and trying to get rid of an ancient being in my blade to worry about sweeping and dusting."

She'd infused her tone with an ingenuous lightness that sounded forced, even to her ears.

Samara's lips quivered upward, and Rhiannon could only stare at her in disbelief. "Are you actually going to laugh right now?"

Sure enough, uncontrollable laughter escaped Samara as she bent over, trying to catch her breath. It was contagious. Rhiannon laughed herself into a fit at the sheer ridiculousness of what her life had become.

And then it turned to sobs.

Samara moved to her side, sliding down to the dirty floor next to her, and locked their hands together.

"You're not a monster, Rhiannon. I was raised by one. I would know. You've saved more lives than you've taken."

"I wish I could believe you, but neither of us really knows the truth of what I've become. We have no idea what carnage might lie ahead."

"But I do know." Samara pressed her palm against Rhiannon's chest. "I know who you are at your core. You saved me once, and you'd do it again. No magic can erase that part of you. The part that's a good friend. You might paint yourself as ruthless and unforgiving, and you can be, but beneath the battle armor you've built around your heart, there's a fierce love that no one can take away. That's why I came here. That's why we're all going to help you escape this fate you didn't choose."

CHAPTER EIGHT

S amara and Kyra returned to the freshly cleaned cottage together and prepared to help her the next day. She tried not to let the disappointment of Tristain's absence dull her appreciation for them making an effort.

Without Jade, they'd become more like sisters.

Jade.

Thinking about the sibling she'd left behind stole her breath. It left a hollowness not even Tristain's love could fill. She'd done well not thinking of her family while she'd been away, focusing on anything and everything else to distract her from her heart incessantly tugging to yank her back to Oakhaven.

She hoped her sister was taking care of their mother. She knew she was. She always took care of others. At least they had each other.

"Rhiannon . . ." Kyra interrupted her wayward thoughts.

"Sorry, yes?"

"I was saying, we've both been asking around about the prophecy. I think there's more to it, like we assumed. But no one could recite anything more from it. And of the few people we found who had heard of it, there wasn't a clear answer to what it meant. They didn't know the actual contents, just rumors. But still, the bits and pieces we were able to gather might get us closer to what we need to know." She glanced sideways at Samara. "Or it could lead us astray."

"Let's hear it, then we'll decide its value."

Rhiannon intentionally smothered her hopes.

"From what I've heard, some think that the prophecy tells of a being that will protect and free them," Samara prefaced. "They believe there is to be a reckoning in the world. A new power will rise and right the ways in which we have currently gone astray. To protect those who have been harmed by the sons who rule the world without respect for the mothers and daughters who sustain their lives."

"And you think that new power, the one that will bring about a new beginning, will be me?" Rhiannon asked.

"Don't you?" Samara exchanged another look with Kyra.

Rhiannon shook her head. She didn't have an answer. The notion that she could truly change the world, that she was supposed to, was too much to wrap her mind around.

"But what I've heard is very different. Some believe that you may be the harbinger for destruction of our world as we know it." Kyra's brow furrowed deeply in thought. "Although now that I'm thinking about these opposing interpretations, it might be that destruction can be construed in multiple ways. If you are meant to free those suffering from the powers that be, perhaps that means destroying what currently stands, not destruction as in the death of innocents."

Rhiannon let out a long sigh. "So, we're no more informed than before, are we?"

Samara tilted her head. "Maybe it's up to who you want to be."

"Maybe. I don't know that I have much of a choice. This entity inside me, the source of my power, is strong. I don't know how to fully control it. It has its own motivations, its own desires, its own plans. I worry I won't be able to make that choice for myself."

"You're the most hardheaded person I know. If anyone can control it, it's you." Kyra let out a sarcastic laugh. "After all, it chose you. That has to mean something."

Rhiannon rolled her eyes, but a genuine smile tugged at her lips. "Maybe."

Kyra sat next to her on the bed, squeezing her hand. "I know that you can do this. You can influence the outcome of this prophecy. You can keep people safe."

Samara nodded her encouragement.

"I don't want to hurt anyone, but I call it my monster because she is hungry. She wants to spill blood. She wants to set this magic loose."

"And . . . what do you want?" Samara asked.

"I want it both ways. I want to be able to protect myself and others. I want to take on threats without fear. But most importantly, I want to be in control of my life again."

"That's up to you." Kyra turned to face her. "You will have to make that conscious choice again and again when you're challenged. It will push you to destroy. These entities, they thrive on chaos. They are greedy and feral, from a different time. They don't understand or respect humanity. But they also have the ability to make a real impact, for better or worse."

"That's a lot of pressure to handle without much to go on. I'm trying my best, but there's so much I don't know." Rhiannon sighed and flopped back against the bed.

"We'll help you figure it out. We just need you to be careful in the meantime." Kyra gave her a knowing look, her amber eyes piercing her.

"I'm doing what I can, but it's digging its claws into me. Day by day, it has a stronger hold on me. I woke up with a heart in my hand and a dead man at my feet the other night. After that, I tried to restrain myself while I was sleeping. They didn't hold me," Rhiannon confessed.

Kyra and Samara exchanged a wide-eyed look.

"That's concerning." Samara gulped.

"You're telling me." Rhiannon huffed as she ran her hands through her tousled waves. "I want to control it. I have no desire to hurt innocent people. But I won't stop it from ending those who would threaten me or someone else. I wouldn't have done that before, and I won't start now."

"Honestly, I wouldn't expect anything else from you." Samara stood.

"We'll try to find out more. But for now, please stay here. I don't want Wispombra to lose anyone else unnecessarily."

Rhiannon couldn't help being defensive. "I haven't killed anyone who didn't deserve it."

A pause lingered as they looked at each other before Kyra let out a deflated sigh. "I know." Joining Samara, she headed out the front door. "We'll be back in a few days."

Rhiannon nodded. While she'd already been enforcing her self-isolation, being told to do it was a whole other challenge. She was already feeling like a caged animal, as the monster thrashed beneath her skin and gnawed at her bones like a restless beast. She hoped they'd find real answers soon. It was only a matter of time before she lost control again.

Not more than an hour later, another knock came at the door. Apparently, she was popular that day. Rhiannon opened the door to a version of Tristain that looked far more disheveled than she'd seen him before. The skin beneath his eyes was purple, and his eyelids were heavy. His hair was even more unkempt than usual, and his voice was hoarse. He hadn't been sleeping.

She wanted to pull him into her embrace as worry wormed its way through her. She refrained, trying to keep her word.

"What are you doing here?" Her throat dried as she struggled to find words. "You just missed Kyra and Samara. Were you looking for them?"

Say no.

Say you miss me.

Say you need me.

Say you don't care about the damnation that loving me would sentence you to.

"The only thing I've ever been looking for is you." He stepped toward her, and she mirrored him with a step back. "Show me."

The words rushed out as his narrowed gaze swept over her.

"What are you talking about?"

"Show me what you've become. I want to see all of you. I need to so that I can say with all honesty how much I don't care."

Rhiannon's legs were unsteady as his words whipped around her head in a rush. She had to have imagined it. He couldn't be saying those words.

Before she could respond, his hand clasped the back of her neck, and he crushed her lips to his.

It was utterly disarming, and nothing could have stopped her from pulling him close against her in that moment. She feared she'd break his bones with her newfound strength, but she couldn't help herself. His desperation was contagious. Without her permission, tears cascaded over her lashes and down her cheeks.

"Hey, why are you crying?" He trapped her face between his palms and kicked the door closed behind him.

When they sat on the bed, Rhiannon pulled away from him. "You came here to get me back?"

It was only a whisper, as if speaking the words aloud would shatter the illusion that everything would be okay between them.

"I did." His lips traveled across her tear-soaked skin. "And I'm not going anywhere ever again." He tilted her chin up. "Do you understand me?"

With those words, all declarations of distance and restraint crumbled into the dust of a monument, a distant memory.

She was weak for him and didn't care.

Rhiannon pulled him to her, and they desperately tried to consume one another. She needed to be closer to him. She needed him to complete her. Fill her. Consume her. Break her apart and put her back together again.

"Fuck me, Tristain." She tugged at the back of his hair, ensuring he was listening to her.

His need matched hers. Tristain furiously scrambled to remove her clothing, and she followed suit. Rhiannon's fingertips traveled across his skin, memorizing every scar, freckle, hard muscle, and softness. Every inch of him captivated her, as if she hadn't seen him naked many times. This was different, though.

His mouth seemed to be everywhere at once, placing his claim on her body and soul. She was ready to relinquish herself to him, consequences be damned.

Rhiannon laid back, allowing him to crawl over her. His large frame shielded her from her own judgment. She was safe in his arms, even from herself. To show her appreciation, Rhiannon reached between them, stroking his glorious, dripping cock. They were both so eager. She was slick between her thighs and desperate for him.

Tristain stilled against her, and she paused. "Did you hear that?" His brow furrowed, and his eyes scanned the space between the bed and door. "I could have sworn I heard someone whispering my name."

"I didn't hear anything." Rhiannon leaned into him and recaptured his lips. "It's probably just the creatures outside."

She worked her hand relentlessly, pulling him back into the moment, dragging husky moans from him. The distraction forgotten, he latched his lips around her nipple. His hand traveled to her other sensitive breast, teasing the hardened peak with gentleness that had her back arching off the bed.

"I can't wait anymore. I need you," Rhiannon breathed out between gasps.

She loosened her grip on his cock, and he notched himself at her entrance, the tip teasing her. Rhiannon bucked her hips, unwilling to show patience. She'd done enough waiting. He chuckled as he slid inside her inch by inch. She groaned with relief at the fullness of him.

The completeness of having him inside her was pure bliss. It was a gift she'd never thought she'd experience again. And then he was gone. The temporary loss of him threatened tears from her again.

"Hey, stay with me," he whispered, bringing her attention back to him. "Am I hurting you?"

"No." She caressed his cheek, then pushed his unruly hair back. "Show me how much you've missed me."

Tristain took the command and pushed into her in one swift stroke. With him inside her, she was whole again, and she refused to let this feeling go.

Rhiannon gripped him so tightly she was sure she'd leave bruises as she pulled Tristain against her and forced him to keep a punishing pace.

"Don't stop." She panted, dragging her nails down his back. She desperately clawed at him, keeping their bodies as close as possible.

Rhiannon needed to feel his weight against her. She wanted to be covered in his sweat. She would ensure he claimed her completely.

"I can't. I'll never stop fucking you like this. I'll never stop loving you, Rhi. Do you understand me?" Tristain gripped her chin, and his hips stopped. Their eyes locked.

"I love you, too," Rhiannon responded and pulled his body flush against hers as she thrusted her hips up to meet his.

Tristain pressed his lips along the curve of her neck and across her collarbone. When his thumb pressed her clit, he circled his tongue against her skin in the same rhythm.

When Rhiannon's legs shook, he pulled out of her. The shock of it made her gasp.

"Where are you going?"

"Turn over. I want to grab that gorgeous ass as I fuck you from behind. I've missed that view." Even his sweet, dimpled smile couldn't soften the sharp desire in his gaze.

Rhiannon turned over and raised her ass in the air. Tristain landed a stinging slap against the plump flesh before sliding his fingers through her dripping pussy. His skilled fingers teasing her clit had Rhiannon pressing into him, Tristain's thick cock hard against her.

"So eager." He laughed as he took his thick length in his hand and pressed it against her needy cunt. "Is this what you want?"

"Fuck, yes." Rhiannon moaned as she pressed back into him and took him fully.

"Take what you want, then."

Tristain's hands were firm on her lush hips as she fucked herself on his cock. He gave her ass another sharp smack before he dug his fingers into the dimpled flesh and gave it a possessive squeeze. "All of this belongs to me, understand?" His voice was gravelly and ragged as he took control and slammed into her over and over.

"Yes," Rhiannon conceded through a moan.

"Yes what?" He punctuated his words with another slap.

"Yes, all of this belongs to you. I belong to you."

Her voice was shaky and desperate as he drove her closer and closer to the edge.

"Don't ever forget that again." Tristain grabbed her hair, pulling her back against him harder.

Her fingers found her clit as he matched his pace that had her orgasm crashing through her seconds later.

Tristain groaned as he emptied himself inside her, his hands massaging her hips. "Being with you now, like this, was well worth the wait." He placed a gentle kiss on her back before he slid out of her.

As soon as they cleaned up and slid under the covers, they let exhaustion pull them into a peaceful sleep.

Despite how spent they were, Tristain wasn't letting her off easily. As soon as she'd opened her eyes, he'd insisted Rhiannon show him more of her magic.

She agreed. Bringing it to the surface was effortless, but keeping it at bay was the challenge. She breathed deeply as she let it come to the surface, blood coating her skin in warmth and mist resting on her fingertips that made them tingle. Rhiannon had to force her eyes open once she'd mentally prepared to take in his reaction.

"You're beautiful." Tristain stood and walked toward her. "You look as powerful as I've always known you were."

She was speechless for once. Rhiannon expected to see fear in his eyes, like the glimpse she'd caught before, but there was nothing but love in his gaze. He saw past the gruesome exterior and saw her—all of her.

Her monster purred with satisfaction. *"He can live. In fact, I think we should keep him."*

Tristain cupped her jaw with his warm hand and pulled her to him. With that action, her fear of rejection melted away.

CHAPTER NINE

A throb of panic jolted Rhiannon from her sleep. Something was wrong. She sat up slowly, noting the chill that spread across her naked flesh and how her hair stood on end. She turned to where Tristain had fallen asleep beside her but found it empty.

Rhiannon froze in the vise grip her mounting fear held her in. She couldn't bear it if something happened to him. Her monster snarled at the thought. Neither of them would accept that option.

Springing into action, she suffocated those emotions, letting her protective, more primal instincts take over. With a deep breath, her glamor fell away, and she crept out of bed on silent feet. Her vision gradually adjusted to the pitch blackness draped over the interior of the cottage. That's when she noticed Morana poised to strike at something—no, someone—sitting at her dining table.

Her breath hitched when her eyes finally focused. It was Tristain holding a dagger.

The dagger.

The black veins that split the cursed silver glinted at her, taunting her. Fear clutched her in a stranglehold. Her heart drummed loudly in her ears. Her vision was tunneling.

"Tristain?"

She forced his name out.

He didn't respond. Something was wrong with him. His eyes were heavy-lidded and unfocused. His chest barely moved. He was asleep.

"Tristain, give me that."

The authority she'd hoped to imbue failed miserably. She was terrified.

His elbow twitched, and within the next blink, the dagger was dragging roughly across his palm. The motion was jagged, and his limbs seemed unnaturally stiff, but it cut deep, pooling blood.

Rhiannon stepped forward, but the twitch of the dagger in her direction halted her once again. Her gaze flicked to his. The hardened eyes that looked up at her were not his. Where pools of fiery warmth usually met her, a distinct coldness took its place.

Something was very wrong with him. The weight of the energy around them turned heavy and oppressive.

"Are you okay?"

The answer was obviously no, but she didn't know what else to say. She needed to make herself nonthreatening.

Her blood ran cold when she found familiarity in the endless depths of the black gaze looking at her.

A cruel smile distorted his features as he took in her realization. "Hello, Rhiannon." His lips moved, but his eyes remained vacant. "Did you really think you could keep me in there? How naive you truly are." He stood, and Tristain's head hung at an odd, lopsided angle as he continued speaking. The soft patter of Tristain's life flooding out of him punctuated his words. "Look where your selfishness has gotten you." His head whipped back unnaturally, then returned forward once again. A long pause drifted between them as a tremor ran through his body. "Protective over you, this one is. What a shame that I will break him because of your defiance."

"Let him go."

Rhiannon's jaw hurt from how hard she clenched her teeth.

"I don't think I will. I think I'll keep him for now. He's quite the valuable tool, especially if I have any hope of getting what I want."

"And what's that?" Rhiannon tamped down her instinct to fight him, knowing it would only result in injury to Tristain.

"For you to set me free, of course."

"No," she spat.

"What a shame." It brought the dagger against Tristain's healing leg. "Stubbornness will get you nowhere, but it will put him in the ground."

"Wait!" Her voice trembled. "If I were to consider it, where would I even start?"

"How lost you are, girl." It took a beastly breath through Tristain's pouted mouth. "If only you'd taken my offer to begin with. How different things would have played out."

"Are you going to answer me or not?"

"Everything you need is in Silas's journals."

Hot shame licked at her as she remembered the last time she'd encountered one of those.

"Where would they be?"

"That's for you to find out, isn't it?" it taunted.

"Fucking hell," Rhiannon groaned.

She had no intention of returning the Volskruga to its true form, but she wasn't going to tell it that. She needed time to come up with a plan to save Tristain without compromising everyone else's safety.

"And, Rhiannon"—it stepped closer to her—"if you betray me, I will force him to rip his own heart out and shove it down your throat as he takes his last breath."

With that gruesome threat, Tristain collapsed in a heap of soft limbs. She scrambled over to him. A cold sweat coated his skin as Rhiannon brushed her fingers over his forehead. She called her glamor back up and pulled him against her to provide him with warmth. Every second felt like years as she waited for him to open his eyes.

"What happened?"

Tristain's voice was hoarse.

"I don't know how, but the Volskruga got to you." She traced the still-bleeding cut on his palm with her finger. "Why did you have the dagger?"

Tristain sat up slowly. "I remember hearing whispering. It wouldn't stop. I couldn't take it anymore. I got up to investigate, but there was no one here. I followed the sound, and it led me to the blade. I only picked it up to look at it. That's the last thing I remember."

"What were the whispers saying?"

"I don't know." His eyes flicked away from her gaze.

A lie, then.

She supposed it didn't matter in the moment. She was just happy he was alive and, for the most part, unharmed. Later, she would ask him again, when he wasn't so shaken up.

Rhiannon got to her feet and extended her hand to help him up. "Let's try to go back to sleep. You need to rest."

She wasn't sure how they could possibly calm their minds enough to rest, but she didn't know what else to do. Adrenaline was still coursing through her, but she knew it would fade.

"I should bandage my hand. You can go back to bed. I'm fine."

"You're not. I'm not going back to bed if you're not. You think I'm letting you out of my sight with the Volskruga lying in wait?" She huffed with disbelief.

It was only a matter of time before *it* pulled something again, and she'd be ready. It couldn't have him. Tristain was hers.

"*Ours,*" her monster reminded her.

Rhiannon bandaged his hand in silence. This terrified her, rattling the fear of losing him loose that she'd temporarily buried when he'd shown up at her door. This was a stark reminder of just how dangerous being with her was. It hadn't even been a day, and his life was at stake. There was nothing stopping the Volskruga from killing him at any moment.

She had to find those journals and fast.

Neither of them could sleep, so as soon as the sun rose, they tore apart the cottage in search of them. They weren't there. Knowing Silas, they were hidden somewhere. Perhaps he'd wanted a backup plan, an out, in case things went sideways. Whatever plan he had, if any, had failed.

After about two hours of scouring every inch of the place, Rhiannon was exhausted. She thrust open the door and sat on the steps that looked out into the mangled woodland. Tristain joined her silently. He scanned their surroundings, as if he were seeing for the first time, and she felt her hackles rising in defense.

"What the hell even happened?" He turned to her.

She whipped her head in his direction, ready to shut down his accusations. But only curiosity filled his gaze. "I let my anger loose." She turned away. "I didn't mean to do this, though."

"How could you have known? This is all new to you, Rhiannon. You have to give yourself some grace. You didn't choose this. It was forced upon you."

She shoved away the warmth his words ignited within her. She wasn't worthy of it.

"Perhaps, but it's my responsibility to control it now."

He wrapped his arms around her shoulder and rested his head atop hers. It was so easy to melt into him and accept his kind words. She could never show herself this same kind of forgiveness, but she would try her best to accept it from him.

"Promise me something, Tristain." She gripped his hand. "Hmm?"

"Promise me that you'll fight its influence. Don't let it take you away from me. I just got you back. I can't lose you again."

"I'll always fight my way back to you, Rhiannon. You should know that by now. I'll never leave you alone in this world if I can help it." He placed a delicate kiss on the top of her head.

The burn of an unreleased sob crawled at her throat, but there was no more time for that. She hated this situation, but this was their reality, and it was only a matter of time before everything came to an end. One way or another. They both needed to be strong. This would test everything they were made of.

With Tristain there, the cabin had become crowded, making it even less habitable for Morana, who had only been sleeping there to watch over Rhiannon. The wolf grew more restless by the hour.

"You don't have to stay here. You should roam if you need to."

Rhiannon spoke telepathically to Morana.

"I can't leave you here with him like this." The wolf chuffed to emphasize the sentiment.

"I can protect myself. If anything, he's the one who needs protection." Rhiannon sank to her knees in front of Morana and rested her forehead against the wolf's. *"I've proven that I can handle the Volskruga. It's him I am worried about, not myself."*

Morana was silent for several moments.

"I promise, I'll be fine here. And if anything does happen, you'll know," Rhiannon assured her.

Finally, the wolf bowed her head in agreement. But not before snarling at Tristain on the way out.

It was difficult to put distance between herself and Morana, but she knew it was in her nature to roam. There was nothing to worry about as far as her safety. Tristain wouldn't hurt her. Even under the influence of such an evil entity, he would fight to protect her, as he always had. And if his strength failed, she was confident she could rely on her own.

Days had passed without incident, but it was only a matter of time before the Volskruga made another appearance, and it was making Rhiannon sick with worry. The small reprieve she'd felt with the return of her friends and Tristain had been stripped away from her just as fast as they'd come back into her life. The few weeks prior had been emotional whiplash, going from suffocating inner turmoil to reviving hope and back again.

She needed to breathe. She needed to get away. With a flustered huff, Rhiannon rose and strode out the door, nearly ripping the rusty knob off in the process. With her emotions in flux, her power became restless, gnawing to get out. That only increased her frustration. She wanted to claw the monster out of her own body, bleed out the magic, and go back to the way things were before. She wanted to be free. But she wasn't. And now, because of her selfishness, neither was Tristain.

That was what was most upsetting to her. He was her weakness, and she was his. Repeatedly, they found themselves in this position. Each time, the consequences worsening. Even still, she wasn't willing to let him go, no matter the outcome.

Her need for him was disturbing. It challenged everything she thought about her own resilience and independence. She'd believed getting her vengeance was all she needed, but that hadn't turned out to be true. She needed him. She wanted him. But what else had she been wrong about? These thoughts tumbled around in a whirlwind of distress that shredded her sanity.

"Rhiannon!" an urgent voice called from behind her.

She halted and looked over her shoulder to see Tristain marching after her through the snow.

"Where are you going?" Tristain ran to catch up to her.

"I'm going for a walk. I needed some air." She continued deeper into the trees, her eyes forward to avoid his.

"Do you want me to go back?"

"I don't know."

It was the truth. Part of her felt guilty for what had happened to him, and it made being around him difficult. But the other part of her didn't want to let him out of her sight. She wanted to cherish every moment for the fear that the Volskruga could take him from her at any minute. The lack of control they now had over his fate had them both on edge. "Don't chase after me. I don't want you to hurt your leg while it's still healing."

"It's healed. I'm fine. Just stop." Tristain rounded on her, forcing her to halt in her tracks. When she looked up at him, he laced his fingers through hers. "This isn't your fault."

He always saw through her.

"I should have never let you stay here. I knew it wasn't safe, but I was selfish in my loneliness. That is my fault."

"You could have never known this would happen." He pulled her toward him. "I don't blame you."

Rhiannon studied his face, memorizing his soft features and the way he looked at her without judgment. "Of course you don't."

It made her sick.

Breaking away from him, she increased her speed. She'd never been this deep in the northern region of the woods. Rushing water could be heard in the distance, and she was suddenly determined to see it.

"Rhiannon."

When she didn't stop, he grunted but followed.

She could see the shape of the stream. The water appeared unusually dark. And the fact that water was moving in freezing temperatures surprised her. Its oddness drew her forward. She was shocked to find that the water was crimson.

Rhiannon was about to kneel to put her hand in it when a gust and body heat caught her attention.

Tristain was standing right behind her.

"Rhiannon, I hope you don't think you can run from me."

It wasn't Tristain's voice.

She turned slowly, dropping her glamor as she did so. Power thrummed across her skin at the threat. Her stomach clenched with dread from seeing the Volskruga peering out from those eyes she'd found so much comfort in. Her fears were confirmed when they were finally standing face-to-face.

Its hold on Tristain had gotten worse. Physical evidence of its presence shown within him. Inky blackness stood out across Tristain's warm skin, trailing down from his eyes. The evil etched into every fine black line on his face was all wrong. It was difficult to look at him, but she resisted the urge to turn away.

"Hello again." The Volskruga peered down at her with disdain. "You don't seem to be trying very hard to find those journals. Time is of the essence, you know. His body will not hold up long if he does not kill someone. And we both know he isn't one to compromise his morals, his own best interests be damned." It leaned closer. "I hope you haven't grown too attached to having him back in your life."

With those poisonous words, she could see it fade into the background, except for the bulging black veins underneath Tristain's skin.

"Tristain?"

Rhiannon's voice was barely audible over the running water, but her throat was so tight that speaking was an effort.

Catatonic, he stared. She slapped him. Still nothing. She shoved him, not considering how close they now were to the water. One minute, he was standing before her; the next, he'd plummeted into the sweeping red water. Without a second thought, she jumped in after him. The shock of it seemed to bring Tristain back to the forefront, but with him off guard, he'd swallowed water and choked, sputtering as he was pulled into the current.

In an act of sheer desperation, Rhiannon's magic overtook her rational thought. Webs of blood shot from her hands and clutched Tristain's torso and forearms, tethering him to her. She breathed out a sigh of relief, even though she was disconcerted that her magic had become second nature already. How long until it had free rein? But that was something to worry about another time, when they weren't drifting through freezing water.

They clung to one another until the river spat them out into a small deep scarlet lake. Rhiannon gripped the back of his hair, forcing his eyes to hers, and was relieved to see the darkness that had overtaken him had fully receded.

Confusion flitted through his brown eyes as he took her in, processing what had just happened. They waded silently, watching one another closely.

Rhiannon kissed him deeply, relieved. At least for now. She'd just gotten him back. She couldn't lose him again. Not ever. Desperation clawed through her, shredding away her common sense until all she had left was need.

They were soaked, and Tristain was shivering, but she didn't care. He was her oxygen, her nourishment, her only need, breathing be damned. All she wanted was to inhale him.

Tristain responded, his hands roaming over her back, her waist, her ass as he embraced her. But he wasn't quite as durable as her, and they knew it. He pushed to his feet to bring them back above the surface. Rhiannon wrapped her legs around his waist as he walked them to the shore and through the thigh-deep water. Finally, he laid her back on the ice-cold ground.

Looking up into his eyes, Rhiannon knew she would never let him go, no matter the cost. Feral need more than just her own flared within her, hot and urgent, but she pushed the monster's possessive nature away. She wanted to be serene in that moment.

Tristain leaned forward, resting his weight on his forearms, sliding a knee between her thighs. Their soft stomachs rested together, their breaths synching.

She reached up, brushing away a grown-out, rogue curl. "Where did you go?"

Silently, he shook his head. Fear bloomed in his eyes. "I was there. I just couldn't do anything. I was submerged in darkness; shadows were restraining me within my mind. Some were holding my body in place. Others were covering my mouth and holding my eyes open. I don't understand how that's possible."

Rhiannon thought back to her experiences with Delphine and Silas. It sounded similar to those interactions. At least then, she'd been asleep, not awake and out of control.

"I know what you mean." She shuddered and placed a hand on his cheek as he leaned into it. "There's something you should know about the Volskruga's magic." He tensed against her, but she continued. "It needs to feed."

"And what does that mean?"

"It means"—she sighed—"that there may come a time when you have to make the choice to kill someone in order to preserve yourself."

"Let's hope it doesn't come to that. We'll just have to figure out how to get rid of it before it reaches that point."

"I will help set you free. It can't have you."

PART 2

Darkness is coming to sweep across the land.
And with it, the clash of good and evil
will come to a boil.

CHAPTER TEN

W hen Morana and Delphine learned of the
Volskruga's new connection to Tristain,
distressed energy rolled off them in waves,
pounding into Rhiannon's head like a raging tide.

*"I told you he was no good for you. Look at what he's done. We
just tamped down the Volskruga's power to something manageable,
and now look what we're dealing with."*

Delphine's voice was shrill in her mind, compounding its
pulsing ache.

"It's not his fault," Rhiannon insisted. "As if you have any
room to talk. If it weren't for you meddling with magic you
don't understand, none of us would be here."

She knew it was sick, but her gut twisted at that thought.

Frustration and worry created a chaotic energy in the
cottage crackling in the air between the four of them.

Rhiannon's monster tried to claw to the surface, eager to
bask in the unease she seemed to thrive in. Rhiannon needed
to reign in the heightened emotions they were all reeling in.

"Casting blame and arguing isn't going to get us anywhere."
She motioned for them to sit at the decrepit wooden table
in the kitchen. "When the Volskruga appeared to me, he
mentioned that the answers were in Silas's journals."

Morana sat directly across from Rhiannon, allowing her
and Delphine to have a more natural-seeming conversation,

even though it was anything but normal. "Why didn't you say that from the beginning?"

"You didn't give me a chance." Rhiannon rolled her eyes.

"My broth—I mean Silas—had spent most of his time back home, scribbling furiously for hours at a time. They must be in Saldova." He and Rhiannon exchanged a concerned glance.

"How are we supposed to retrieve them? What if what we're looking for isn't ther—"

"They're not here. Where else could they be?" Delphine stated.

"To answer your first question, we'll have to travel by ship." Tristain tapped his fingers on the table.

Rhiannon could see his wheels turning as he jumped right into planning.

"Thank you. I didn't realize we'd need a ship to cross the ocean." She paused to glare at him. " I meant"—she gestured between them—"how are we, two people with erratic and highly dangerous magic, supposed to travel that far safely?"

"I don't think we have any other choice than to figure it out." He shrugged as if it were obvious. "Plus, Samara and Kyra will be there."

"Why would you assume that? We've already pulled them away from their families once. We can't ask them to do it again."

"If you think they're going to let us go alone, you're in serious denial." He huffed.

"Even if they did go, there's only so much they could do. They couldn't stop me on their own—or together."

"You act as if you haven't always been volatile." He leveled his gaze at her. "Yes, you can do more damage now, but I trust you to tread carefully, given how important this is."

Rhiannon ran her hands through her hair, letting out a long sigh. "I guess we have no other choice. Maybe we'll get lucky, and Silas will have known something about the prophecy as well. The Volskruga seems to think he held a lot of knowledge about how this magic works."

"He must have if he was able to survive so long as its host," Delphine weighed in.

Rhiannon didn't bother relaying her thoughts to Tristain. They were all on the same page, it seemed. They needed to break the news to Samara and Kyra; the thought alone had her stomach in knots.

Instead of having Tristain return to the village in his unpredictable condition, Morana went to fetch Samara and Kyra so they could fill them in. When the wolf returned with her two friends, tension blew in with them.

In unison, Kyra's and Samara's gazes swept over the room, taking in the scene, like they expected disaster. Morana strode over and sat at Rhiannon's side.

"Okay, so you haven't ushered in a new age of darkness, and you both seemed to be in one piece. What was the urgency?"

Samara tried for humor but fell flat.

Kyra's lips turned up ever so slightly before her eyes seemed to rest on Tristain. Then that shadow of a smile quickly inverted. "What did you do to him?"

Rhiannon scoffed. "For once, actually, this isn't necessarily my fault."

Tristain stepped forward. "It wasn't anyone's fault. And if it was, it would be mine." His fingers twined through his hair, pulling the rogue waves taut. "I was lured by the Volskruga. Part of its magic lives inside me now."

Kyra and Samara gasped, exchanging a horrified look.

Tristain put his hand up so he could continue speaking. "It somehow called to my subconscious while I was sleeping and convinced me to offer myself up to it—"

"I thought hosts had to willingly tie themselves to the Volskruga," Kyra said, her voice low and tense.

"I guess it didn't force me, not really." Tristain's voice wavered with uncertainty. "Somehow, it made it work, because the magic definitely took."

"He sliced his own palm. My guess is that, since he held the knife and drew it across his own skin, he was considered a willing participant." Rhiannon shrugged.

"I thought he was asleep." Samara voiced the unease around that important point. "He couldn't have consented if he wasn't awake."

"He wouldn't be the first to be taken advantage of when his mind wasn't coherent, but his body was an active participant."

Disgust thickened Kyra's voice.

Silence fell upon the cottage that felt suffocatingly small with this conversation drifting in the air. They were all trying to parse together what this meant for Tristain, what it meant for them. Because, even though they'd had their differences and falling out, they hadn't abandoned each other after all. They were in this together, for better or worse.

"Whatever the case may be, Tristain can't remain like this. We need to find a way to separate him from the Volskruga's magic—and soon. His life hangs in the balance as long as he's tied to it." Rhiannon subconsciously shifted closer to him, as if she could shield him from the danger he was in.

"And how are we going to do that? We're no closer to finding a way to help you. And now we have this to contend with," Kyra stressed.

"Tristain is my first priority. All of our first priority," Rhiannon insisted.

Delphine spoke into Rhiannon's mind, causing her to jump, since she'd almost forgotten the witch was present. *"I think the answers we find will help put us on the right track toward helping you. It makes sense that what you learn will help you understand your own connection to the prophecy and the entity that now resides within you. Hopefully."*

"I guess that makes sense," Rhiannon answered. *"I just hope we find answers for him in time."*

"You should probably make your travel plans, then. Morana and I will stay behind. We can venture to the Vrugian Woods to see if there are any answers there. I should be able to communicate with the souls of the Volskruga's victims, since I am one myself."

Morana whined her discontent at being so far from Rhiannon.

She bent down in front of the wolf who had become such a vital part of her. "I'll be okay. I have them to watch over me. And most importantly, I'm not an easily breakable human anymore. You helped make sure of that." As much as she wished Morana could come, there was no hiding her magic. She ran her hand over the wolf's billowing form in reassurance as she stood.

Finally, she turned back to the group. Everyone had stood by silently, watching Rhiannon, as if her having conversations with someone they couldn't hear or see was completely normal. Perhaps it was one of the least outlandish things they'd had to deal with throughout this entire adventure.

"The Volskruga mentioned that there is a way to break the tie that he and Tristain share. Tristain thinks that information is in one of Silas's journals back at their home in Saldova. Delphine agrees that it's our best lead. And she and Morana will go to the Vrugian Woods to speak with the lost souls to see if they can find answers for me while we're gone," Rhiannon said.

"You're not going alone, just the two of you." Samara swung her finger back and forth between them.

Tristain stepped forward. "We agree. That's why we were hoping you'd come with us."

Kyra worried her lip. "How long is the trip there?"

"Only a few days by ship. Then, we'll have to travel the rest of the way by horseback. It'll be less than a day's ride from the port." Tristain's brows shifted as he checked his mental math.

"Wait, you have to travel there by ship?"

Samara's voice wobbled.

"How else would you expect us to cross an ocean?" Rhiannon rolled her eyes.

"I've never been on a ship. I've heard awful stories about what lurks at the bottom of the ocean." Samara chewed at her already-short nails.

"You don't have to come. I don't want to ask you to do anything you're not comfortable with." Rhiannon moved in front of the two women, holding their gazes.

"I'm not staying here. I've been stuck on this continent my entire life. I want to see what else there is." Samara rolled her shoulders back, straightening her posture. "I just wish we didn't have to take an unreliable ship to get there."

"Don't worry, the sailors who travel this route know what they're doing. They've faced many a storm on this unruly coast. There's nothing to be afraid of," Tristain reassured her.

Samara swallowed thickly but didn't protest.

"And what about you? Are you afraid of the monsters that lurk beneath the ocean?" Rhiannon turned to Kyra.

"Who has time to be afraid of monsters that might not even exist when I've already faced my fair share on land?" She shrugged.

Rhiannon had no doubt that Kyra meant it. She felt the same but still wasn't enthusiastic about being trapped on a ship in the middle of miles upon miles of water, surrounded by people she couldn't trust. But that was the least of their problems.

Tristain cleared his throat. "So, it's settled. We'll go to Saldova to try to find the journals and, hopefully, figure out how to separate the Volskruga from me before it kills me." He let out a nervous laugh.

Rhiannon put her hands on his shoulders. "It will not kill you. I already told you I won't let that fucker have you." Her hand wrapped around his chin firmly, and she didn't release it until he nodded.

"When should we plan to leave?" Samara asked.

"As soon as possible," Rhiannon answered as she turned toward them. "It's already changing him, and it's only going to get worse. From what I know of the Volskruga, he's not safe and neither is anyone else until we break the hold once and for all."

Kyra and Samara exchanged wary glances but nodded back to her.

"Can you be ready in two days' time?" Tristain asked.

"Yes," Kyra answered.

Samara nodded her agreement.

"Meet us back here, then. We'll travel north up to the coast where there's a busy port. There should be at least a ship or two with open rooms that we can book passage on," Tristain explained.

"We'll see you then." Kyra's gaze moved between them. "And, you two, be careful in the meantime."

They nodded, but Rhiannon knew that would be easier said than done.

CHAPTER ELEVEN

T hick plumes of crimson hovered above her spread fingertips as she watched Tristain through narrowed eyes. His heaving sent white clouds into the air as he waited for her to strike. She hesitated, giving him a moment to recoup after the last blow she landed. It was Tristain's idea that they should use the remaining days in Wispombra to try to learn to control the magic they'd both had forced upon them.

She saw his reasoning but was hesitant. Even with the additional strength he had from the Volskruga, there was still the risk that she might harm him accidentally. Rolling shadows brought her attention back to the present. There was no more time to waste weighing the pros and cons. Tristain made the decision for her. Magic sparked to life within her veins and heated her hands as red mist floated up in wisps from her fingertips.

When the dense blackness came within a foot of her, she unleashed the tether on her resistance. Red clashed with black, forcing it back inch by inch, until it swarmed Tristain in angry plumes. It pulsed and quivered, a snake ready to strike. But she was familiar with the venom of this beast. Another wave of crimson burst from within her and charged him, breaking up the deep blackness engulfing him and chasing away all remnants of the magic he'd wielded. When

Rhiannon commanded the sea of red to disseminate, Tristain looked back at her with those veins of black writhing beneath his skin through his cool onyx eyes.

She shuddered but not out of fear. It was something far more disturbing. The way he looked now, and the way he looked *at* her, coaxed the lingering lust that had always simmered between them into a full-blown inferno. Rhiannon swallowed thickly, and his lips quirked into the semblance of a smile. But those dimples she loved didn't make an appearance. The air around him was different, too.

Darker.

More predatory.

A weighty seduction with claws.

And she wanted to know if the thrill of danger that bore from his eyes into her marrow tasted as good as it felt.

Her lingering human instincts told her to run. But the monster within Rhiannon straightened her spine and forced her to hold her ground. The cloud of his breath fanned over her face, and his fingers grasped tightly into her thick brown hair.

A gasp tumbled from her lips, but she didn't trust herself to speak.

"Does seeing me like this turn you on?" He took a half ragged, half snarling breath. "If I slip my fingers between those delicious thighs, will I find you wet and wanting?"

Time stood still as he unwound his fingers from her tresses and slid it down over her sleeved arm, along the curve of her waist, and across her hips. When he reached the ridge of her rounded lower stomach, she reacted. Thick strands of blood sprung from her flexed hand and shoved him against the tree several feet away. They strapped him to the trunk, securing him in braided garnet ropes.

Shock shifted to amusement as Tristain let out a low laugh. "You're scared." He tossed his head back, another bout of laughter escaping him. "Oh, Rhi. There is no hiding from this." His gaze landed on her once again, and she fought the urge to punch his obnoxious face.

"I'm not afraid of you. I'm afraid *for* you. There's a big difference." She returned his smirk with a scowl and a glare as she approached him. Running her fingers under the thick bloody bands, Rhiannon admired her handiwork, a quite useful skill.

Tristain bit her ear, and she yelped. She hadn't realized how close she'd leaned in while she was captivated by her creation. Irritation burned through her, and she pulled her knife from her holster. Rhiannon held it to his throat, admiring how the light of the muted red sky caught the gleaming silver.

"As if you'd need that to shut me up," he taunted.

"It's not a matter of need, Tristain. It's a matter of want. And right now, I *want* to see you bleed." She pressed the tip of the knife just under his jaw and watched eagerly as scarlet pearls dotted the skin of his neck.

Something about the vibrant red soothed her. It was a reminder he was still here with her, even if he wasn't fully himself. That thought was enough to restore clarity to her lust-addled mind.

Rhiannon stepped back and retracted the bindings. "Either we continue practicing, or I'm going to take a nap. Neither of which require you to put your hands on me."

"Who knew you'd ever be the responsible one."

Rhiannon swallowed her frustration in favor of productivity. Idle hands and all that. It wasn't that she wasn't curious about what it would feel like to be with him like this, but it didn't feel right to act on it without his consent. And he wasn't in the right mind to do that. The only way that was happening was if he expressed his curiosity when he was back to himself.

Focusing, she felt the blood shift around her forearms and coat her fingertips. She willed it in his direction, aiming to suspend him, but the force she used threw him backward. At the sound of the harsh thud, her eyes sprang open.

Menacing shadows curled around his figure as she continued her attack on him. Rhiannon struck again and again with the same results, but, finally, she executed just the right amount of power to lift him off the ground. Webs of red extended from her and wrapped around his neck. His gloved hands tugged at the substance restricting his airflow. She held him there for several more seconds before lowering him to the ground.

While her smile broke free, Tristain's brow was creased, and his jaw was flexed. It was clear he was battling with the force occupying him. He was himself, but he wasn't. The real Tristain would have been impressed. This one was competitive and frustrated by her power. Her heart throbbed—for him, for herself.

"Let's see what you can do against the shadows," Tristain called as he approached.

"I don't think that's a good idea." Rhiannon watched him carefully. "After all, I'll be dealing with humans—no other magical entities. Right?"

He stopped in front of her, sizing her up. "Who knows what the future holds. Isn't it better to be prepared for anything? Besides, it would be fun, wouldn't it?"

That new hungry smirk was back.

Chills raced down her spine, and it wasn't because of the cold.

"Fine. But only for a few minutes."

"Whatever you say. You're in charge."

With that, shadows unfurled from his body, crawling across the white landscape in her direction.

Rhiannon stood her ground, having to remind herself that it wasn't Silas as her heart raced at those unwanted memories. Within seconds, Morana was by her side, sensing her distress. *"I'm okay."*

"This isn't a good idea. You shouldn't encourage him to use those powers," Delphine answered instead.

Rhiannon rolled her eyes and refocused her attention on Tristain. She circled him counterclockwise, waiting for him to make a move. He followed her from the corner of his eye. When a gust of wind tousled her hair across her vision, he made his move. A shadow knotted around her ankle and dragged her to the ground. She launched her hand toward it, sending a red mist to chase it away, but it didn't stop. Instead, it kept going until it knocked Tristain unconscious. When he hit the ground, a heavy puff of air exhaled out of him, sending her heart pounding with worry.

Before she could react, his eyes flicked open. Darkness pulsed beneath the skin around his eyes in warning. He was up and marching over to where she lay frozen before she recognized that look.

Rhiannon scrambled to get her bearings and shoved her hands into the snow. Webs of blood slithered toward him. Where they met his boots, they traveled up his body, wrapping him in their sticky trap that kept his arms at his sides, his legs unable to move.

"Stop," Rhiannon called, halting the magic before it suffocated him. The magic listened, but she could see it tightening around him like the coils of a deadly snake. "I said *stop*." The movement ceased, and she took a deep breath again.

Taming her magic that was so eager to take was exhausting. It was almost as if it matched her stubbornness. Perhaps that's what she deserved.

"Are you going to release me?" Tristain asked, his voice too low.

There was a grit to it that both unsettled and called to her.

"Not until you settle down. It's flourishing under the competition between our magic." Rhiannon stepped closer and placed her hand over his heart. "I don't like this for you. It's not safe."

"It was never safe, but it was necessary." He closed his eyes, breathing deeply. When he opened them again, his tense facial muscles had softened slightly, the veins receding. "Better?"

His bitterness was uncharacteristic, but he was trying.

She called the extension of herself back, and it unwound from him. "No more for today. I'm . . . not feeling well."

Part of her held back from telling him how tired using her power made her. The impulse to lie to him worried her. It didn't feel like a step in the right direction. He insisted this was the only way, but she feared it would be their undoing. How could they trust one another like this? How could she be sure he was still him? That thought chilled her to the bone. It was unnerving, yet she couldn't deny she was truly worried.

All she could do was hope the journals held the answers.

She needed to be rested for their impeding trip the day after tomorrow, but sleep wouldn't come to her. Instead, she was taunted by an incessant pull in her gut. It was as if invisible ropes were tugging her toward an unknown destination.

Something similar had happened the night she'd heard the woman screaming in the village, but she didn't hear anything. Rhiannon dressed silently, trying her best not to disturb Tristain.

When she stepped outside into the brisk night, Morana was already waiting for her.

"Stay here and watch over him," Rhiannon whispered.

"No. He will be fine. He isn't helpless in this form," Morana shouted.

Rhiannon gritted her teeth but set on the path. Morana was right, but she didn't like it. It wasn't that she wanted him to be vulnerable; it's that she didn't trust the Volskruga's influence.

With each step, the draw became more intense. She traveled quickly through the snow, seeking out the mysterious source. Nothing in the woods. Nothing in the town. Her path led her out of Wispombra and onto the trail they'd taken to get here. Just a mile or so outside of the border, she heard it, the distressed neighing of horses.

"You go left, I'll go right," she urged Morana.

The wolf obliged.

Rhiannon took in the scene as she got closer. One man held the reins of the horses gathered in one hand, while another fisted a woman's cloak. She listened closely, trying to determine how many people were present. Someone else seemed to be rummaging through the contents of the carriage.

"Please don't take those. That's everything I have for the winter festival. I need that money to see my family through the rest of the season," the woman being held by her cloak pleaded.

The man grunted.

Hot anger pulsed through Rhiannon as she calculated her next move. Roiling air caught Rhiannon's eye from the edge of the trees on the other side of the carriage.

Morana was sitting in wait. She decided approaching from behind the man was her best bet.

No sound came from her footsteps as she crept forward. The other man's attention was on his partner as they waited for the looter to exit the carriage with their stolen goods.

Rhiannon was able to send webs of blood discreetly across the distance between them. She watched as it reached their feet and made its way up their legs. They noticed the hot stickiness when it was too late. Their fear sent the magic into urgency as it wound the rest of the way up their bodies. This time, she didn't tell it to stop. She watched, transfixed, as it coated their faces in red, covering their eyes, noses, and mouths. They couldn't breathe, much less scream for help.

Rhiannon shook her head at the woman who looked on the verge of shrieking herself. "I'm here to help you," she mouthed, hoping the woman understood.

However, she was frozen in fear.

Morana appeared at her side. The wolf's fur stood on end, shadows drifting high into the air, becoming the terrifying black mass of her truest form.

The two oxygen-deprived men fell to the ground at their feet, and her magic receded from their corpses, having accomplished its job. The third person was still unaware of her presence. When Rhiannon peeked around the open carriage door, she saw an unconscious girl lying on the floor while the man tore through their belongings, stuffing what he found valuable into two large sacks.

She sent mist slowly into the carriage, but the young girl yelped upon waking, alerting the man of her presence. He took off into the night through the other door. Unfortunately, for him, there was no outrunning Morana. The wolf pressed him into the snow, gnashing and growling furiously in his face.

Rhiannon was torn between going after them and comforting the shocked and terrified woman and child. The woman shrank back as she approached.

"Take your things and go. You have nothing to fear," she urged her.

The woman rushed her child to help close and ready the carriage to keep moving, but she never took her eyes off Rhiannon.

This worried her.

"Do not tell anyone what you saw." Rhiannon allowed her mist to whip around them but did not move to harm the woman. She backed away and mounted the carriage once more. Once they were in motion, Rhiannon approached the man Morana had pinned.

She leaned down, hovering over him beside the wolf. "What did you think you were doing? Taking what doesn't belong to you. How cowardly. Can you not provide for yourself?"

"Why should they get to come here and steal our business? They bring their goods and take away our customers. How am I supposed to thrive when they're preventing money from finding my pockets?"

His eyes were hard with greed and absent of any remorse.

Rhiannon felt confident that the world wouldn't miss a man like him.

Morana rumbled her agreement. "Finish him."

The man's broken screams followed her on the wind as she returned to where the two dead bodies rested in the snow. Everyone would be angry with her if they found out about this. She sighed deeply. Discarding of them shouldn't be difficult out here, but she didn't want to risk them being found. She sent out a call to the twisted creatures she'd created, hoping some of them would be eager for their stomachs to be filled without any hunting. To her relief, a small gathering of them crept along the outskirts of the woods.

With the confidence that they'd dispose of the bodies, she hustled to return to the cottage before Tristain noticed their disappearance.

CHAPTER TWELVE

Watching Tristain's chest rise and fall was the most relaxing thing Rhiannon had ever done. They were the closest they'd been to the possibility of making a future work between them, yet they were the furthest from safety. Their fates hung in the balance. He'd accepted her, but she couldn't accept him as this. It wasn't right, even if they'd temporarily accepted it. But this moment, with him sleeping peacefully while she watched over him, gave her some comfort.

"Haven't you two ruined one another enough?"

Delphine's voice shattered that illusion.

"We were both already broken. After everything, I can't help but think that maybe it was always supposed to be this way."

Delphine's brittle huff was a scrape against the walls of her mind.

"I know you don't approve, but I did everything I could to keep us apart." A warm smile curved her lips. "You can't deny that he's good for me. I've tried. And maybe I don't want to deny it anymore. If I am to be the dark night that falls upon the world, then he is the starlight that guides my path."

"How poetic." Delphine sighed. "It's not that I begrudge your love, but caring for someone that way makes you vulnerable. It leads to pain. It leads to betrayal. We both know that. You can't trust him like this."

"He would never hurt me. It's the Volskruga I don't trust."

Rhiannon ended the conversation as Tristain stirred. At the first sign of his wakefulness, Morana vanished into the woods.

She could have melted into the warm pools lovingly gazing at her that morning, when he was most at ease, just coming to, unburdened by her or the day.

He pulled her against him. "Good morning, beautiful."

Tristain's breath tickled the shell of her ear.

Rhiannon turned to face him. Her fingers traced beneath his eyes where the skin was currently unmarred by the Volskruga's magic.

His thumb smoothed over the crease of worry furrowing her brow. "Why do you look like you're going to cry?"

"I hate this." She mumbled into his chest as she buried her head under his chin. "I can't stand to see how it's influencing you. I'm afraid for you. For us."

"What are you afraid of?" His large palm cupped the back of her head in a comforting gesture.

"Of losing you." She took a deep breath. "Of you turning into Silas."

She hated to say it, but she needed to voice the ugly truth that had buried its roots in her thoughts.

Tristain gently fisted her hair, bringing her gaze to his. "I will never become Silas. You have my word. I would drive a sword through my heart before I ever hurt you like that."

Sensing her need, his lips forged a path, chasing the tears down her cheeks. Her lips hovered over his, but the door whipping open interrupted them.

Samara stepped inside and nearly tripped over her feet at the sight of them in bed. "So much for keeping your distance." She scowled and shook her head. "But that's not why I'm here. What the hell happened?"

Kyra followed Samara, flicking between surprise, then annoyance.

"You're going to have to be more specific." Rhiannon begrudgingly stood from the bed, tugging a blanket around her.

"The missing men. Don't bother saying you had nothing to do with it. It has you written all over it," Samara accused.

"If you're referring to the three men that were robbing a woman and her child of their goods on their way into town, then they're not missing. They're dead." She walked past them nonchalantly and poured herself a glass of water.

"Oh, just dead? That's all?" Samara chimed in sarcastically.

"What the hell does it matter to you?" Rhiannon turned to the other woman. "The world is a better place without them, I can assure you."

"We've had this conversation before. You can't just be the judge, jury, and executioner whenever you please. That's not how things work here." Kyra balled her fists at her side.

"I didn't have much of a choice. I wasn't just going to leave her there. Who knows what else they would have done to keep them quiet."

"Rhiannon, I'm begging you. Please stay here and try not to kill anyone else before you leave." Kyra ran her hands down her face. "You're going to stir a pot you are not going to enjoy boiling in. Trust me."

"What the fuck is that supposed to mean?" Rhiannon gritted her teeth with being treated like an out-of-control child.

"Many people have seen things in these mountains. You know what lies between here and Norhavalta. If maimed bodies start piling up, they will want to get to the bottom of it and deal with it accordingly."

Rhiannon rolled her eyes at how dramatic it all sounded. If someone else had apprehended them or even stabbed them because of what they were doing, it would have been the right thing to do. But *her way* was never the right way.

"I can see those wheels turning. Just don't do anything we wouldn't do, and we'll be fine." Samara crossed her arms and arched a severe brow.

"Well, that doesn't sound like any fun, but I'll do my best." Rhiannon smirked as she walked up to them and ushered them out the door. She loved riling them up. She had no intention of leaving again until they were ready to make for the port.

When she slammed the door, a heavy warmth pressed against her back. She inhaled the rich, woodsy scent that made her knees weak.

Tristain felt up the ample bend at her waist and caressed her full thighs. He didn't give her an inch, forcing her breasts and stomach to rub across him tauntingly as she turned to face him.

"I want you. In that bed. Now." His lips feathered against hers with each word.

Rhiannon's body flushed with heat that chased away the coolness of the wood pressed against her back.

"Tristain, I don't think it's a good idea." There was no authority in her voice. "What if you lose yourself in the moment? What if you slip into the background and this new side of you takes over? That wouldn't be right."

"Why not?" Tristain's large hand pressed into the wood above her, while the other slipped under the edge of the sheet wrapped around her.

Determined fingers roamed across the expanse of her stomach and teased the sensitive skin just above her cunt.

"Because you're not able to consent for yourself. What if I do something you wouldn't normally be comfortable with? I would never want to do something you didn't enthusiastically agree to." Rhiannon chewed on her lip.

"What if I wanted to lose control for once?" His warm hand cupped her firmly. "But that won't happen."

Her breath hitched, but she forced the words out. "You don't know that."

"I do. When the Volskruga isn't actively forcing himself in my consciousness, I'm there. I'm participating." He inhaled deeply as his thumb circled her clit. "When I'm wielding the magic, there's an edge to it that flips on another part of my brain. The part that so many of us try to tamp down in order to be the best versions of ourselves. But with its essence coursing through me, that resolve slips away, like the barrier was always as thin as a wisp of smoke."

"Do you want me when you're . . . like that?" Rhiannon stuttered as two wide fingers slipped inside her.

"You have no idea," Tristain gritted out.

"Why?"

"Because I want to see what it's like when we're on even ground, when your darkness faces off with mine, and we tangle in the depraved web we've woven in our grief and denial."

It wasn't the reasoning she expected. She hadn't known what to expect, but the sentiment made her heart clench. Her pussy mimicked the sensation, squeezing around his fingers that methodically dragged in and out of her like they could lure the answer he wanted out of her.

"I need to think about it," Rhiannon forced out on a moan.

His fingers instantly froze, and his gaze burned into hers. They stood there staring at one another, neither willing to bend as the seconds ticked by.

Finally, Tristain broke the silence.

"Okay."

She gasped at the sudden absence of his fingers. The emptiness burned as much as the dismissiveness of his response.

"You can't be serious."

Tristain glanced over his shoulder, a knowing smile taunting her. "I'll let you come when you're ready to embrace all of me like I have you."

"That's not fair," she called after as he disappeared into the white landscape.

A muffled "Don't I know it" was his response.

Sexual tension had pressed upon Rhiannon from every direction over the course of the day. The restless energy it created made each task more irritating as she prepared for their journey. And Tristain knew it. Every opportunity he got, he pinned her with a heavy, knowing look. She did her best to ignore him, but that was nearly impossible in the small quarters, much to his satisfaction.

"You seem a little tense. Is there anything I can do for you?" Tristain taunted as he crowded her space while she poured herself a glass of wine.

"As you can see, I'm already handling it myself."

A smug laugh grated on her ears.

"We both know that's not what you need." Tristain dragged his knuckles down the side of her neck and across her shoulder, then paused to drop a kiss on the sensitive, exposed skin.

Rhiannon drank deeply from her glass, then set it on the table harder than necessary. She focused on the burn of the rich blend as it clung to her dry throat. Another long sip filled the silence, hanging over them like an executor's blade.

There would be no taking this decision back. But if Tristain said he was in his right mind and consented to it, maybe it was okay. Maybe she owed it to him to let him lose control. To let him explore this side of himself.

Tristain's fingers grazed the soft underside of her breasts, sending a shiver down her spine. She melted into him and raised the glass to her mouth once again, but he pulled it away and set it gently on the mahogany table. Rhiannon tried to turn to him and pull his mouth to hers, but Tristain clenched his arms around her sides, holding Rhiannon in place.

Tristain brought his mouth to her ear and said in a low voice, "I want to hear you say it."

Rhiannon whined, but his hold only tightened. A frustrated sigh slipped through her clenched teeth. "Okay, I'm willing to try."

He tsked. "That doesn't sound very *enthusiastic*." He smirked down at her as he used her own words against her.

"I'm yours to do with as you please." The words sounded like a concession, but her blood thrummed with satisfaction and excitement.

"You might just regret those words." He nipped her ear, startling Rhiannon as she turned toward him.

When she looked up into Tristain's handsome face, that crooked grin she'd come to love turned sharp—wolfish, even—in its predatory nature. A shot of fear snaked up her spine as she watched him observe her. Tristain blinked, and his eyes went pitch black, followed by the equally dark veins webbed in his skin. She knew it was wrong, but she was instantly dripping at the sight of him like this.

Like this, he was as dangerous as she was, as hungry as she was, as terrifying as she could be. Her pussy throbbed as she waited for him to make his move.

"Come here."

Rhiannon shook her head. The thrill of pushing him in this state was too intoxicating to resist. It would be terrifying if she were her old self. Defenseless. But this? This was a safe way to play with the ancient magic that had taken everything from her.

They were equals in this scenario. She didn't need to be afraid of him. In fact, Rhiannon was curious how their power would interact when put in opposition of one another and fight for dominance.

"Rhiannon. It wasn't a request." Tristain ran his tongue along the ridge of his teeth, as if he could taste her excitement in the air.

"And you don't command me." She quirked her brow, sitting on the bed.

A sinister chuckle was the only warning Rhiannon got before Tristain was on top of her, with her wrists gathered in one of his sword-roughened hands as he pressed her into the mattress until her lungs struggled to expand.

"Are you trying to scare me?" Rhiannon gave him a mock pout. "I think you forget who you're toying with."

Rhiannon ripped her hand out of his grasp and wrapped it around his throat, her sharp nails digging into the skin until droplets of blood cascaded his neck like the fountain she loved back home.

Drops spattered softly on her face, and Tristain's eyes followed them. Ever so slowly, he drew closer to her, his tongue slithering out as he licked it off, never breaking eye contact. It nearly drove her over the edge, but he wasn't going to make it that easy for her.

Mischief danced in Tristain's gaze before he struck. She shrieked when he bit her neck. A growl erupted from Rhiannon's throat as she bucked against him, but that only gave him the opportunity to press a knee between her legs and spread them. His thigh against her cunt provided pressure that was just short of what she needed.

He smiled wide as he leaned down, then grazed his lips across the shell of her ear. "Beg for me. I want to hear how badly you need me. How you can't live without me." He wrapped his free hand around her throat, applying pressure as he dropped his voice an octave. "Tell me that you will never leave me again. Say you belong to me and only me, no matter how dark it gets. We travel through the abyss together. We light the way for one another."

Rhiannon bit her lip to hold back tears. She could hear the fear and desperation, the plea, buried under the gravel Tristain infused in his tone. Those words couldn't be said. She couldn't make that kind of promise, not knowing what lie ahead of them.

She rolled her lips together tightly and shook her head slowly, denying him.

He wasn't having it.

Tristain moved his hand from her throat to her cheeks in an instant, forcing her mouth open. "Say it, Rhiannon."

She started crying but not from pain. Everything within her wanted to believe this would all work out, like he did. That they could have a happy ending. To put her faith in them, consequences be damned. But she'd learned not to trust this cruel world. How could she promise something that was so wrong? She believed in equal parts that they did and did not belong together. They brought one another so much comfort. He brought out the best in her. At least the old Rhiannon. This new version of her? She could only bring pain and destruction into his life. Given Tristain's current state, that was undeniable.

"We're destined to go up in flames, always have been. We both know that." She tried to turn her head, but he held her firm.

"At least we'll be together when our ashes settle into the ground."

Darkness crept out of Tristain's gaze with his soft words. His inner warmth shone through as he looked down at her with the undeniable truth of his love.

There was no escape for either of them. Whether they made it through the other side of the fire or were burned in the unwieldy flames of their love, she couldn't run from this, and they both knew it. It was fucking terrifying, but she was ready to give in. For him. For her. For them. There was no more running from it. He simply wouldn't allow it, and she was tired of going in circles.

Rhiannon nodded, loosening her grip on his throat. "Into the ashes, then."

"Fucking finally," Tristain growled.

Possessiveness inhabited every inch of his being, the shadow magic rushing back in. He was horrifyingly beautiful. While it was only temporary, it was a visual testament to the darkness she'd brought into his life. Tristain's acceptance of it had loosened the guilt that had wound itself tightly within her. She found peace in this chaos.

His hand crept up her shirt, the roughness of his palms grounding her in the moment. "I'm going to fuck you now, and it won't be gentle." Tristain watched her carefully as he waited for her okay.

Even like this, he would never truly harm her.

Rhiannon smiled and nodded. She was eager to see this untamed side of him. Who would he be when the darkness took over? She was ready to find out.

Tristain released her hands and sat up, removing his tunic in one swift move. "Stand up."

She stood in front of him, peering up into those pitch-black eyes, daring him to do his worst.

"Turn around," he commanded.

She did.

Tristain grabbed the blade from her bedside table and jerked it upward, tearing her shirt in half and leaving a sting along her spine where the sharp metal grazed her skin.

She hissed as she became impossibly wetter.

His tongue glided over the line, soothing the sting, sending chills across every inch of her skin. It was juxtaposed by the yank of her pants coming off. All the sensations were making her dizzy with pleasure. She didn't know what to expect from him next, and it thrilled her.

"Step out of them and turn around."

The command rumbled against her ear with his closeness.

When she turned, there was no more than an inch between them. His chest was rising and falling quickly as he looked down at her in only her panties.

"Those are next." He fisted the material at her hip and cut one side.

A grunt left her when it dug into her skin. He repeated the motion on the other side, then ripped them away. Small drops of blood ran down the front of her thighs. He proceeded to lick the flowing scarlet up one leg and then the other, making sure to blow heated breaths across her dripping cunt as he switched sides. The sight of him on his knees before her, the most powerful he'd ever been, made her weak.

The left side of his lips slowly curved into a crooked smile, a single dimple greeting her as he took note of the effect he had on her. He peered up at her with wickedness in his gaze as he lifted one of her legs and put it over his shoulder, forcing her on her tiptoes, given his height. Rhiannon was shaking from anticipation, so ready for him to make her scream his name, to beg him not to stop.

Tristain pressed his nose against her center, parting her just slightly as he inhaled with a growl. "Do you know what you smell like?"

She shook her head silently, hanging on his every word.

"You smell like my damnation, and it's the sweetest thing."

His tongue delved inside her before she could utter a response. She slammed a hand on the small table next to her, the other fisting his hair.

His hands pressed between her thick thighs, pushing them further apart as he feasted on her. But that wasn't enough for him. It was as if he was trying to devour her from the inside out as he lifted her other leg on his shoulder and braced his arms under her. His palms splayed across her lower back as he brought Rhiannon closer to his face. Within minutes, she came on his relentless tongue, her release coating his lips, facial hair, and nose. Marking him as hers.

He pulled back and slowly licked around his lips, taking in her essence gratefully. His gaze was feral as he dropped her legs back to the ground and slowly rose, skimming his teeth along the softest parts of her.

When they finally stood face-to-face, he rubbed his forehead against hers, his features pulling into a grimace. He seemed afraid of taking it too far. But there wasn't anything he could do that would be too much for her. There were no lines he couldn't cross, not when they both had descended into the darkness together.

"What are you waiting for?" she taunted as her fingers wound tightly into the grown-out hair at the nape of his neck. "Take what you want. No one is going to stop you. You won't hurt me, no matter how hard you try."

Black shadows slithered around her. Silky smooth tendrils lifted her arms until they were high above her head and tethered to the aged chandelier. It swung as she struggled against them, testing their strength. She didn't miss how the candles tipped, and their fiery wicks flickered wildly with the movement.

He lifted her legs, wrapping them around his wide waist as he lined up his cock with her slick entrance. A devious light in his gaze was the only warning before he thrust into her to the hilt.

The shock of it had her tugging on his shadowy bonds, which caused the chandelier to tip. Hot wax splattered between them, coating them in stinging droplets that cooled quickly but left red splotches in their wake. Rhiannon shivered, the acute pain heightening her pleasure.

It was her turn to be devious. She shifted herself up and down his length, tilting the chandelier once again. They both groaned with the second splash. They exchanged a wicked smirk between one another as Tristain palmed her ass and lifted her before slamming her down, tugging the makeshift restraints. With each splash and sting, Rhiannon was driven closer to her end. She became mindless, moving herself roughly up and down his cock, as he met her with punishing thrusts. They were both so lost in the connection of their bodies that they didn't hear the creak of the chandelier coming out of the anchors. It wasn't until a cascade of blistering wax flooded down their bodies that they realized what had happened. Tristain moved quickly, slamming her back into the wall. The chandelier barely missed them as it hit the ground and cracked the rotting wood slats.

Candles rolled in all directions, and within seconds, flames shot out across the floor. Tristain sent shadows sprawling across the cottage, snuffing out the fire.

The scent of smoke, sweat, and sex hung heavy in the air as they panted against one another. When Rhiannon looked back up at Tristain, his eyes had gone soft, and the remnants of the Volskruga's magic had been chased away. He was back to himself for the time being.

"Are you okay?" He pushed stray hairs away from her sweat-soaked forehead.

Rhiannon nodded and pointed to the bed. "I think we've let you play enough for today."

He went to lift her off him, but she gripped his hands, halting him. "We're not done, but I'm taking over."

He walked them back to the bed and sat with her poised on his lap. His cock had gone soft in her, but with a few swivels of her hips she could feel him hardening once again.

Tristain let out a groan and leaned back on his palms. "Drop your glamor. I want to see you. All of you."

Her breath shuddered, and her heart raced. She hadn't considered being intimate in this form. Would the feel of her slick in his hands disgust him? Would her monster chase him away?

His hand gripping the back of her neck brought her back to the moment with long soft strokes of his thumb. She conceded with a nod. When she let go, she could feel the magic ripple across her skin. It was painful as the shards of armor poked out of her skin once more, spilling fresh blood down her arms. A thick coat of blood traveled over her skin, but it didn't turn back into the dress. It spread out evenly across her skin and into her hair, her eyes the only thing untouched.

All she could hear was the pounding in her ears as Tristain's eyes traveled over her, taking in her truth. He didn't pull away or grimace in disgust. Instead, he gently grazed her wide thighs with his fingers, up the rolls at her sides, over her breasts, and up to her face.

He cupped her cheeks and pressed a soft kiss to her lips. "You can't scare me away. I love every version of you." He waited until she nodded and then his hands traveled down to her hips, encouraging her to resume riding him.

Her hands found his, holding them tightly as she shifted up and down his length cautiously. Part of her was waiting for him to pull away from her, but each time he sank into her, she became more confident in the depth of his love.

"Don't stop," he begged as he kissed her forehead. "Let go, Rhiannon. I won't let you get too far away from yourself. You can trust me."

Rhiannon pressed him back into the mattress. Her hands rested on his chest, steadying herself as she ground herself against him.

He remained still, simply holding her legs and maintaining that connection. He was at peace, and it allowed her muscles to relax. Letting go, she hung her head back. Her movements became jerkier as she chased her end aggressively. She used him to get herself off without any guilt, and he let her. When she finally crumpled forward in the glow of ecstasy, he sat up with her on his lap and thrust up into her hard and fast. Her hands wrapped around his shoulders, causing the sharp points on her arms to cut up his chest. He didn't flinch away. Instead, he pulled her against him, blood smearing across him. He pounded into her relentlessly until he filled her with his release. When they finally finished, he was a bloody mess. His chest, his face, his hair, all slick with red. It felt like they truly were one in this moment.

Rhiannon pressed herself into him, as if she could force them to disappear into one another.

"I love you."

Those were the final words that passed between them before they collapsed into sleep.

CHAPTER THIRTEEN

The violent clash of churning water was nothing like the slow, sloshing waves Rhiannon was used to hearing when she visited the coast closest to Oakhaven. Much like the freezing temperatures, the sea here was harsh and likely to kill you if you weren't careful.

When they came out the other side of the thick expanse of trees, gray sand greeted them. Large jagged rocks peppered the shoreline and continued out into the surrounding shallows. Heavy fog sank low, making it difficult to make out what lie ahead. If it weren't for the sound of men calling to one another, the scuff of boots on wood, and the groaning heavy cargo being loaded, it would be difficult to imagine there was a port to be found.

"You're sure this is a good idea?"

Rhiannon had never sailed anywhere before, and she wasn't eager to do so. In her nearly thirty years, she'd heard many stories about how unforgiving it could be. She might be more powerful than any man, but she knew she was no match for the force that was the open sea.

"It's the quickest route. We don't have time to waste." Kyra charged ahead toward the docks in the distance.

After several minutes of clumsily walking across the uneven sand, they could finally see the bustling sailors preparing twin ships for their voyages.

"Let's get to it, then." Rhiannon went to take charge, but Kyra gripped her wrist.

"It would be best if Tristain made the arrangements." She continued quickly before Rhiannon could object. "Sailors are not eager to have women aboard their ships, nor are they used to making deals with them. It's absurd, but it will make things much easier."

"Fine." Rhiannon flexed her hands at her side as she let Tristain by.

The idea of having to deal with this level of misogyny for the next several days was going to be the ultimate test of her patience. She had good reason to play nice, though. If they were going to be able to find the answers they needed and free Tristain from his ties to the Volskruga, they needed their help.

Rhiannon watched Tristain carefully as he discussed their passage with whom appeared to be the captain.

The pale, dark-haired man had a strong, proud posture and an air of authority, even from afar. Rhiannon was probably going to hate him. The captain sent several disdainful glances their way as he conversed — or, more aptly, had a heated exchange — with Tristain. Finally, money exchanged hands. It must have been a handsome sum, given the wave of shock that washed over the man as he looked from his hands to Tristain more than once.

She supposed it was worth the cost, whatever it was.

"He agreed?" Kyra asked him when Tristain was in earshot.

"He did." Tristain averted his gaze as he rejoined them.

"Impressive. You must be quite persuasive to convince one of the most superstitious sea captains to allow not one but three women aboard his ship." Her sharp brow arched in accusation.

"Are you insinuating something?"

His tone was brittle with guilt.

Kyra shook her head and turned to Rhiannon. "You're a bad influence, but I guess, in this case, it works in our favor."

"How do I have anything to do with this?" Rhiannon protested.

"I think Tristain learned the art of intimidation from someone."

"Tell me you didn't." Rhiannon turned to Tristain. "How? We didn't even see anything."

Tristain shrugged. "It was just a quick flash, nothing he could prove. But it worked, didn't it?"

"You shouldn't be using your powers. What if it gives the Volskruga a stronger hold on you?"

Worry throttled Rhiannon's vocal cords.

"He wasn't going to allow all three of you. What other choice did I have? I did what I needed to." With finality, he picked up his bag and headed toward the ship.

They followed him, but Rhiannon was disturbed by the ease with which he was using the magic and how it seemed to chase away the warmth from his demeanor more each day. The man she loved was starting to slip away, and it solidified the urgency to get on with this.

Once they'd settled into their two cabins, Rhiannon immediately headed for the deck. Being in the ship's belly was unsettling. Plus, she wanted to observe the crew. Despite Tristain's successful intimidation tactics to get them on board, she wasn't under any illusion that they'd be given a warm welcome.

As suspected, Rhiannon was greeted with grimaces and sideways glances. She paid them no mind as she studiously took in her surroundings. The water below was a bit choppy, but if the clouds rolling in were any indication, it was going to become much rougher as the hours passed.

"Can I help you with something?" a cold voice asked from over her shoulder.

Rhiannon turned to find the captain watching her through narrowed eyes.

She pulled back the black hood of her cloak. "No. Just familiarizing myself with the ship." She made to turn, but he stepped closer.

The urge to pull her dagger was strong.

"No need to get too familiar. You won't be aboard for too long." His gaze rested pointedly on her dagger. He hadn't missed the reflexive movement of her hand.

"I'd say a week or so is a generous amount of time when you're in such tight quarters." She crossed her arms over her chest.

"When you've spent most of your life at sea, that's nothing." He raised his chin in retort.

"Mmm. Well, lucky for me, it'll be but a small stain in my memory." She held out her hand. "We should get acquainted nonetheless. Rhiannon Savatia, you'll be seeing a lot of me."

He sneered down at her hand, as if she were reaching out with a dead fish. "Captain Vadir. I don't think we'll be seeing much of each other. Passengers—especially those of the more delicate variety—are encouraged to remain below deck when possible. It can get dangerous up here."

Waves smacked aggressively against the ship, accentuating the hostility of their exchange.

"Thank you for the suggestion, but I'm not one to shy away from danger. You'll find I'm perfectly capable of defending myself *and* any others who might need protecting." She replaced her hood and turned to leave, casting a dismissive glance over her shoulder as she walked across the deck.

Everything about that man made her hackles rise. Magic stirred beneath her fingertips, restless and keen to fight. But she needed to avoid conflict if possible. They had no other options for getting to their destination, and she didn't want to put them in harm's way by getting them kicked off the ship.

However, if anyone caused trouble, she wouldn't hesitate to make them regret that decision.

Turned out, there wasn't much to see. The crew was busy at work, racing against the angry clouds unfurling across the bruised sky, and two uninhabited coastlines bordered the narrow channel through which they were traveling. With no creatures to be seen below, birds avoiding the clouds, the others resting below deck, it seemed she had no choice but to entertain herself until dinner.

On her way back, she heard raucous laughter erupting from the kitchen, so she decided to investigate. She didn't make her presence known once she was close enough to hear what they were talking about.

"Three women! One is enough to send the ship sinking, let alone three. What was he thinking? He's losing his mind with age."

"Aye. And there's already a mean storm rolling in. Barely came aboard and, already, our luck's gone to the fish."

Rhiannon rolled her eyes at the superstition, as if they hailed in a storm that had been brewing for over a day now.

The first man spoke again.

"Maybe if we throw one overboard, it'll appease the rulers of the deep."

Laughter followed.

"They're not harsh on the eyes, though. Maybe we should keep them for ourselves?" another chimed in.

Rhiannon's hands shook, anger coming to a boil. They were worried about angering whatever lurked below and surviving violent storms. Little did they know she was a lethal entity. And her wrath was a much more immediate concern.

"Maybe the lithe one with the braids and the small blond one. The other one, though—somethin' isn't right with her. Sooner rip your balls off than offer up a kiss, I'm sure o' it."

A wicked smirk curved her lips. At least one of them had some wits about them. Still, she'd need to keep an eye on things.

She'd be damned if one of them hurt her friends. Although, she was confident they could take care of themselves.

Rhiannon had heard enough, not surprised at the pigs they'd be stuck with over the next few days. Sometimes, she truly wondered whether Tristain and Idris were the only good men left. They were the only two she'd ever personally met anyway.

Disgusted but letting it go for now, Rhiannon returned to the room she was sharing with Tristain. Hand on the knob, she halted, hearing the echo of voices coming from Kyra and Samara's room. She knocked quietly, and the door opened almost immediately.

"The crew is full of scumbags. Watch yourselves around them." Rhiannon shut the door behind her and leaned against it. "We can't trust anyone but the four of us."

Kyra nodded. "Figures. The sooner we get off this ship, the better. One of them already inferred that they wouldn't hesitate to throw us off the boat if the storm came down too hard." She rolled her eyes. "I would like to see them try."

"Itching for a fight?" Rhiannon teased.

"I'll leave that to you. Unless I'm attacked, there's no reason to put myself in unnecessary danger. I want to make it back to my family in one piece. I hardly got to enjoy settling back into life with them."

Her gaze became wistful.

"You'll see them again." Rhiannon squeezed the other woman's shoulder. "I wish you would have stayed behind with them. You didn't need to take the risk."

Kyra shook her head, her braid swishing gently with the movement. "You know why I'm here. I want to see this through. I need to make sure the people I care about are safe. There's too much that can go wrong, and if we don't find a solution, it's my people who are in the greatest danger."

Rhiannon didn't miss the sheen blurring her amber eyes, but she simply nodded and then turned her attention to Samara.

"I wasn't about to stay behind. But my reasons aren't as selfless. I've been trapped my whole life. I want to see what's out there—even if it's a dangerous journey. I need to do this. I've been the dutiful daughter so long that I don't even know who I really am." Samara twisted a lock of hair around her finger. "It's not that I don't miss my family. It's just that I need time to be me."

Rhiannon could understand that. She'd never been one to thirst for adventure, so content with her own life . . . before. However, this thing within her made her restless. She wanted answers, and she needed to take action. She couldn't just sit around anymore. Looking at the two women so different from her—different from each other, even—she truly appreciated them for what they brought to the table. Kyra's commitment to her priorities and unyielding self-assurance. Samara's determination to find herself and hunger to learn about the world she'd been blindfolded to.

Kyra was hunting.

Samara was searching.

Rhiannon was chasing.

But they were all headed in the same direction, and that was what mattered. With a shared goal, she was confident they could figure this out. For themselves and for the ones they loved.

Rolling thunder shook the boards beneath their feet, tearing Rhiannon out of her comforting thoughts. The storm was coming.

From above, the crew yelled commands to one another as they prepared for what came next.

A harsh knock came from outside.

Rhiannon cracked the door open to see the captain.

He grimaced. "Stay in your rooms unless we tell you otherwise. You'll be more of a liability on deck. We'll bring dinner to your rooms." Without waiting for their agreement, he turned on his heel and headed up the creaky wooden stairs.

Following him out, Rhiannon returned to her and Tristain's room. She would be lying if she said she wasn't worried. She didn't fear any man, but the ocean was a whole other story. A force of nature like that didn't bend to shadows or blood. They were all, equally, at its mercy.

CHAPTER FOURTEEN

T he storm hadn't been as tumultuous as they'd
    expected, but the choppy waves and rain lasted the
    next few days of their voyage. Trying to stay out of
the way of the crew and their spiteful captain, the four of them
had remained below deck in their rooms for the most part.
They only had to make it two more days without incident,
and Rhiannon was becoming increasingly optimistic.

That was until Tristain fell ill. It wasn't sea sickness but
something else that left him lethargic and weaker at an
alarming rate. He drifted in and out of sleep, and a sheen of
icy sweat coated his skin. He could hardly eat, only waking to
consume just enough to sustain him.

The night before, he'd groaned and moaned all night,
vocalizing his pain and torment. They even had the ship's
resident doctor look at him, but he chalked it up to an
unknown virus.

Rhiannon did everything she could to comfort him. Her
heart tugged at the purple-gray rings around his eyes and
his uncharacteristic disinterest. Without any answers or
authority, all she could do was hope he would start feeling
better soon. If he wasn't recovering by the time they made
shore, it would drastically complicate their plans. He was
the only one familiar with Saldova. More than that, though,

Rhiannon worried it could be something potentially life-threatening.

By sunset, his skin had become paler, and his teeth were chattering constantly. He seemed so frail she decided to venture above deck to see if there were more blankets and anything else she could use to make him more comfortable. Rhiannon ran into a crew member who directed her to the captain's quarters for accommodations. Despite her disdain for him, she was willing to ask him a favor if it was for Tristain.

She rapped her knuckles against the thick oak door that featured a brass helm.

"Come in," the low voice from the other side beckoned.

Rhiannon braced herself, plastering a pleasant smile on her face, then entered.

His gray eyes flicked up at her from the parchment and coins on his desk. "What do I owe the . . . pleasure?"

"I wanted to request more blankets and perhaps another visit from your doctor."

"You don't look ill to me." The captain turned his attention back to the task in front of him.

"Yes, well, one of my companions is, and I would like to ensure that they are taken care of, especially because we have a fair distance to travel after we make shore tomorrow."

"Who?" His attention returned to her.

"What's it matter?"

The hairs on the back of her neck prickled to attention. She didn't like his prying.

"Do you want what you've asked for or not?"

"The man I'm sharing a room with."

"Mmm." The captain rose from his seat. "Worried you and your companions will be left to your own defenses?" He rounded the desk, taking several measured steps that forced her uncomfortably close to the wall in the small dark space.

"We're perfectly capable of caring for ourselves, I assure you." She watched his expression change from thoughtful to menacing.

"I doubt that very much. But what say we get to the truth of it?" He lunged forward and fisted his hand in the back of her hair.

Rhiannon flinched despite herself. His anger had taken her by surprise, and she hadn't come prepared. Finding herself in this position, where someone was trying to make her feel small, reminded her of that fateful day.

Once again, she was cornered by a man who thought it would be easy to take from her. She found those old feelings of shame and weakness stirring with her. Rhiannon held them beneath her composure.

Unlike with Silas all those months ago, she wasn't helpless against him. She could easily overcome the captain, but such an action would set off a chain of events that could end poorly for everyone aboard this ship.

While her mind raced through the paths forward, she allowed him to push her through the door and out onto the deck. She expected him to stop once he made it to the center and caught his men's attention, but the disgruntled captain kept walking until he reached the side of the boat. He forced Rhiannon over until her chest was pressed against the wood and her head was facing down to the turbulent water below.

"It would be so easy to throw you overboard, to rid this ship of your cursed presence. Have your friends follow you next. I'd save your sickly companion for last and make him watch you all suffer." He spoke through gritted teeth. "Or I could take you here and make an example of you to my men. Drag him out here and make him watch. Prove to them that we cannot be bought or intimidated."

Rhiannon's pulse hammered so hard it was nauseating. His vile threat rang in her ears like chimes caught in a storm. No one spoke about her like that. No one threatened her like that. Her head spun as images of her ripping out his tongue for the way he spoke of her and decimating this ship to a sea of scattered planks bombarded the failing barricade of control she was trying to hold up. The magic thrashed so violently within her it threatened to tear its way out.

Impatiently, he pushed her harder against the wood, and his forceful handling sent her failing restraint over the edge. Rhiannon twisted herself out of his hold with ease, faced him as she dropped her glamor, and allowed her true form to take over. Magic at her fingertips and skin coated in blood, she grabbed him by the throat and lifted him off the ground. Her clawed fingers twitched with the urge to puncture his throat and watch him choke on his own blood, then force him to repeat those filthy words back to her again and again until he drowned. Such a pretty picture. It soothed her enough to bring her boiling rage back to a more manageable simmer.

For now.

"I tried to warn you." Rhiannon assessed him at her mercy, while he dangled from her fingers like a foolish puppet. "You couldn't just let us be. You had to push your luck." Rhiannon sighed. "I didn't intend to shed blood. I was trying to be on my best behavior—really, I was—but here we are."

Unsheathed metal sung through the air as several members of the crew drew their swords and circled her and their captain.

"I wouldn't come any closer if I were you." She flicked her gaze over the surrounding group. "I can crush the life out of him before you reach me. And then, well"—Rhiannon laughed—"then I'll be forced to make an ultimatum that you'll, of course, reject. One thing will lead to another, and this deck will be littered with bodies. And while I'd take great pleasure in making you sorry you ever considered laying a hand on me, it would put a quite a wrench in my plan to prove to my friends that I'm in control of my anger." Rhiannon slowly applied more pressure to the captain's throat until he was kicking and clawing desperately. "So, what do we say? Your captain pays for his indiscretions, and you lot make sure we reach our destination safely?"

"This crew is loyal. We don't sway to the whims of witches." A gray-haired man stepped forward, his sword raised.

"A witch?" She laughed, the simplicity of the title amusing her. "I'm the fucking embodiment of a lifetime of swept away injustices and pent-up rage. I'm you worst nightmare come true, *a powerful woman* who isn't afraid of a single one of you. And you'd do well to grovel for my mercy."

The man lunged as the last word left her lips.

Rhiannon pivoted, holding the asphyxiating captain off to her side while the other hand directed bloody tendrils to the man's sword, ripping it out of his hands and sending it flying to the other end of the deck. His lips quivered as he faced her, stripped of his weapon. Just like most men, he crumbled when he no longer had tools of violence at his disposal.

Rhiannon gripped him by the shirt collar and pulled him to her face. "You should have chosen mercy." She slammed her fist through his chest and ripped his cowardly heart from its cavity.

Satisfaction melted the tension within her as she watched the tragic expressions flick across his face as his brain caught up with what just happened. His mouth gaped uselessly in his final moments. Finally, the light left his eyes, and she tossed aside the organ. She shoved him backward, and his body landed on the moist wood with a thud that resounded among the silence settling around her.

"Would anyone else like to put on a show of bravado or have the tides of loyalty changed?"

One by one, the men around her sheathed their swords, casting apologetic glances at their captain, who had long since taken his last breath. Rhiannon walked to the edge of the ship and held him over the crashing waves. She grabbed the feathered hat off his head and stomped it beneath her boot before finally dropping him into the raging water below.

"Now, who will be in charge of ensuring we make it to Saldova without delay?" She turned in a slow circle, waiting for someone to volunteer. When none of them did, she pointed to the short red-haired man closest to her. "You'll take up the captain's responsibilities."

He shook his head wordlessly.

Rhiannon took his tanned cheeks in a tight grip, her long sharp nails cutting into the freckled flesh. "You'll do it, and you'll do it well. Remember, we make it the rest of this journey undisturbed, and you all get to keep breathing. Try anything, and, well, you've seen what happens to those who don't heed my warnings."

With that, she turned on her heel and left them to scramble among themselves. Rhiannon didn't let her magic go back to sleep just yet. First, she'd get what she had come up here for.

She stopped the next man who walked past her. "Send down the doctor, more of that vegetable soup with *fresh* bread, and any extra blankets you can find."

He nodded so vigorously she could have sworn she'd heard his teeth clack.

Before he was out of earshot, she called over her shoulder, "And don't try anything foolish."

His eyes widened.

Finally, she allowed her power to slip back beneath her skin. A smile tugged at her lips as she strutted down the stairs.

Fire ale paled in comparison to the way their fear made her head swim. However, her glee was chased away when she entered her room to find Tristain sitting on the edge of the bed with his head in his hands. When his eyes met hers, Rhiannon went cold, seeing that the dark veins beneath his skin had become much more prominent, draining his warm brown skin to an eerie gray pallor.

The puzzle pieces seemed to come together for them. The lethargy, the sickness, the change in demeanor. It was happening, just like the Volskruga had warned. She just didn't think it would take hold of him so quickly.

CHAPTER FIFTEEN

T he next afternoon, they made port on the northern coast of Saldova. The vibrant landscape of multi-colored flowers and bountiful green trees spanning as far as Rhiannon could see would have been a warm welcome if it hadn't been for their dire circumstances. Tristain was so weak he couldn't walk on his own, but between Rhiannon and Samara, they could support his weight as they set out to find the nearest inn. With plentiful accommodations for the busy port, it didn't take them long. The lodgings were modest, but the beds were made up with their freshly washed linens, and they'd get two meals with their stay. Once Tristain was settled in the room—albeit clumsily—Rhiannon prepared to head back out. Watching Tristain fade from her these last few days had occupied her every thought. She'd explored every potential source of his affliction, and there was one possibility she needed to rule out. She couldn't ignore the similarities between how Silas had begun to break down and how Tristain was withering away before her very eyes. If this sickness was due to the Volskruga's need for sustenance, then she would remedy the situation. If that didn't fix him . . . No. She couldn't think about that.

Impending despair tried to claw its way above the undercurrent of her wayward thoughts so it could drag her down into its depths. But she had to stay focused. She wasn't losing him. Whatever had to be done, Rhiannon would do it.

Yet, her conscience stirred in the back of her mind. Tristain wouldn't willingly kill someone, not even if it meant saving his own life—*especially* not if it was to save his life. His moral compass would point him over the edge of a cliff, and if it were what he deemed the right and good choice, he would step off without regret. She loved his pure heart, but not when it threatened to stop beating for her.

Being faced with that decision would be heartbreaking for Tristain. He wasn't selfish enough. So, Rhiannon wouldn't give him the choice. She'd make it for him. Her hands were coated in blood, permanently stained with it. A bit more wouldn't hurt. Taking lives had become a natural part of existence for her. Rhiannon didn't lie awake at night, haunted by their faces; she couldn't even remember most of them. And if she had to choose between losing Tristain or him being angry and disgusted with her, then so be it. It was a price she was willing to pay. He would continue living, and he could breathe easier and sleep more peacefully if he had her to carry most of the blame.

With her decision solidified, Rhiannon closed the teal door softly behind her and set out to find someone for Tristain to kill.

The fine white sand crunched and shifted beneath her boots as she traveled back toward where they'd come into port. Rhiannon didn't approach the swarms of sailors busy unloading their ships. Instead, she stopped where she would be cloaked by the surrounding lush greenery. Waiting, she observed them closely as she looked for someone she could pick off and use as a test for her theory. Her heart sped up as two men walked over, but they stopped just a few feet short of where she lurked.

"How long till your next voyage?" an older man with rich brown hair and similarly toned skin asked his much younger companion.

"Ship out first thing in the morning. How about you?" The man smiled, creating creases in his reddened yet pale complexion.

"I'll be sticking around a while. Money was good enough to take care of the necessities, and I want to spend some time with the wife and kids. They grow so quickly."

The younger man laughed. "Well, if that's what suits you. I'll be spreading my seed along the Larindian coast. The ladies will be lining up to see if all those songs about charming sailors are true."

Rhiannon rolled her eyes at the comment. He wasn't the worst of the men she'd encountered, but she needed a quick solution, and he was as good a pick as any. It was nothing personal, but with his sailor's lifestyle and no family waiting for him back home, it was safe to assume it wouldn't raise too much concern if he went missing.

She waited until the two men said their goodbyes. When the older man was out of sight, she made her move.

Rhiannon wrapped her arm around his throat and shoved a dagger against his back while he was distracted by watching his companion walk away. He gasped, but no one could hear them as she pulled him back into the dense cluster of trees. He grunted, kicked, and sputtered threats all the way back to the other end of forest, but his protests were no match for her inhuman strength.

Rhiannon hesitated, looking around to check that no one was coming, before shoving him forward toward the inn. "If you try anything, I will gut you before a scream of pain leaves your lips." She gripped his cheeks until her fingers ground against his teeth, forcing him to face her as she allowed magic to flash in her eyes. His skin paled. "Now, walk." She shoved him up the stairs.

Luckily, no one was around, since it was between mealtimes.

After opening the door to her and Tristain's room, she thrust him through, sending him flying to his knees. He glared up at her from the floor but didn't say anything.

"Get up."

He didn't budge, so she strode over to him and grabbed a fist of hair, forcing him to his feet. When she did, his fist connected with her rib cage. If this had been before, the blow would have knocked the air out of her, but it just pissed her off.

Rhiannon picked him up by his throat, crushing hard enough to make him gasp and kick. When his face went blue, she threw him on the ground next to Tristain's bed.

Finally, he roused.

"What's going on?" His unfocused, black-rimmed eyes were swollen slits as he looked at her, confused.

"I'm fixing this." She threw her dagger on the bed next to him. "Stab him."

Tristain sat up slowly, concern pulling at his features. "I'm not stabbing an innocent man."

He was speaking to her as if she'd completely lost sight of reality.

Rhiannon growled and fisted his collar. "Stab him. Now. Don't play the hero. You have to do this to save yourself."

"Why would this help anything?"

"The Volskruga needs sustenance, and you haven't provided. Without another source, I think it's started siphoning from you."

Tristain's eyes lit with understanding, but he still didn't move. His resistance wasn't a surprise, but it shredded the last of her patience. How could he not see that there was no other way?

Her mind was a destructive storm of emotions, driving her determination to become frantic. The lifelessness in his gaze was infuriating and terrifying. Rhiannon desperately wanted Tristain to fight for his life. She wanted him to fight to keep her. But this was his limit.

Rhiannon couldn't accept that.

I will not lose him. I will not lose him. I will not lose him.

She released him, detangling her fingers from the rumpled fabric, and returned her hand to the man's throat. "I will torture him to the brink of death over and over until you do it. Do you want that on your conscience?"

Tristain shook his head silently as he watched Rhiannon strangle the man. When his eyes rolled back, she released the pressure, allowing him to gulp air. As soon as his breathing returned to normal, she started again.

"Enough!" Tristain commanded, his hand latching around her wrist.

The pressure was barely noticeable.

She didn't stop. Instead, she watched with relief as the black veins coursed beneath his skin under the duress, and his firm grip became much more effective. "That's it. Get mad. Fucking fight for your life."

"This is too far. I won't do it. There has to be another way." His eyes pleaded with her.

"I wouldn't ask this of you if I thought there was. For fuck's sake, please do it. You've lived a lifetime of good, and you can spend the rest of it helping others if that's what you need to do to live with yourself, but I swear it right now, none of us are leaving this room until he's dead. If I'm wrong, you can be furious with me later. I'm certain I can live with your anger, but I know that I can't bear this greedy, shit world without you. If you leave me to spare this man's life, I will be sure to take ten, a hundred times that, just to spite you." She watched the emotions war within him. "Do this for me, please."

Desperation clawed out of her, tearing her tough skin and reaching deep into that bleeding heart of his.

Tristain wavered, picking up the blade and turning it over. But there was no conviction in the act, only more uncertainty.

"It's the only way, I'm sure of it," she coaxed.

Another long moment passed, and he didn't move. Her nerves were frayed, and she could see him slipping further away. Before he was lost on her, she took matters into her own hands—like always. Before Tristain could register the motion, Rhiannon had gripped his wrist with her superior strength and forced him to plunge the dagger into the man's throat. Blood spouted and coated their hands in the heat of his fading life force.

When the man had finally bled out, she let him drop to the ground and released Tristain's wrist. He glared down at her, horror and anger lighting a fire within him. His lips quivered.

She could accept he was enraged with her. It was a small price to pay. But what he couldn't do was make her feel guilty for saving his life. They didn't have the luxury of guilt and regret in the harsh reality they found themselves in.

"You had no right to do that. That man was innocent," Tristain grit out.

Already, there was more vitality in his voice, but the accusation made his words heavy.

"We were all innocent once." Rhiannon dismissed his irritation and ripped her blade from the man's throat. "You're innocent in all this. Aren't you? Just a pawn in this twisted web of destruction."

Tristain whipped his gaze to hers, a flash of spite and denial greeting her. "This wasn't necessary. It wasn't your choice to make. You crossed the line."

"Don't you dare fucking do that. You asked me to choose you. And I did. You asked me to give myself fully to you. To promise you forever. And I did. I'll be damned if I allow you to pretend you didn't know what that meant. I showed you my razor-sharp edges, my monstrous heart, and my unyielding mind, and you told me you loved it, that you loved all of it. So, tell me you were lying. Were you?" Rhiannon's voice cracked. She knew that wasn't the truth but asking it still split that crack in her heart a bit wider. "You can't. You won't. Because if there's one thing you are, it's good and honest. And even though I taint the honor you bear so proudly upon your shoulders, you can't deny that you love me exactly as I am. Brutal. Unforgiving. And merciless."

Her nail stabbing into his chest accented the end of her furious speech.

Rhiannon took a steadying breath and turned her back to him, desperately clinging to the last of her control. Knowing how betrayed he would feel and seeing it in his gaze and feeling it in the weight of his words were two completely different things.

She'd stolen a choice from him, and she wasn't proud of it. He had every right to be furious. She would be. Yet, it was so much worse than that because she'd hurt him.

"I . . ." she started.

"Don't. I need you to leave. I can't be around you like this. Not right now."

Tristain felt as distant as he sounded in that moment. The usual warmth in his tone had frozen over.

Frustration, anger, rejection, hurt, and a twinge of guilt created a flurry of uncertainty within her. But she locked it down, refusing to show vulnerability. She didn't deserve his comfort and couldn't stand the idea of him not offering it.

"You should clean that up." Without a glance back at him, Rhiannon left the room, her hands shaking at her sides.

She needed a fucking drink.

Tristain could fight it all he wanted, but the fact that he was able to stand on his own after days of barely lifting his head off the pillow justified her actions in her own eyes, and that was enough. It had to be.

The full dining room buzzed with energy as people tucked into their meals. The room was welcoming with its driftwood fixtures, vibrant blue-and-green hues, and sea glass accents. The air carried the scent of warm bread and the savory saltiness of the fish most guests were eating.

Rhiannon was preoccupied with the sweetness of the cooked yellow fruit in front of her. Despite the surrounding obnoxiousness, Rhiannon felt at peace for the first time in days. She didn't just think that had to do with the change in Tristain's circumstances. It was lighter here. But that peace was disrupted by two plates clattering on the table in front of her. She looked up to find Kyra and Samara sliding onto the bench.

Rhiannon noticed both had brought garb made for a warmer climate.

Kyra wore a light-yellow sleeveless linen top that emphasized her toned muscles and complimented the reddish hue of her brown skin.

Samara wore a slate-gray tunic that stopped just below the elbow and complemented her ivory pallor.

While a breeze came off the water, it wasn't anywhere near the frigid temperatures they'd come from.

Rhiannon noted that she'd need to check her bag for something more appropriate or find somewhere to purchase what she needed for the next few days.

Returning her focus to the present, she asked, "Did you two finally get some sleep?"

"Thankfully," Kyra answered before she sipped from her dry red wine. "It's amazing how much easier it is to drift off when your bed isn't swaying beneath you."

Laughing, Rhiannon nodded.

"I asked the innkeeper whether there was a doctor around," Samara chimed in, tucking a strand of blond hair behind her ear.

"Oh." Rhiannon smirked at them, swelling with pride. "We won't be needing one. Tristain is feeling much better."

Both women looked at her suspiciously.

"It appears that, even though the Volskruga doesn't have quite the same hold on him as it did on Silas, it's still powerful enough to drain him if he doesn't meet its needs."

"Tristain killed someone in his condition?" Kyra leveled her with an arched brow.

"Technically, yes, with some help," Rhiannon admitted.

Samara scoffed.

"Would you have rather I let him wither away?"

"No. But you can't just force your decisions on people." Samara stood and slammed her palms down, earning them concerned looks from several people.

"I can do whatever I want with what's mine. If Tristain won't do what needs to be done, then I will." Rhiannon dropped her voice but matched her posture. "I will not let the man I love slip through my fingers because of his own hardheadedness."

"An honorable death is his to choose," Samara shot back.

"That death would have been anything but honorable. Could you imagine Tristain's soul confined to the Vrugian Woods in eternal servitude to the Volskruga? That is not what he wants. And he was not in his right mind to make that decision for himself, so I did. If you have a problem with that, then that's too damn bad. He belongs to me, he *promised*, and I will act accordingly."

Samara snarled her disgust. "You two are sick. I wish he left when he had the chance." With that, she left the dining hall.

Rhiannon turned her attention to Kyra. "Are you going to berate me, too?"

Kyra shook her head. "There's no point. What's done is done. I just hope we can free you both from the grip of this cursed magic once and for all, for all of our sakes."

Rhiannon knew she should voice her agreement, but she didn't know if she wanted it to be gone. Did she want to control it? Yes. But be rid of it completely? She wasn't so sure after how things transpired on the voyage. Perhaps there was a way to wield it more purposely. But she couldn't tell Kyra as much, so she simply buried her nod in a gulp of wine.

Kyra was too observant to miss the lack of an answer, but she didn't press it. They all had their own interests to protect and plans in motion.

"Will we go to Tristain's home tomorrow, then?"

"He should be back to his normal self. I don't think it's far from here. Saldova is a small country." Rhiannon fought back the twang of anxiety she felt at the thought of meeting Tristain's mother and father.

What if they hated her? Would he abandon her? Would he be proud to have her by his side? Nothing in his actions had ever indicated it would be any different, but she knew how much he loved and respected his family.

When she lifted her gaze from her half-eaten plate, she was met with Kyra's knowing smirk. "What's so funny?"

"You're nervous."

A teasing lilt sprang in her words that bristled Rhiannon's pride.

"Nervous? Me? Absolutely not. What would I have to be nervous about?"

She didn't even sound convincing to her own ears.

Kyra laughed at Rhiannon's expense, her bright smile easing the tension in Rhiannon's shoulders. "You were willing to face the Volskruga and Silas on your own, but you're worried about meeting his parents? This will be interesting."

"I've never done this before." Rhiannon shrugged. "What if they don't think I'm good enough for him?"

"Rhiannon, you're not going there to ask for their permission to marry. We're there to find Silas's journals. I don't think it's going to be an issue. Maybe they won't even know you two are together." She leaned forward. "Besides, would it even stop you if they didn't approve?"

Humor danced in her golden-brown eyes.

Kyra was right. That was their purpose of coming here. *That* was their priority.

Still, part of her even wanted their approval. Maybe then, she'd feel deserving of him.

CHAPTER SIXTEEN

They hadn't spoken the night prior, but Tristain watched her closely as she got ready. A mixture of appreciation and apprehension swirled in his demeanor.

"What happens now?"

"We do what we have to do to keep you healthy until we find out how to end your connection to the Volskruga." Rhiannon turned to him, needing to see his reaction.

As expected, he grimaced. "I don't know if I can do that."

"Then, I will be the hand that guides your blade."

He stood and approached her. With a heavy sigh, he leaned his forehead against hers. "I can't ask you to do that."

"You're not asking, I'm offering. I already have so much blood on my hands. What's a few more bodies?"

Tristain's calloused thumb stroked her cheek as he held her stare. "I don't want that for you."

"I lost the choice in what I wanted before we met, but I've embraced what I've been forced to become. Let me take care of you. That is what I want. That is the choice I've made willingly." She placed one hand around the back of his neck and the other against his heart. "Anyone who tries to take you from me will die a painful death, and I will eagerly take on that task."

Those warm eyes assessed her, searching for the signs of a lie. For anything that might turn to resentment. But the truth of it rattled in the depths of her soul. She would gladly sacrifice whoever she needed to keep him safe. She might have lost herself to the Volskruga's interference, but she would not lose the man she loved.

Tristain's lips found hers as he pressed her back against the wall. He wrapped one of her legs around his waist, grinding into her, so she could feel just how much he appreciated her. "When you talk like that, it makes it impossible not to want to worship you."

Rhiannon's eyes flicked open, the feral monster within her purring. That internal satisfaction radiated, bringing a smile to her lips.

She raised her hands to his shoulders and pressed him downward. "So, worship me, then."

He obliged with a satisfied gleam in his eyes. She loved how Tristain was always ready to please her.

Chills erupted over her at the sight of him on his knees for her. She forced her magic forward, and her clothes shifted to the warm film of blood that now felt like a second skin. Rhiannon felt powerful like this but even more so as Tristain embraced her form, hands caressing the sides of her dimpled thighs in rapt devotion.

He dug his fingers into the fat of her legs as he positioned her to bury his face in her cunt.

She dug her toes into his back as he licked her from entrance to clit with a reverence that made her eyes roll back.

Patient strokes quickly turned into desperate devouring as his tongue delved deep inside her, and his thumb rubbed her clit in punishingly delicious circles. Her hands dug into his curls as she pressed him against her, forcing him to give her everything he had.

"Don't you dare fucking stop," she gasped out as he followed her lead.

"I wouldn't dream of it," he whispered, the words vibrating against her flesh. "All I want is to make you feel like I do when you take care of me."

It was his final prayer before he returned to his task. Tristain brought his thumbs to the side of her pussy, stretching her wider for him, allowing him to work his tongue over every inch of her.

The skilled attentiveness had her back arching off the wall and her hips rolling against his handsome face.

Understanding how desperate she was to come, he placed a harsh bite on her clit that had her falling apart, weeping grateful tears of blood. He didn't retreat, gently licking and sucking at her pussy, until the aftershocks of her orgasm had come and gone.

When strength returned to her, she used his hair to drag his face away. What she saw had her clenching air.

His face was covered in blood.

Her blood.

Her power.

Rhiannon fisted the collar of his shirt, and she hauled him to his feet. She licked up the center of his lips, tasting herself. All control unraveled from within her as she switched their positions, pinning him to the wall. She shredded his shirt from his body in one swift move. His pants suffered the same fate as she freed his thick cock and ran her blood-coated fingers up and down the shaft.

Tilting her head down, she let her spit drip onto the head before she dropped to her knees.

"A devout worshipper always earns their goddess's favor." Rhiannon tore her gaze away from his and ran her tongue along his length, savoring the taste.

Circling the tip of his cock, she gathered the moisture beading there before taking him fully. Her head bobbed, and her cheeks hollowed as she sucked him with the same fervor he'd shown her. It wasn't just that he pleased her; it was that his trust and love for her shone through with every touch. She wanted to show him how grateful she was for all he'd given to her.

Every moment he stood by her, every time he chose to love her unconditionally, it was all that ran through her mind as she took his cock deep inside her throat and worked eagerly to bring him to his end. And when he did come, she drank down every drop of him, enjoying the taste and evidence of how alive he still was.

When she finished, Tristain brought her in for another crushing kiss that made her knees weaken. "I'm not finished showing my gratitude." He pushed off the wall and sat at the end of the bed. "Come here."

She approached him, but with a spin of his finger, he instructed her to turn around. Facing the mirror on the wall across from them, she lowered herself onto his lap, slowly taking the thick head and length of his cock inch by inch. When she was fully seated, he lifted her thighs over his legs and used his hands on her inner thighs to spread her as wide as he could.

Rhiannon was transfixed by the image of them covered in blood, and her cunt stretched around him as he filled her so perfectly. Tristain's eyes appraised every inch of her full figure as he slowly pumped into her.

"Put your hands here." He moved hers to replace his own.

Rhiannon gripped her thighs until skin was peeking out between her fingers with the pressure.

Meanwhile, Tristain rested one hand on her lower stomach, pressing against the plush roll. The other wrapped gently around her throat in a reassuring, possessive hold. She admired how he held her, his arms flexing with exertion.

"Look at how well we fit together." His breath tickled her neck as he thrusted forcefully into her. "Do you see how well I can support you? How I can uplift you?" Another thrust had her moaning desperately. "How I belong to you and will gladly devote myself to following you to the ends of this world, love you without judgment, and fuck you exactly how you need every single time."

The last three words were punctuated with thrusts that left her shaking.

She nodded, closing her eyes as he slowed once again, allowing her to revel in the sensation of him gliding in and out of her.

"Open your eyes, Rhiannon. I want to see the truth of it when you say it."

She did, burrowing her deep brown gaze into the fiery orange of his. "Yes." She choked out the words. "Yes, I see it."

He pressed harder against her lower stomach. "Can you feel it like I can? I was made for you."

"Yes." The words fell effortlessly from her lips as she watched his hand wander down to her clit where his thumb circled. "Fuck, yes. You were made for me."

Her eyes were drawn to the straining muscles of his thick thighs as he pounded into her from below, picking up his pace to rapidly drive her to the edge.

Rhiannon's hands left her thighs and traveled to her nipples, which she tweaked harshly. She screamed out in pleasure as he placed a synchronized bite against her throat, her orgasm ripping through her.

When she came back to herself, she wrapped her arm around the back of Tristain's head, her nails digging into his scalp as she circled her hips. Within moments, Tristain's movements became choppy and rushed as he spilled into her.

They sat there like that, with him sunk deep inside her, watching themselves breathe heavily. Tristain wrapped his arms around her soft middle and pressed a kiss to her shoulder. "Never doubt my love for you, Rhi, because that is the one thing that could undo me. The one thing I can't continue to forgive."

"I won't."
It was a whisper on her lips but a promise she would keep.

Chapter Seventeen

T ristain's family home was only an hour on horseback from where they'd been staying. They were able to secure a few horses they'd paid extra to have someone fetch in a few days' time.

Rhiannon's stomach was a battlefield of warring emotions as they traveled. What would his parents think of her? They were so important to him. What would it mean if they didn't like her? She already knew she didn't deserve him. What if they saw that, too?

She worried over the impression she would make on his family, yes. But more than anything, the looming terror of what awaited them in Silas's journals was of far greater concern. Even after his death, he still held sway over her emotions and actions. It disgusted her, but that didn't stop the unease swimming through her gut when faced with relying on his words to help her find answers.

Kyra's voice broke her train of thought. "Why do you look like you're going to be sick?"

"What if we don't find any answers and are stuck yet again?"

"If the answers aren't here, we keep looking." Samara came up to her other side and squeezed her hand in a brief but comforting gesture.

Her stomach settled ever so slightly. Despite their disagreements, it was reassuring that Samara and Kyra always had her back. The only other people who'd ever been here for her like this were Jade and Idris, and the distance she'd put between hurt something fucking awful if she lingered on it too long.

Instead of responding, Rhiannon enjoyed the soothing balm their steady presence in her life had become. As they passed through endless trees, she took in the landscape of Saldova. It was lush with vivid greenery, and the rumbling of waves could be heard every so often as they ventured southwest. A balminess hung in the air that made her legs heat in her boots. She was glad she'd had the forethought to pack sleeveless tunics.

Finally, a beautiful home came into view. It wasn't nearly as big as her family's, but it wasn't modest, either. It was a single-story structure comprising a rust exterior with soft cream accents, complemented by the rich green plant life surrounding it. The soft, sound nature of the place resonated with so much of who Tristain was. He carried this place with him down to his marrow.

They crossed an open gate that was only a few feet taller than they were on horseback. Not a means to keep people out so much as a welcome to the stunning property that the Terrowin family resided on. The warmth radiating from the land embraced her, and it made Rhiannon wish they were here for other, happier reasons that would give them an excuse to extend their visit.

Maybe someday. It was a dangerously hopeful thought.

Tristain rode up next to her. "What do you think?"

His gaze was tentative as he awaited her answer.

"It's beautiful. I can see why you speak so fondly of home," Rhiannon answered honestly.

She was rewarded with a bright smile that touched his eyes. *Fuck.* That was the smile that had undone her. The one that had claimed her heart. She didn't see enough of it these days.

They stopped in front of a stable area off to the side of the property. Once they'd all dismounted, the stable hand greeted them, whom Tristain embraced affectionately and introduced to them as Stefan. They then made their way to the main house.

Rhiannon didn't miss the way Tristain's shoulders tensed. "What's wrong?"

He stopped dead in his tracks. "I hadn't thought about the fact that I was going to have to tell my mother that Silas was"—he swallowed hard—"gone. She's going to be devastated. Even though he was distant and unkind, she still loved him. He was her son. She didn't know just how horrible he'd become."

"Will you tell her that Rhiannon killed him?" Samara chimed in unhelpfully.

Rhiannon glared at her but squeezed Tristain's hand. She hated how she wished he wouldn't.

Selfish. Selfish. Selfish. She chastised herself.

Surely, then, his mother would hate her. But she didn't voice her opinion. That wouldn't be fair to ask of him. She'd already taken so much from him, from *them. Fuck.* Surely, they couldn't love her like he did. They'd see her for what she was. *Murderer.* Just like Silas had said. They'd warn him away. They'd save him from the impending destruction that was her love.

"No. I won't tell her the details. I don't want to decimate her memory of Silas with visions of his death that will only haunt her. She's suffered enough in her life. I'll tell her it was an accident. But I'll wait until the right moment."

The three women exchanged a glance, clearly uncomfortable with the situation, but they followed Tristain's lead as they entered his home.

A stunning middle-aged woman with red-mahogany hair and a generous figure sat in front of the window across the room with a book in hand and tea sitting in front of her. The creak of the door drew her eyes up, which transformed from surprised to elated when she saw Tristain. Within seconds, she had crossed the room and thrown her arms around his neck, embracing her son in a warm hug. He lifted her off the ground and kissed her cheek, returning her excitement.

"You didn't write home. We weren't expecting you." His mother looked around at Rhiannon, Kyra, and Samara, assessing his companions. "And you brought company. Please introduce us."

"Sorry, Mother, it was a bit of a last-minute decision." He hugged her against his side. "This is Kyra, Samara, and Rhiannon"—he pulled Rhiannon toward him and placed a chaste kiss on her lips—"the woman I'm in love with."

Rhiannon felt her face grow hot at the unexpected introduction and display of affection, but she tried to recover quickly.

"It's so nice to meet you." She extended her hand, but his mother pulled her into a hug. Rhiannon told her limbs to relax when they stiffened.

She didn't want to make a bad impression, but she didn't know how to hug casually. Besides, hadn't she wanted this kind of approval?

When Tristain's mother released Rhiannon from her embrace, she kept her hand. "I am so happy to see my son smiling again. The pleasure is all mine, dear. I'm sorry his father couldn't be here to meet you, but he had to tend to a trade matter up north."

That heat crawled down Rhiannon's neck and chest, uncomfortable with the attention and endearment, given what she'd done to her other son. "Thank you. I'm sorry we sprung this visit on you."

"It's fine. We have plenty of room." She turned to Tristain. "Your companions can stay in Silas's room. We're not expecting him back."

Rhiannon's gaze whipped to Samara and Kyra. She felt bad for them, but she wasn't going to be the one to say something about how uncomfortable that would be. They were hoping they'd be here only a few days. They would have to make do, but that would be Rhiannon's worst nightmare. She was grateful when Tristain's mother insinuated they'd be sharing his room. Although, that was a separate issue for Rhiannon. She wondered if there would be reminders of Leylah or if he would think of her as Rhiannon lay next to him. She knew it was unfair, but that didn't stop the insecurities from taking root in her mind. Leylah had been with him his whole life, and then she'd been taken from him. You didn't just forget that. She didn't want him to. It didn't make it easier, though.

Tristain squeezed her hand, pulling her attention back to him. She'd clearly missed parts of the conversation as her mind spun.

"I'm sorry. I'm just tired." She gave a weak smile.

"Of course. You must be exhausted from your travels. Have a seat and some tea. I'll prepare the room for you quickly and then you all can rest for a bit." With that, his mother exited the room.

Rhiannon sat, a wash of guilt rushing over her. She didn't feel remorseful about killing Silas, never would. She did, however, feel like a lying snake under his mother's roof, with her thinking he was simply out living his life. But she had to trust that Tristain knew what he was doing and would tell her when the time was right.

When his mother finished preparing their rooms, they followed Tristain to the other side of their home, where his and Silas's rooms sat back-to-back.

"If there's anything you two need, just let me know. I'm sorry the accommodations aren't more . . . comfortable." Tristain grimaced.

"It's fine," Samara insisted, but she flexed her hands at her sides as if steeling herself.

"We'll be fine. Maybe we'll have an easier time finding what we need now that we'll have easy access to his things," Kyra said, ever level-headed.

Tristain nodded and then led Rhiannon into his room before closing the door behind them. He took a deep breath. "Well, this is it."

Rhiannon allowed herself a moment to take it in. The room was furnished with light wood and soft browns, accented with touches of forest green. It was all very calming and warm, like Tristain. She didn't see anything that was an obvious feminine touch, and there weren't any keepsakes to be found. Maybe it was wrong that she was relieved, but some of the tension finally left her as she turned back to him.

"It's very you," she concluded as she leaned into his chest.

Tristain chuckled, but it was hollow.

Rhiannon leaned back, gazing up at him. "What are you thinking?"

He nodded. "It's just hard to know when to tell her, that's all. I hate to be the one to break her heart. It's been months since I've seen her, and I just wish I could enjoy the brief visit. But there's no avoiding it. It has to be done. I can't leave here with a lie sitting between us . . . not with the circumstances as they are." He sighed and walked them back toward the bed.

Smooth wood beneath plush fabric met the back of her legs as she fell back into the thick green blanket on the bed. He crawled over her, placing a gentle kiss on her forehead. "I think I need some sleep before dinner."

Rhiannon nodded.

Since they'd stopped moving, she could feel the exhaustion sinking in. Her body felt heavy, and she groaned at the thought of removing her clothes.

Tristain was quick to relieve himself of his sweaty clothing, and when she didn't move, he did the same for her, starting with her boots and working upward.

"Thank you."

"It wasn't a completely selfless act," he mumbled against her hair as they pressed close together under the soft cream sheets that smelled of floral cleanliness.

CHAPTER EIGHTEEN

Stepping into Silas's room was like a punch to the gut. The earthen scent of him had seeped into the floor and buried itself into the walls. It was cloying, clawing its way into Rhiannon's sinuses and burning her throat. Kyra and Samara watched her carefully. Her discomfort likely matched theirs when they'd first set foot in here.

There wasn't much that was personal in the room, nothing that made this space feel distinctly like Silas had lived a full life here. But his distinct energy hung in the air, thick and oppressive. Rhiannon's shoulders sagged with the weight of him as she allowed her gaze to wander the room. The only thing noteworthy was the desk in the corner, strewn with papers and clutter.

Samara followed her line of sight. "We went through a few of the loose papers. It's hard to read."

Her throat bobbed.

Rhiannon forced herself to fully enter the room and close the door before they began the conversation.

"What is it?"

She struggled to keep her tone even as the air grew tense around her.

"A lot of it is fairly nonsensical, at least to us." Kyra spread some of the loose pages across the desk. "But we didn't get very far yet. The writing is messy, like it was frantically scribbled down."

"That would make sense. Tristain mentioned that Silas was not in his right mind when he'd last been here. Before . . ." Rhiannon battled with the barrage of memories that came back to her, including the day he tried to take her life.

"He does rant and rave quite a bit about how he was betrayed and how he'd make them pay. Isn't it odd to think that 'them' included us in the end." Samara shuddered.

"But look how grandly they failed." Kyra crossed her arms.

Rhiannon didn't know if she necessarily agreed. He'd derailed her entire life, but she didn't bother arguing. "We should try to do as much digging as we can now. We don't know how long it'll take to go through everything."

"I'll start with these." Samara grabbed a stack of papers off the well-used desk.

Kyra followed suit, picking up one of the journals. Rhiannon did the same, taking a deep breath and unlatching the brass closure. The three of them sat in silence as they read Silas's notes, desperately searching for answers.

"Wait," Kyra said, breaking the long silence, "I think I have something."

When Rhiannon looked up, she noted the sun had already set.

"What is that?"

Disgust painted Samara's voice as they looked down at the disturbing images on the page torn out of what must have been a book older than them combined.

Rhiannon shook. Her throat instantly dried. Tears sprung to her eyes. There were horrific scenes drawn out in front of her. Worse than what she'd imagined, which was unsettling enough. The brittle paper crumpled as she grabbed it out of Kyra's grip.

"Do you think Silas drew this?" Kyra's voice was quieted with caution.

The series of images depicted an evolution—no, devolution. A rudimentary drawing of a woman painted in red showed a powerful energy coming off her in waves. In the next, magic radiated from her still, but it had shrunk significantly. Then she was weakened, on her knees in sorrow, with a duplicate of herself in shadow before her. The two figures appeared to be in a standoff.

The next drawing showed the red woman rising to her feet and opening her arms in acceptance. In the fifth, the shadowed figure drew closer, just slightly out of alignment with her own body, within and without. The final two illustrations were what made her blood roll through her in cold shivers and her hair stand on end.

In the sixth image, she held a man by the throat with one hand, his head pulled back at a sickening angle. Her other hand was feeding his heart to the shadow. Finally, the woman walked into a new day, into a serene landscape. It would have been a beautiful scene if there hadn't been a severed head hanging from her slumped wrist and a trail of corpses lining the path behind her.

Her breaths were shallow. Her knees went weak. Her head was spinning. Rhiannon threw the paper to the ground, as if simply touching it would bring it to fruition.

For what felt like minutes, no one moved. They simply stared at one another, all keeping their distance from the cursed parchment that lay on the ground.

"Please tell me this isn't supposed to be you?" Samara finally asked.

Kyra hesitantly picked it back up and turned it over, revealing text they hadn't previously seen on the other side.

Another punch to the gut.

Bile rose in her throat as she tried to keep her composure. Rhiannon couldn't answer Samara. The lump of fear in her throat had grown so large words couldn't get past it. It was just as well because Kyra confirmed it for her with the passage she read aloud.

When the father of greed and desire is awakened, he will spread a poison through our soil.

Darkness is coming to sweep across the land.

And with it, the clash of good and evil will come to a boil.

If untamed greed and indiscriminate death, one day, walk hand in hand, in the end, that will be all that stands.

An era of death and blood it will bring. It will come for all of our lives and feast on our screams.

But if one is strong enough to resist temptation and stop the wheels that have been set in motion, these predictions of terror will simply die as harmless dreams.

Stunned silence filled the room. Until Samara finally spoke.

"So, that's the full prophecy, then?" She ran a shaky hand through her blond hair. "That sounds potentially devastating . . . but also . . . promising."

Rhiannon glared at her and held out her hand for the paper. She read it over and over until the words were carved into the walls of her mind. Her monster, the supposed harbinger of an era of death and blood, vibrated with a force that threatened to split her skin open and spill out the contents that made her who she was.

This confirmation made her feel more in control and completely out of her depth. Who was she to stop a prophecy?

"Hey"—Kyra gripped her shoulders and shook her—"this confirms what we talked about before. There are two potential outcomes of this prophecy. The most obvious path of destruction doesn't have to be your end. You want to resist the temptation of your magic, and we will help you do that."

"You've seen the drawings, haven't you? How can the end be anything other than this?" Rhiannon's voice was shrill as her finger thwacked the last image. "I don't see any that depict the more hopeful outcome. Do you?"

"What if those drawings are just missing?" Kyra challenged.

"Maybe. But what if everything I do to try to stop this" — another thwack—"only drives me toward this end, anyways?"

The words tumbled from Rhiannon's lips, nearly outpacing her thoughts.

"You need to sit down." Samara eased her onto the bed.

Cold sweat coated her skin in a sickly sheen, and her breathing was uneven. Everything around her swayed, unsteady, as her mind spun in a violent, flooding whirlpool of inner turmoil that threatened to engulf her sanity.

"I know this seems hopeless, but this proves that it doesn't have to be. You just have to stay strong, Rhiannon." Kyra sat next to her, lacing her fingers between Rhiannon's. "I still believe that however we help Tristain is the answer—or at least part of the answer—to your situation."

Samara leaned down in front of her, their gazes meeting. "We just need to keep looking. But to do that, we need you to remain calm."

Anger coursed through Rhiannon as her hands whipped out and latched around Samara's throat. A low growl spawned from her as her sharp nails pierced her ivory skin. "You would do well not to threaten to get rid of me."

"Please, stop," Samara croaked out as she shook in her grasp.

Rhiannon could hear the other woman's faint whimpering, and she wanted to let go, but she wasn't in control, not completely. She was fighting with her monster for dominance.

The singing of metal was enough of a distraction for Rhiannon to wrestle back the reins. The moment her monster's attention deviated, she forced her grip to relax. Samara's gasps brought her fully back into the moment.

Rhiannon bent down to where the other woman kneeled and dragged in deep, disjointed breaths.

"Don't," Samara choked out.

Rhiannon shifted back. All she wanted was to utter comforting words. She needed to beg for forgiveness, but she understood her friend's need for space. That sickening feeling was back, but it turned on herself. She hated what she'd become. Was heartbroken over the violation of trust she'd just committed. And there was nothing she could do about it.

If she could have been rid of her monster right then, she would have done it, just to erase the hurt in Samara's eyes, which looked far too similar to the way she'd looked at her father as he held her over that river one last time.

When Samara stabilized, Rhiannon turned her attention to Kyra, who still had her dual swords drawn and pointing in her direction.

"It was a moment of weakness. It was an accident. I didn't mean to harm her." Rhiannon stood to full height, backing away.

Kyra's gaze flicked over her features and down her body, scanning for any signs of aggression. Slowly, she turned her back to Rhiannon, confident that the threat was gone. The whisper of metal on leather sounded as one sword, then the other, was returned to their sheaths on the aged dresser.

Tear-rimmed blue eyes gazed up at Rhiannon from the floor, making her feel as much a monster as the one residing within her.

"I'm so sorry, Samara. I don't know how she took control so quickly."

Samara nodded but refused to meet her gaze, and her posture was tense. She rubbed her throat, fueling the gnawing guilt creeping under Rhiannon's skin.

"I think this means we're getting closer to our answers." Kyra shuffled through the papers once again. "If it feels threatened, then there must be a way to change the course of things, like the prophecy insinuates. A way to get rid of it."

"Her." Rhiannon joined her side.

Sifting through the old paper reminded her of days spent in the library back in Oakhaven. Days lost to escapism and taking the adventures her father never brought them along for. The journey she found herself on was nothing like the excitement she thought had waited out in the world. It was a much crueler place than young Rhiannon could have ever imagined.

The woman at her side stilled. "Don't humanize it. It's not some pet you're going to keep."

Rhiannon rolled her eyes. Nobody understood just how attached they'd already become. For better or worse, they were one. Who knew if they would ever be separated again? She was afraid to hope for that. Worry blossomed in her gut, vines of foreboding tangling with her organs and clenching with a possessive reminder.

"Here, look through these." Kyra handed Samara loose papers with a gritty substance blurring the surface.

Rhiannon opened another journal. Supple leather grounded her as she dove into the uncertain waters that were the inner thoughts of a man unraveling.

"Keep it happy. Keep the power. Keep it fed. Keep my strength. Keep it in the dark. Keep myself alive."

The unsettling, repeated mantra filled three pages.

Of course Silas had been obsessing over keeping the Volskruga's power for himself.

She moved on, stumbling across line after line of useless spewing of vile hatred for the women in his life.

> *My mother was an ungrateful whore. She defaulted on her duties for a handsome face and pretty words.*

*Imagine my surprise when I arrived at her new home
to find it was nothing to blink twice at. She insisted
they lived humbly to enjoy other enrichments. All I
saw was disrespect as she shoved how little it took
for her to abandon Father and I into my face."*

Rhiannon flinched at how twisted Silas's view of the world
had been. How little he thought of what mattered most to
the people to be loved. But his harsh words were a reminder
of the cruel lens he'd cast upon people without even giving
them a chance. A warm tap on her shoulder interrupted the
tangent her mind had wandered.

"You're going to want to see this."

Samara's face was ashen, and Rhiannon suspected it wasn't
from the newly hatched unease between them.

CHAPTER NINETEEN

R hiannon strode over to where Samara and Kyra had spread out a series of dirtied pages. The weight of the letters was heavy, and the scrawl slanted to the left. Whatever this was wasn't written by Silas. She kneeled on the ground, careful to keep space between her and Samara as she brought her face close to the parchment. She noted the flecks of dirt embedded into the paper and the rich scent of soil hinting that it had been safely tucked beneath earth.

"What is this?" she asked in a hushed tone.

"I think it's some kind of spell." Kyra pointed to the middle of the page.

> *What is bound can be undone. But only by one who is strong enough. They must follow the instructions within these pages exactly to break the bonds that tie. A letting of blood and a return to the soil can force the submission of an entity to where its spirit must toil. To begin, the possessed must gather—*

The passage ended abruptly, and Rhiannon's heart rate matched the speed with which she turned it. It was the previous page.

"Where is the rest?"

"We sorted through all of the remaining pages that look to have come from the same text. There's nothing that fits logically to be next in the sequence. We think that's the last page he had."

Rhiannon shook her head. "Silas would have been clever enough to separate the most valuable piece of information."

"But why?" Samara sighed.

"Either he planned to use it for himself. Or he wanted to ensure it couldn't be used in a way that would interfere with his plans. Maybe he wanted it for leverage. Who knows." She paced, her eyes darting around the room. "I just don't believe it's conveniently missing. It feels purposeful."

It's Silas.

The creaking door behind her sent adrenaline coursing through her veins. If Tristain's mother caught them going through Silas's things, it would be difficult to explain. It would mean she would have to lie to the woman who opened her home to them.

It was just Tristain. At the grief that pulled at his features, the spike of fear crashed into a wave of sadness. She was responsible for the pain tormenting him.

Rhiannon would never feel guilty for taking Silas's life, but her sympathy for the hardship it caused Tristain was at odds with the satisfaction her revenge had given her.

The sentiment passed between them, unspoken, when his eyes found hers. It didn't change anything. They'd always sit at this stalemate.

Within the next breath, he'd crossed the room to where they all sat at the edge of the bed, poring over the weathered parchment.

"What's this?" Tristain bent at the waist, leaning over to read it better.

"A lead," Kyra answered.

"But not enough." Rhiannon stood before him.

Her muscles twitched, but she stilled her fingers yearning to tuck a stray strand of hair away and soothe the weary bags beneath his eyes. It could wait until they were alone. He was on the edge and trying hard not to tip into a well of sorrow.

"We'll finish going through the last journal tonight. But it's likely that Silas has hidden the rest of what we need. If he took the time to separate it, it wouldn't make sense that he'd keep the rest of it so close by." Kyra pulled her braids into a bun atop her head, then secured it before rolling the tension out of her shoulders. "Now we just have to figure out where—"

"Unless . . ." Rhiannon chewed at the fraying, rough skin around her nail bed that became increasingly painful with each passing day. "I know of one other journal. There's one back at home that Silas forgot in his haste."

Humiliation prickled hot across her neck and cheeks at the memory. All eyes were on her at the revelation.

"Let's plan to set out first thing in the morning." Tristain turned his attention to Samara and Kyra. "If you don't find anything in that journal, we'll go to Oakhaven. If we get our answers, we'll go back to Wispombra. Either way, our time is done here." With that decision, he abruptly left.

Rhiannon wordlessly followed him.

When they were in his room with the barrier of the door between them and the others, she wrapped her arms around his wide torso, sinking her weight into his back. "I'm so sorry that you had to have that conversation."

His body turned to stone beneath her cheek but then melted against her just as quickly. "You have nothing to be sorry for. What's done is done, and she needed to know. Hopefully she can come to peace with it, and next time, if there is one, I will be able to visit with her on happier terms."

"There will be a next time. I told you, anyone who tries to harm a single hair on your head will have to go through me, and I will not lose you." She forced him to face her and gripped his chin. "Do you hear me?"

He nodded slowly, sadness melting into affection.

"The only way anyone will ever harm you again is if I'm in the ground. You will see her again, and it will be a reminder to both of you that she still has the better son left."

Tristain nodded once more and swept a thumb across her cheek.

No more words passed between them as they readied for bed. The weight of knowledge and grief was heavy from that day, and it pulled them into slumber with little resistance.

Rhiannon wasn't surprised to find that the last journal Silas had kept here had been no help. The disappointment she felt when leaving Tristain's family home, however, was unexpected. The peacefulness of the land radiated from the very ground you walked on and into the air that filled your lungs. Even with the moisture latching onto your energy, that serene feeling couldn't be touched. She knew it was against her better judgment, but each time she glanced back over her shoulder, at the warm house buried within the dense foliage, a fondness grew that would have her wishing to come back for many months to come.

It wasn't promised that she'd get that chance, but it was a nice thought to entertain while they set off on their uncomfortable ride toward the southwest shore.

CHAPTER TWENTY

The sun-soaked landscape quickly became rain-sodden during their journey. It was clear why everything was so lush. Even beneath the widespread canopies of trees under which they passed, unforgiving rain drenched them. Their clothes and hair clung uncomfortably to their skin and would send a chill over them whenever the wind picked up. It was positively miserable for Rhiannon.

"Do you smell that?" Kyra asked with a broad smile spanning her face, her amber-brown eyes aglow with happiness.

Rhiannon inhaled. "Dirt?"

Samara's laughter chimed over her shoulder, while Tristain shook his head at her.

"No." Kyra rolled her eyes. "Life. There's so much of it here. The musky bitterness of the battered plants that have been chewed by passing animals, the rich scent of damp earth, the sweetness of flowers blooming." She looked at Rhiannon expectantly.

Rhiannon shrugged. "I suppose I didn't notice. I have a lot on my mind."

"Are you so worried we won't find the rest of the spell? It makes sense it would be there if he left some of his belongings behind." Kyra maneuvered her horse to stand beside her.

Samara had caught up to Tristain, so it was just the two of them. She'd seemed to forgive Rhiannon, but she also didn't seem eager to be close to her just yet, which she could understand.

"Yes. What if it was on him when he died? I didn't search his corpse. I didn't think I needed to." She sighed. "That, and I'm not sure how I feel about seeing my family again like this." Rhiannon swept a hand over herself.

"Will it really affect anything? You don't look any different. Not most of the time, at least." Kyra searched her face carefully.

"What if I lose control again? What if I hurt one of them? What if they see what I left them to become?"

Shame was heavy on her shoulders.

"We won't be there long, right? You know where it is?"

"I do."

"You don't even have to see them if you don't want to. One of us can grab it, and we can continue on our way back to Wispombra," Kyra suggested.

"No, I need to see them. Who would waste a second chance to say goodbye?" Rhiannon chewed her lip.

"Don't think like that. We're going to free you both from this."

"We don't know that." She held Kyra's gaze. "My priority is Tristain. If it comes down to it, and I succumb to my monster's nature, you know what to do."

Kyra nodded, her eyes growing somber at the turn in conversation.

"We have another hour or so until we reach the port," Tristain called over his shoulder. "We may have to make camp for the night if no ships are taking sail that late, but we may be fortunate."

Silence fell among them with the thought of having to sleep outside in this weather. The rain was a constant reminder of how potentially miserable their night could become if they didn't find a ship out. It served as an effective motivator for picking up their pace.

As the trees became sparser and the sun-bleached sand came into view, Rhiannon let out a heavy breath of relief. There were three ships.

One in three was pretty good odds, right? She'd never been a gambler, but she'd spent enough time in taverns to allow hope to blossom in her chest.

Once again, Tristain handled their arrangements. But this time, there was less resistance to book their passage. They asked for a higher payment up front. She'd gladly give up more coins if it meant they'd hold back the hostility. They boarded shortly after, and to Rhiannon's relief, the sun parted through the clouds, and the turquoise water slowed to a calm, rolling pace. She was tempted to take this as a good sign for the next part of their journey, but she was no longer that naive.

While the seas were much more peaceful this time around, she was just as unsettled but for very different reasons. The stress of everything ripped the seams of her barely stitched heart. Anxiety over seeing her mother and sister again gnawed at the sensitive lining of her stomach. The weight of the prophecy looming over her crushed her bones with each hour.

Unfortunately, this all meant she still wasn't getting any sleep.

"Are you awake?" she whispered into the darkness of their cabin.

"I am." Tristain wrapped an arm around her bare waist and pulled her closer.

The familiar scent of him enveloped her in comfort as she took a deep, slow breath to ground herself.

"What's wrong? Afraid of the dark?"

His breathy laughter tickled her neck.

"No. I . . ." She sighed. "I'm terrified."

Warm, strong fingers prodded the knots in her neck. "Now I'm worried. You're never afraid. Is it about what you found in Silas's room? We still haven't talked about it, by the way."

"Yes. And we haven't exactly had a good opportunity to talk." She groaned as his fingers worked to ease the tension out of her muscles.

"Good thing we're stuck in the middle of the ocean with nothing but time to waste." His thumb traced gentle circles across her stomach. There was no suggestion in his voice, but she was determined not to have this conversation, so she took it as an invitation.

Rhiannon turned into him and pressed her yearning lips to his, savoring the moment.

"You can't avoid this." Tristain stroked her hair with a featherlight touch.

Silence dragged out the seconds while Rhiannon searched for the courage to explain the drawings they'd found and the duality of the prophecy. He didn't rush her.

"We found it, the full prophecy." She recalled the inky scrawl imprinted on her mind but opted for the most basic of summaries. "It's foretold that I will bring in a new era. One of bloodshed. One that is sure to be filled with destruction and loss. That is, unless I can find some way to change the course of my path. And how to do that, of course, was not specified." She let out a long sigh. "Kyra thinks that spell could be the answer to both our problems, but who knows if we'll even find it." Rhiannon closed her eyes, preparing for his panic to match her own.

"But we already knew that was a possibility. The Volskruga said so back in the woods that day." He shrugged. "But like you said, that's not the only possible outcome. There is a chance you can stop that from happening. We just have to find the rest of that spell."

"Who am I to change a prophecy? I don't know how to prevent these events from unfolding. I'm already in so deep. What if wanting to stop it isn't enough?"

"A prophecy is a prediction. A calculated one based on a sequence of events, but if that sequence is interrupted, then there is room for change. We just have to make sure you don't fall into pace to complete the final steps." Tristain pushed back the hair framing her face and cupped her rounded cheek. "If there's one thing I know about you, it's that no one will stop you from doing what you've set your mind to." The warm pressure of his lips on her chilled nose soothed her.

Rhiannon could feel his pulse pick up beneath her fingers. "You make it sound so easy." She scoffed.

"I don't think it will be easy. Not at all. But look at all of the difficult things you've done. Look at all the impossible choices you've had to make," Tristain encouraged.

A glimpse of yellow light slipped in as someone walked by, revealing the sincerity in his gaze. It was painful to see the hope she wished she could have so effortlessly alight within him.

"And look at what I've become." Warmth flashed across Rhiannon's skin as blood crept over it. It was gone just as fast as it came. "I don't know if I have it left in me to defy fate."

"You are the most powerful woman I have ever met. I believe in you."

Tristain's voice was firm with conviction. Those words lit a spark within her.

She turned away. She wished she could close her ears. It was hope like this that got people killed. Confidence and optimism had led her into Silas's trap in the first place. Rhiannon didn't want to go back to that place. She wasn't ready to have her heart broken again when it all went wrong.

"If we find a way to break your ties to the Volskruga, you should go back to Saldova. You should all go your own way. I don't want you in my path of destruction."

Her voice was hollow and cold.

"We're not doing this again." Tristain gripped her chin with authority. "You said you would never leave me again. I'm staying by your side, no matter the outcome. Do you understand me?"

His words, accompanied by the slosh of rolling waves, sent chills skating across her skin.

Rhiannon nodded.

That wall of resolve she'd built collapsed into dust at the reminder of his boundless love for her.

Tristain's voice deepened, and with the absence of light, she could feel his darkness reaching out to her. It seeped through her skin and filled her lungs.

"You promised to set me free. But I could never be free without you. Both of us make it out of this, or neither of us do. I won't face another day of this life without you." He gripped the back of her neck and parted her lips with an invasive tongue. "The sun has no warmth without you. It only burns. Time has no meaning. It only drags. My heart doesn't beat without you. It only forces blood through my veins." Cool shadows caressed her sensitive skin, punctuating his words with a featherlight touch that had her arching into him. "An existence that doesn't include you is a burden. It would simply be unbearable. Do you hear me?"

A current of ferocity flooded his tone she'd never heard before.

Rhiannon nodded, words failing her. His proclamation was an echo of her own feelings. The reason she was so intent on liberating him at any cost, even if it meant sacrificing herself. She knew he wouldn't understand.

Even still, she believed he would find reasons to smile under the summer sun, although they might be given up begrudgingly.

Losing her would break his heart. But at least it would still beat.

And if time dragged, so be it. She could take comfort in the slow passage of time that would delay his march toward death.

Because, for Rhiannon, giving everything up, losing herself to this damned prophecy and the destruction it would wreak on her mind, body, and soul could only remain tolerable if it was in exchange for his endurance.

And how he'd endured for her through every test of fate, every time she erased a line from his moral code.

Rhiannon refused to be the darkness that consumed him. She would shove him back into the light with her final breath as it swallowed her whole. Of that, she was sure.

Tristain's sudden grip sent a sting across her scalp. "Rhiannon, I mean it."

"I know."

And she did. But nothing he could say would sway her decision if it came down to it.

Rhiannon pressed her lips to his once again to chase away the impending grief threatening to shatter her.

Recognizing her need, he pulled her closer, and his other hand wrapped her thigh over his. When he deepened the kiss, she ground herself against him.

Tristain's fervent words. Their closeness. His enveloping essence. A heady cocktail that sent her depressing thoughts retreating. Rhiannon desperately wanted to believe that, one day, moments like this were all there would be.

She and him.

Them.

Together.

A time when they could get lost in one another. No vengeance to fulfill. No lives to save. No prophecy to defy. But she didn't know if that day would ever come, so she lost herself in this one. Rhiannon gave herself over to the fantasy, and what a beautiful one it was.

The creaking of the boat, the chill in the salt-filled air, and the gentle rocking fell away until they were in their own world. One that made it safe for her to give into the lure of hope that he'd cast into the murky waters of her despair so long ago.

She latched on and let the darkness pull them into its velvet cocoon. The shell of stubbornness that had stunted their disastrous love from fully evolving softened. Once it burst open, the hungry new parts of themselves devoured those helpless feelings one by one until they were nothing but a memory.

The anguish.

The fear.

The uncertainty.

It all sloughed off like old skin ready to be shed. But it hadn't gone to waste because it was what had nurtured them to this point. Breaking down those final barriers in the safety of one another's embrace allowed them to metamorphize into something new.

Something stronger.

Something enduring.

Something hopeful.

Something they were both prepared to fight for.

For Tristain, that meant complete and utter trust.

For Rhiannon, that meant accepting his love and defying the odds for it.

Her monster gnashed and writhed within her, reminding Rhiannon of just how hard of a fight it would be. It shook her from the safety of the moment, and she pulled back in response. Her palm against Tristain's chest put distance between them, briefly severing the depth of their connection.

But he'd been endowed with the makings of a monster, too. Smoky tendrils coiled around her waist and throat, juxtaposed by the heat of his tense fingers that walked up the inside of her thigh. His thumb brushed her exposed cunt, causing her to suck in a needy breath.

"There's nowhere to run. Stay here with me." Tristain's teeth sank into the full pout of her bottom lip.

The tang of blood was intoxicating as it spread against her tongue. And once again, she was drunk on him. Like all other kinds of inebriation, liquid night filled her veins, distorted the space around her, and quieted her mind.

Once again, the world fell away.

Silken blackness engulfed her until they were just two bodies and souls clinging to one another as they continued down the wayward path and into the unknown.

Tristain breathed into her body, his darkness snaking out and burying itself so deeply within her that she'd surely lose something vital if she ever tried to remove it.

With his knowledgeable fingers, he explored the canvas of her skin and traveled the landscape of her body, carefully navigating her dips, rolls, and scars. With his other hand, he masterfully stroked her pussy. His thumb rolled against her clit in smooth circles while two fingers slipped inside her, causing her toes to curl and a moan to spill from her lips. He captured it greedily, swallowing it whole.

"Mine. For now. Forever." He pressed harshly against her clit, and her body bent into him obediently.

She would agree to anything as long as he didn't stop.

"Say it."

The shadows tightened.

"Yours. Forever." Rhiannon gasped.

"I will make you say it again and again until it's sounds more like a promise than a prayer."

Those hungry lips traveled down her neck, still restrained by his dominant shadows, and continued their pursuit until the peak of her nipple was caught between his teeth. Without hesitation, he took a teasing bite, then soothed it over by a slick tongue. Shadows multiplied in response to Rhiannon's whimper, pressing gently over her mouth. She sucked in a cool breath as his fingers and tongue synchronized in a heady rhythm that her body quickly succumbed to, arching and writhing at his insistent command.

Fuck. She'd never been so full yet achingly empty.

The way he unearthed her pleasure was an artistry that put his devotion on full display. His reverence for every inch of her body was something she would never get enough of.

The shadows slipped away from her mouth once more.

"Tell me again," Tristain demanded as he pumped his fingers into her.

"I'm yours." She gasped as a third finger entered her. "I'm yours. I'm yours. I'm yours. I'm yours." She chanted with his rhythm, squeezing her eyes shut, her control shattering.

His fingers didn't leave her cunt as she came around them.

When her breathing became steady once again, he didn't hesitate to command, "Say it again, Rhi."

"I'm yours. For now. Forever." She panted, and maybe her orgasm-melted mind actually believed it.

As strength returned to her limbs and her magic spread across her skin, Rhiannon began her own journey of adoration as she tasted his. His salted sweat and sweet essence revealed a decadence no meal could ever match. Her determined tongue painted possessive symbols of ownership and devotion that claimed him irrevocably.

He was hers. For now. Forever.

Rhiannon gripped his thick cock, her blood covered hand sliding up and down with slick ease that rang audible pleasure from him with each stroke. She alternated pressure and played with the head as her lips sucked at the bend of his neck, over his collarbones, and across his chest. Her elongated nails slipped into his hair, tugging at the roots, earning a desperate moan from his lips.

"Rhi, I need to be inside you."

Tristain's words were slurred with need. His fingers dug into the thick rolls of her hips as he pulled her closer.

Rhiannon couldn't resist when he asked so sweetly. She was never one to deny him.

And when he pressed into her, her body welcomed him home. With each pump of his perfect cock, he staked ownership that could not—and would not—be questioned.

It was dangerous. It was liberating. It was everything she needed and more than she deserved. But if Rhiannon was allowing herself to dream, she wanted to claim it all. Their bodies molded together and crested the hill as their climax approached, and she dove over the edge and into the unknown waters below to chase forever with him.

CHAPTER TWENTY-ONE

The wind lifted Rhiannon's hair into the salty air when she emerged onto the ship's deck. Voices rose over the breeze, drawing her to the alcove where the crew had gathered for breakfast. A long oak table had been set with an arrangement of brightly colored fruit and an assortment of breads. Rhiannon's stomach grumbled in anticipation as she filled her plate. The activities of the night before had worked up an appetite.

Once she'd grabbed her orange slices, pear, and bread covered in butter, she took a seat out of earshot from the sailors. While the slowly rolling waves and cloudless sky were the picture of peace, the serenity Rhiannon had found in Tristain's arms didn't last long once her companions joined her at the far end of the table.

"We didn't finish our conversation last night," Tristain reminded her in a hushed tone as he handed her a sweet-smelling red spread for her toast.

"If I recall correctly, we certainly both finished." A wry smile twisted her lips as the transformative experience of the night before flashed through her mind.

"I'm serious, Rhiannon." Tristain took an unnecessarily aggressive bite of his own pear and held her gaze the entire time he chewed. "I need to know what we're facing. I need you to tell me the specifics of the prophecy."

"Can't you just trust me that it's absolutely dreadful and we're almost certainly all fucked?" She fixed her stare to the food in front of her and ignored the bustle of the men cracking jokes just feet away.

"It's not a matter of trust. I want to know exactly what it says, not just your morbid interpretation. Keeping me in the dark isn't going to do us any good. You can't shield me from everything."

He sounded tired.

"Fine. You can read it for yourself. It'll be easier that way," Rhiannon told Tristain as she pushed her wind-tousled hair out of her face with a frustrated huff. She turned her attention to Kyra, who was in possession of said vital information. "Will you let him take a look after breakfast?"

Kyra nodded. "I think that's a good idea. Maybe he'll interpret it differently than we did. Possibly even see something we didn't."

"Its like six sentences long. There's not much to misinterpret." Rhiannon huffed.

She knew she was frustrating them, but batting away their optimism was all she could do. If she voiced her hope, it was sure to slip between her fingers, like the grains of sand washing away on the beach. "Pretty sure the impeding doom was the most logical conclusion." She didn't wait for a response. Instead, she walked over to the nearby railing.

The Larindian coastline was visible. Barely, but it wouldn't be much longer until they docked. "The next afternoon, at the latest," the captain had said when she passed him on the stairs. The sunlight glimmering off the surface was a lit-up path leading directly to their destination. It was beautiful, but the thought of setting foot on solid ground so soon sent a swarm of bees buzzing through her insides. The rapid tumbling worked its way up through her stomach. And up. And up. At the last second, she leaned over the railing and emptied the undigested breakfast she'd just finished.

Snickers nearby forced her to recover quickly. Hot anger rippled through her, boiling her blood and rattling her bones. It shook her monster awake. The waves were moving impossibly in all directions as her vision swam, and her head pounded while she fought to keep the magic at bay. In her vulnerable state, her control was difficult to grasp. Her lengthening nails dug into the thick wood of the railing. The old structure groaned under the pressure.

A steady hand on her lower back allowed Rhiannon to slowly come back to herself. Labored breaths dragged in and out of her, as if she'd been training for hours. A cold sweat coated her brow. Several more seconds passed before she gathered her control. She wiped her mouth on her sleeve, then turned to meet Tristain's cautious gaze.

"Are you all right?" He gently cupped her cheek.

"Maybe I'm just not cut out for sea voyages." An insincere laugh passed over her lips.

"Mmm." Tristain examined her closely. "Or maybe bearing all that worry alone is taking its toll." He leaned an elbow against the railing and shifted closer to her. "Why don't you tell me what's really turned your stomach?"

"I'm . . . afraid."

Her body and mind were at war as the words dueled with her tight lips to free themselves.

Tristain didn't laugh at or discourage her. Instead, he brushed his fingertips against her cheek. His patient touch coaxed more information out of her.

"What will they think of me?"

His brow furrowed, not following her train of thought.

"When they realize how much worse I've made things. When they see me for what I really am."

A wildfire of flames blazed through her chest, searing her charred heart.

"And what is that?"

"A selfish coward."

The sloshing waves tried their hardest to drown out her words, but when Tristain placed his other hand on her face, it was clear he'd heard them.

"Have you always lied to yourself so much?" Tristain's jaw tensed, and his eyes narrowed at her, trying to see what she did.

"Your love for me blinds you. Always has." Rhiannon moved to leave, but Tristain was quick to counter the action, positioning his arms on either side of her and pressing her back into the hard wood. "No. I see you exactly as you are. And so do your mother and sister. That's why they won't think those things about you. Because they know you did what you did out of pain. They'll understand that there was no other option for you. And most importantly, they'll trust that you will do the right thing." His fingers caressed her chin. "That is if you decide to tell them, which you don't have to. You could simply enjoy the short time you have with them for now. And then, when it's all said and done, you can come back and tell them how you've changed the world. Or I will."

Rhiannon's composure was failing her. Her hardened pessimism and crushing doom melted away. All that was left was the image he'd painted of her. It left her speechless.

"Tristain, Kyra went back to the room. She said you could find her there when you're ready."

Samara's approach disrupted the tender moment.

Rhiannon was relieved. Otherwise, she might have had to admit there was a possibility he could be right about everything.

"Go. I'll see you later. The more time you have to sit with the information, the better. Like Kyra said, maybe you'll see something we didn't," she urged.

Tristain kissed her forehead and then departed, like he hadn't just turned her world on its axis with his kind words.

"You two make me sick."

Samara's voice was light and teasing, their frustrated words already forgotten.

"Don't be jealous," Rhiannon said through a smirk as she rolled her eyes.

"Jealous?" Samara laughed, but it wasn't unkind. "I could never endure the storms you put each other through. If I'm going to let another man in my life, all I want is sunshine and blue skies. Laughs and adoration. I want someone who makes life easy."

Her gaze flicked conspicuously toward the young man, who was busy cleaning up the dining table. His sun-kissed arms bulged as he gathered heavy platters strewn from one end to the other. When he turned to go back to the kitchen, his green-eyed gaze caught Samara's, and even from here, Rhiannon didn't miss how his lips fought a smile under her friend's attention.

"You wouldn't happen to have your sights set on a certain someone, would you?" Rhiannon teased.

Samara's light demeanor was infectious, as always.

"Of course not. But I do have eyes." Samara waggled her brows. "I'm not going to be surrounded by handsome, strong men and not at least look my fill. You're not the only one who gets to have some fun, you know?"

"Mhmm." Rhiannon laughed, turning back toward the approaching coastline.

Samara followed suit, leaning her head on Rhiannon's shoulder, as they watched the ship eat up the waves and close the distance between their next destination.

Rhiannon had paced the short length of their cabin for what seemed like hundreds of times at this point, and Tristain still wasn't back. Would he think differently of her after seeing those chilling scenes drawn out in harsh detail on the parchment? Her heartbeat was pounding in her ear, the repetition grating on her nerves. When the knob finally twisted open with a sharp metallic sound, Rhiannon was a walking bundle of stress.

"Are you okay?" Tristain shut the door cautiously behind him.

"Are you?" she deflected.

"Yes, why wouldn't I be?"

His brow furrowed as he sat on the bed and removed his shoe.

"I wasn't sure how you would feel about . . . everything."

She hated how fearful she'd become. That's what happens when you let yourself be vulnerable.

"The drawings were something." He grimaced. "But like we've all talked about, there are two potential outcomes of the prophecy. I believe that's just depicting one of them—the one I believe much less likely to come to fruition."

She couldn't have heard that right.

Tristain held up his hands. "At least now we have something more to go."

"But we don't."

Rhiannon was utterly confused about how he came to this conclusion. She'd expected him to be more concerned than her.

"We know your purpose, or the prophesied purpose, at least. But most importantly, we know there's a way out of this. A way to break the ties that bond us to these monstrous beings. A way that we can safely be together."

"We don't even know that we're going to be able to find that spell. Not to mention death and destruction is a much more likely outcome."

"Well, your cynicism isn't helping," Tristain said pointedly.

"And your optimism is dangerous." Rhiannon slammed the door behind her, unable to bear the absurdity of his inability to be realistic. She stomped up the small set of stairs onto the deck.

An endless sea of black peppered with silver stars floated above them. Below, the turquoise waters had turned a deep blue under the night sky, breathtaking yet eerie.

It was times like these she remembered the world was so much bigger than her. There was so much out there she didn't understand. So many things she'd never seen. Who knew if she ever would?

Rhiannon rested her elbows on the railing and stared into the abyss beyond.

Her frustration with Tristain rapidly cooled to a simmer. She didn't want him to be completely overwhelmed like she was. She loved that he was always able to find hope, even in the face of such dire straits. But Rhiannon also meant what she'd said: his persistent hope was dangerous. Hope means you aren't prepared for the worst possible outcome. Hope risks letting your guard down. Worst of all, hope like that could get you killed.

Rhiannon couldn't wrap her mind around why he wasn't more concerned about the first half of the prophecy. Yes, he was a generally optimistic person, but he was smart and even-keeled. He didn't dismiss danger. And maybe it wasn't danger. Maybe he was just as afraid as she was of the end that felt like it was running toward them. But maybe his desperation to avoid it, his need for her to see another outcome as a possibility, was forcing him to lock his own doubt and trepidation away. Perhaps his persistent optimism was his shield against her inevitable pessimism. That, Rhiannon could understand. That loosened the noose her panic had been tightening around her all morning.

As Rhiannon stared out into the rolling waves, she tried to envision the fear flowing out of her and away into the vast ocean. It was drowning her just as surely as the frigid water would if she were to get caught below the ship. She couldn't think clearly when it was filling up her lungs and depriving her brain of oxygen. She needed to exercise it, get it all out of her system. Rhiannon needed a breath of fresh air to refocus. She hoped seeing her family would be that for her.

Boots clunking on wood had her casting a glance over her shoulder. She was relieved it was Kyra and not Tristain. Rhiannon wasn't ready to apologize.

"I didn't peg you as one for wishing on stars," Kyra quipped, taking up a spot next to her as she tilted her head to the sky.

Rhiannon snorted. "You'd be correct. I needed some fresh air. But it is beautiful out here. It feels like we're at the edge of the world and everything around us is so filled with possibility."

"Maybe it is."

"Tell me he didn't get to you, too. That optimism of his is infectious." Rhiannon shook her head, looking at Kyra from the side of her eye.

"No. But there's nothing wrong with having a bit of hope. Otherwise, what keeps you pushing forward when you find yourself in a dire situation?"

Kyra's voice was sincere as she watched Rhiannon carefully.

"Spite."

They laughed at that.

Kyra bumped Rhiannon's shoulder with her own. "Come on, Rhiannon, be serious. I'm terrified for you. For all of us, truthfully. But I won't give up hope for a future where we might all be happy. Where we get to see the ones we love again. Not when it's just as likely as the alternative."

Her eyes misted over with emotion.

"I want that for you, too." Rhiannon put her arm around the other woman's slim shoulders and pulled her closer.

Kyra only stiffened for a moment before relaxing into her. "What future do you hold out hope for, then?"

"One where I spend the rest of my days surrounded by my loved ones and community. Where I find someone who cares for those they cherish like I do. Where I find someone who loves me as I deserve." She gathered her brown braids gleaming with silver in the moonlight and shifted them around in her hands, her gaze darting as she spoke.

"Describe this perfect man to me."

"It doesn't have to be a man. Just someone caring. Someone with a good soul," Kyra admitted with upturned lips and a dreamy look in her eye. "And what about you? What hopes are you begrudgingly holding in that dark little heart of yours?" she dared to ask.

Rhiannon sighed. "My hope is that the people I love will make it through this, no matter what happens to me. My hope is that Tristain will find happiness again when I'm gone. His capacity to love knows no bounds, even after the kind of heartbreak he's seen. He was made for it."

"Don't talk like that, Rhiannon. You act as if this prophecy has sealed your fate when you have the ability to veer off the path if you have it in you to forge a new one. You can't discount one half of the prophecy and not the other." Kyra gripped her arms. "You need to accept that we'll find a way to break these bonds and stop the warnings of destruction from coming true. Will it likely be gruesome and painful? Yes. But we believe in you. And you need to believe in yourself. We can't do that for you."

Rhiannon was taken aback by the passion Kyra infused in her speech. She swallowed the ball of emotion swelling within her. "I'll try."

"I mean it."

"I promise I will."

"I'll hold you to it." Kyra kept a pointer finger trained on her as she retreated several steps, then disappeared below deck.

Rhiannon inhaled. Already, the air flowed more easily.

PART 3

What is bound can be undone. But only by one who is strong enough.

CHAPTER TWENTY-TWO

W hen her boots hit the sand, Rhiannon took a deep breath. Mixed in with salt and sand was the scent of rich foliage and floral notes carrying on the breeze. She was so close to home. While she was waiting for the others to make their way down, she saw a familiar face.

"Sabine!" she called as she sprinted to where the talented tailor who'd always made her clothes was loading a wooden cargo box into her carriage.

It had been so long since she felt the comfort of seeing a familiar face.

A broad smile greeted her as Sabine turned toward Rhiannon. "You're back?"

"For a short visit." Rhiannon bent down and helped her gather several smaller packages. "It's so good to see you."

And it was. Sabine has always been kind to her.

"I'm glad to see you. It looks like you've been on quite the adventure. I'm glad to see the pieces I made are holding up." Her fingers ran over the seam of her pants.

"Yes. Everything was perfect. Thank you for the care you took making them."

Rhiannon's attention drifted as her companions approached.

"Are you going home?" Sabine asked, her curious gaze sweeping over the other three who'd joined them. "I can give you all a ride. It's no trouble."

"We'd appreciate that," Rhiannon answered.

Sabine motioned for them to get in. Once they were all seated, they were on their way back to Oakhaven.

"Thank you so much for the ride. I think we were all dreading a long walk." Tristain smiled warmly at the woman.

"Of course, anything for my favorite customer." Sabine squeezed Rhiannon's elbow. "So, tell me, what have you been doing all this time?"

Genuine interest heightened her voice.

The question was so simple yet so difficult to navigate. Rhiannon didn't miss the way Samara's eyes darted to hers in panic, but she ignored it. There was an easy, harmless answer she could give, so she would. Still, she let her eyes linger on the grand trees and stone-crafted homes outside the window as she said it.

"A lot of traveling. I've seen so much more of the world since I've left."

Sabine nodded. "I'm sure you have. Your appetite for life was always so much bigger than Oakhaven. But your mother will be so happy to see you, even if it's just a short visit. She—"

"Jade?" Rhiannon asked, not hearing the end of that sentence because she'd flung open the carriage door and jumped out, landing on her feet—which she credited to her newly gifted reflexes—and sprinted toward her sister, who was walking along the path just a few minutes away from home.

She choked on the dust that she'd kicked up, but she didn't care as she flung her arms around her frozen sister. Jade dropped the basket of supplies she'd been carrying and wrapped her slim arms around Rhiannon's waist. Twin streams cascaded their cheeks when they finally pulled apart.

It hadn't truly hit her that she was back home till then. Jade was her home, and everything else that she'd been worried about fell away as soon as her sister's arms wrapped around her. And when they stepped apart, it hit her how much she'd missed her best friend. How had she gone so long without her? The deep wound of her absence itched.

"How are you here right now?" Jade's voice was breathy with disbelief.

"It's a long story. I'm only here for a short while, but I'll tell you about it later." Rhiannon skirted around the questions.

The scuffle of footsteps sounded behind them as they watched each other carefully. Tristain interrupted their stare-off when he slung his arm around Rhiannon's shoulders. She was grateful for the stability as she reeled from the onslaught of emotions that came with seeing her sister again.

"Jade."

He greeted her with affectionate familiarity in his voice.

"Tristain, it's nice to see you again. I'm assuming you've kept your promise about keeping my sister safe."

Rhiannon felt him tense beside her, and she was sure his expression matched. He was a terrible liar. Even though she was technically safe—for now—he couldn't pretend everything had been fine.

Jade slapped the canvas against Tristain's arm. "Whatever that look was for, you're going to tell me about it later." She narrowed her eyes before turning her attention to the rest of Rhiannon's companions with a bright smile. "Hi, I'm Jade."

"Kyra." Her friend hastily wiped a hand on her pants before extending it.

Rhiannon noted the way her eyes bounced around, not quite meeting Jade's gaze. When their hands parted, Kyra took a distinctive step backward.

Odd.

"Samara." Her other friend leaned forward excitedly.

Their exchange was notably easier.

Rhiannon would have to ask Kyra what that was all about when they were alone next.

"Nice to meet you both. I'm assuming you'll all be staying with us?" Jade turned back to Rhiannon, curiosity burning in her gaze.

"Just for the night. I left something important here that I needed to retrieve."

She rushed the words out, anticipating the disappointment that followed.

"Oh. I just thought . . ." Her sister tucked a strand of black hair behind her ear with shaky fingers. "Never mind. I'll see you at home, okay?" Jade rushed to collect her basket off the ground and was already several feet away before Rhiannon could respond.

"Okay . . ."

As they climbed back in the carriage, Rhiannon's regret soured their reunion as she berated herself.

"Your sister is so pretty. I can see the resemblance."

"She takes after our father. I take after our mother."

Rhiannon was half listening as worry tormented her once again.

Samara nodded. "She's nice, too. Too bad that those genes didn't pass onto you."

Mischief danced in her blue eyes. Samara was trying to get a rise out of her.

Rhiannon rolled her eyes and laughed at her friend's teasing, but her gaze was stuck on Kyra's uncharacteristic fidgeting as she rubbed her hands up and down her pant legs. She didn't say anything and let the others take over the conversation, becoming preoccupied with how she'd responded to her sister and what their mother would think. She hadn't meant to be harsh but didn't want to get her hopes up. The rest of the ride went by quickly as she picked apart their conversation.

When they finally stopped outside of Rhiannon's family home, the knots in her stomach loosened slightly, and she smiled fondly. It looked just like she remembered. She bid Sabine goodbye and thanked her for her help, then made her way up the stone steps, like she had countless times before.

The rest of her companions followed suit, but she stopped at the precipice, wondering if she should knock. It was so foreign, being back here after all these months. Especially given the fact that she'd upset her sister. Before she could make the decision, Tristain leaned around her and turned the handle. The door swung open, and Rhiannon was greeted by the sweetness of rye bread, her favorite. The savory scent of chicken and rice followed soon after.

Clearly sensing her apprehension, Tristain took her hand and walked them inside. "It smells delicious."

He spoke loudly enough for her mother to hear, bringing her out of the kitchen and through the dining room with eager steps.

Her embrace was strong enough to crush Rhiannon as she held her against her, like any give would allow her daughter to vanish into thin air. Rhiannon rubbed her hands gently against her mother's back until her hold finally loosened, and they parted.

"It's so good to see you. I've missed you."

"I know. I've missed you, too." Rhiannon smiled fondly at her mother, noting how her eyes were misted, and her lip quivered.

Instead of letting the tears fall, her mother rolled her shoulders back. "Come into the dining room. The food is almost ready. I'm sorry we haven't been introduced yet." She turned to Kyra and Samara. "I'm Elena. Welcome to my home."

They introduced themselves in tandem.

"Nice to meet you. Please sit. I'll be back in just a few minutes. Jade is bringing wine."

Rhiannon almost told her not to, but she didn't want to dampen her mother's joy. She'd already made that mistake with her sister. They all sat around the table, Tristain choosing the chair closest to her, while Kyra and Samara were across from them, leaving the two end seats for her mother and sister. It was odd being back here; the domesticity of it didn't suit her anymore.

The quiet and safety of it unsettled her and made her restless. What did that say about who she was now?

Rhiannon had become a dangerous and feral thing, and she didn't necessarily begrudge herself that. She'd changed, but she hadn't had a choice. She was doing the best she could with the circumstances she'd found herself in. Yet, she shifted nervously in her seat, her feet restless.

Tristain's foot tucking against her own stirred her from her thoughts. "Are you okay?"

Rhiannon nodded and grabbed the glass of wine she hadn't noticed Jade had placed before her. "Yes."

Not quite. She took a long drink.

Her mother and sister came in, carrying several plates of food, then went to fetch their own. "I'm so happy to have you here, but Jade mentioned it would only be a short visit?" her mother questioned.

"Yes. I left something important here that I need. But I'm very grateful that I'm getting the chance to see you both."

"How long will you be here?"

Hope sparkled in her mother's eyes.

"Just a day or two. We have to get back to Wispombra." Rhiannon cleared her throat of the guilt clogging it.

"Wispombra? What's it like there?" Her mother redirected the conversation graciously, and Rhiannon sat back, letting others share their stories.

Time passed quickly as they all got to know each other. Wine flowed, and dessert was served. Rhiannon chimed in here and there, but the question she needed to know piqued her mind as the clock ticked.

Was the missing page in the journal Silas had left behind?

CHAPTER TWENTY-THREE

Sunrays snuck between the familiar heavy, black curtains, revealing glittering dust particles that drifted peacefully in the air. They'd stayed at the main house far too late and drank their way through several bottles of her mother's favorite wine, but it had been comforting to disappear into a semblance of warmth with her family—both the one she was born into and the one she chose.

The one that chose her.

A grateful smile graced her lips, but the reminder of why they were there quickly chased it away.

A dreadful pull forced her to roll over to face the nightstand on the other side of the bed. Notably absent was Tristain. She sighed contentedly, assuming he went to get them something to eat. She never would have expected to be so enraptured by one man again, but here she was. Committed. Attached. In love. And he was everything she could have hoped for and more than she deserved. He knew her so well, including the fact that she was not the most pleasant when her stomach was empty. If she closed her eyes, she could already smell the fresh fruit and whatever breaded delight her mother would predictably prepare just for her.

With that motivation, she sat up and crawled across the bed, pushing the sleep-warmed blankets out of the way. Her feet touched the worn floor, and she let it ground her as she slowly pulled the drawer open. It groaned in protest as stubborn, swollen wood grated one another.

The brown leather looked soft and unthreatening, but she knew the words inside were sharper than any weapon. Her fingers flexed hesitantly over the small book. It was silly to be terrified of such a thing, but maybe she would ask one of the others to read through it to see if the missing page was there. While Rhiannon wanted to believe she was strong enough not to care what Silas said about her, some wounds were best left untouched. She'd barely stitched herself together, and she didn't know how well it had healed. She didn't want to find out.

With finality, she slammed the drawer shut and looked away in embarrassment of her weakness. That was when she noticed the blood drops creating a path to the door. Worry gripped her, sending a cold sweat of fear across her skin and a dizzying ringing in her ears. Rhiannon stood from the safety of the bed and walked cautiously alongside the vibrant splatters, following them outside.

Rain poured from above, but she didn't go back to put on more clothes. Her night dress was quickly soaked through, clinging to her skin. She couldn't feel the cold, but the chill of dread wrapped around her bones and threatened to shatter them.

Following the path, she soon realized it continued through the garden and behind the house. Within a cluster of trees, she saw Tristain's large form hunched over. Her feet tore the slippery ground beneath her as she ran toward him, her mind and heart sprinting even faster.

Please don't be hurt. Please don't be hurt. Please don't be hurt was all she could think as she approached him.

Tristain wasn't alone. A dead man with rust-colored hair and freckled, lifelessly white skin lay in front of where he kneeled. Rhiannon's breath caught in her throat as she stepped around him and got on her knees beside the body.

Carefully, she placed her hands on his wet cheeks. Crimson was smeared across his moist skin. Some of it was pouring from his nose—the source of the dripping—but the rest was splattered across him as if it had sprayed from below. Her dagger was clutched in his shaking hand.

"Tristain, give me the knife," Rhiannon requested in a soothing voice, the antithesis of everything she felt. She suffocated the emotions gasping for air. If she let them out, they'd drown him, too.

Tristain didn't move his head, but his eyes rolled upward to meet hers. Deep obsidian veins pulsed under his skin, and there was no telling where his pupils ended. Two voids stared into her, unseeing. Her lips parted on a quivering breath as she moved painstakingly slow toward the knife, never taking her eyes off his unsettling stare. When cool metal pressed her fingertips, she peeled his hand away. Tristain let her take it before his fingers curled back in on themselves and fell in a fist at his side.

"Tristain." Rhiannon snapped her fingers in front of his face. Nothing. She shook his shoulders. Nothing. "I need you to say something. Tell me what happened."

She was desperate for answers. She looked around, searching for anything that would help her piece together the details of what happened. When Rhiannon returned her focus to him, his hand snapped out around her throat, and he shoved her back with the brunt of his weight. Tendrils of shadow wrapped around her wrists and fought to pin them against the dirt. His other hand joined around her neck, and her monster tore through her barriers to meet the attack.

She snarled and hissed as she thrashed beneath him. Rhiannon's elongated, talon-like nails slashed at his skin, shredding long gashes into his muscular forearms. When he didn't release her, she dragged them across his face. Still nothing. She needed him to let go, but she didn't want to permanently harm him.

"Get off of me," she growled as she got her knees up under his torso and pushed off as hard as she could.

He fell back off her, and she used her magic to restrain him against the nearest tree. The ropes of blood quivered with tension as Tristain struggled to break free. Before, he hadn't even been able to move in their grasp, but Volskruga's magic was stronger now. She froze, waiting to see if they would hold. Bark cracked beneath the strain, and the bindings shifted slightly, but they didn't snap free. After several minutes of fighting, Tristain slumped, and his eyes slid closed.

Rhiannon remained still, not daring to approach for another minute. But when he didn't stir again, she got close enough so that, when she released her hold on him, he would fall gently against her instead of slamming down to the ground.

Tristain didn't wake, so she wrapped him in the security of loose bindings and left him there to sleep while she disposed of the body.

Rhiannon concentrated, sending her mist to descend upon him. Within seconds, the man's body had been dissolved by her magic and eradicated from existence. Even without a body to contend with, the evidence was all over Tristain. That would need to be dealt with.

The worry that swept over Rhiannon at the agonized look on his face nearly brought her to her knees. His brows were pulled tight, and his jaw was tense. The pout of his lips was more pronounced. She wanted to be the one to chase away the demons haunting him. Rhiannon would do whatever it took to make it so.

A twig snapped beneath her as she sat in front of Tristain, prompting his eyes to open. Gentle brown eyes looked back at her, and she sighed with relief.

All markings of the Volskruga had retreated. She called back her magic, and it eased away from him.

Tristain clutched a hand to his head as he wavered where he sat. "What happened?" His eyes widened when he pulled his hand away and noted the blood staining his fingers and palm. "What did I do?"

Fear quaked through the words.

Rhiannon swallowed thickly, debating whether she should tell him. She didn't want to lie, but he didn't seem like he was in the best state to handle the truth. He was on the brink of shattering.

"I remember walking back here" — his eyes traveled across the surrounding area — "and then I saw someone, a man. He was watching the birds. I had the sudden urge to attack him. I tried to resist but then everything faded away. The next thing I remember is waking up here." Tristain's voice was unsteady. "What happened?"

Rhiannon searched his gaze, confusion and apprehension etched across his features. "You . . ." She hated to be the one to confirm his fears, but there was no way around it. "You killed him."

"You mean we?"

The hope in his voice tore away at Rhiannon's composure.

"No." She wanted to glance away so she wouldn't have to witness the damage of the blow, but she couldn't do it. "*You* did."

The way his throat bobbed and his eyes shimmered pulled at something inside Rhiannon that felt like failure and regret. She hadn't protected him from this. She'd been callous to his soft heart. She hadn't thought through how immensely painful this would be for him.

Unlike Rhiannon, Tristain didn't take lives easily, even if it meant his own survival. Tristain was the type to defend himself when absolutely necessary, but he'd take every precaution to avoid death. While she, on the other hand, would deliver death first, then find forgiveness within herself later. She could excuse her actions, but for Tristain, this would weigh so heavily on his soul, and she was watching it shatter him beneath the burden of it.

One tear. Then two. Then three, four, and five. Within seconds, his sorrow had painted his cheeks, inseparable from the rain that came down on them. The once-dried blood mingled with the tears and the snot pouring from his nose. Sobs racked his chest as he gasped for breaths. It was ugly and heartbreaking. She never wanted to see him like this again.

Rhiannon was frozen in horror as she watched the man she loved fall apart. She knew it would be difficult for him to process, but she'd refused to imagine this.

She should have. It wouldn't have changed anything, but maybe she would have been better prepared to give him what he needed.

With a deep breath, she steeled herself, bracing to bear the whole of his sorrow, as she tried to put him back together. Slowly, she crawled through the pooling mud and wrapped her arms around Tristain, pulling him to her chest. The force of his emotions took everything for her to withstand as she cradled and soothed him.

When Rhiannon lost feeling in her legs, she pried them apart and stood, extending her hand. He took it but didn't look her in the eye. She wrapped her arm around his shoulder and allowed him to lean his weight into her as they followed the path home.

She prepared a bath with hot water to chase away the chill that had surely burrowed deep within his bones. As Rhiannon went through the motions of preparing the water, undressing him, and helping him get in the tub, Tristain barely reacted. His gaze was distant, his limbs were stiff, and his breathing was slow. When Rhiannon pushed his shoulders, lowering him into the basin, he hissed at the high temperature that was a stark contrast to the frigid surface of his skin. Rhiannon was thankful for the small reaction.

Once he was seated fully, she kneeled behind the tub and wet his hair. With gentle motions, she worked soap into the dirtied strands, cleaning the matted blood and grime in his curls. When it finally rinsed clear, she lathered his limbs slowly, trying to reconnect him with his body that had betrayed him as he stared past her.

When it was time to wash his torso, she stripped out of her night dress that was ruined with blood and mud and stepped into the tub with him to straddle his lap. She moved her hand in smooth, circular motions across his toned chest and soft stomach. Her fingers kneaded his tense shoulders and his arms, trying to work out the memories of the rise and fall of the blade that would surely haunt him. After rinsing him, she washed herself, then pulled him up to stand for one final rinse with the extra clean water she'd brought in. Still, he barely acknowledged her presence.

Rhiannon's heart sank farther as Tristain shuffled toward the bed under her direction and slunk under the covers. He pulled his arms around himself and closed his eyes, shutting out the world. Shutting out Rhiannon. While it wasn't about her, she still felt another crack web a jagged line running through her increasingly fragile heart.

Once, she'd believed loving him had made her weak. That needing him would soften her dangerously. But with his broken spirit leaning on hers and his trust resting safely in her hands, she felt strong. Like she could hold his entire world with sheer will as it tried to crumble around him.

With gentle hands, she covered him with the sheets and blankets, then laid on top of them, cocooning him in his own safe space while she used a separate blanket. She tucked herself against his back but left a few inches between them, providing support but not overbearing him with her touch.

She'd never felt more determined to end this. Rhiannon was up against forces far larger than she'd ever expected, but she wasn't alone. Whether they found that journal, she was done allowing unchecked evils and greedy magic to dictate their lives. As the man she loved lay, broken in her arms, she renewed her vow of vengeance.

She would bring the corrupted powers to their knees. Not for herself. And not just for the women of Larindia and beyond. But for everyone who'd had the misfortune of being a victim of the darkness that moved in silence, unseen as it lurked among them.

The world was cruel. It stole love and life. It dragged innocent beings beneath the ground before they were ready. It allowed men to build pyres with the bones of those weaker than them and then it stoked the raging fire that would set the rest of them aflame with its wayward embers.

But through all of this, she'd learned that, to overcome an unwieldy fire threatening to wipe out everything that matters, you must become a roaring flame to devour it whole. Perhaps she'd burn out with it, but she'd always been prepared for that. The ones she'd come to love were worth laying it all on the line for.

CHAPTER TWENTY-FOUR

The rustling of paper, followed by the sound of her name, roused Rhiannon earlier than she would have liked.

"Rhi. Rhi, wake up."

Tristain's voice was strained and gravelly, but her heart fluttered at the sound of her nickname on his lips.

It was something so small yet so much more than she thought she'd get from him. The deep wounds on his conscience wouldn't heal overnight, but his resilience was inspiring.

Rhiannon turned to him and had to bite the inside of her cheek to prevent herself from reacting upon seeing the evidence of yesterday's struggle.

Tristain's eyes were haunted by dark circles, and scratches marred the ridge of his nose and cheeks. Scratches she'd made by fighting him off. With everything that had happened, she'd almost forgotten about that.

Rhiannon had been trying to protect them both in that moment, but as it replayed in her head, her muscles tensed as she remembered the way his hands tightened violently around her neck. It hadn't been the reassuring and possessive weight she was used to, the kind she craved from him. It'd been meant to force the life out of her. Those hands that had touched her so gently, the ones that had held her, supported her, pleased her, tried to kill her.

Unease settled in her stomach, but that was something she'd need to dissect another time. She needed to make sure he was okay.

"How are you feeling?"

The words weren't sufficient for the emotional trauma he'd endured, but she needed to know.

"Tired." There was a pause as he sifted through his thoughts. Rhiannon waited patiently. "Guilty. Sorry. Regretful. Angry." Tristain let out a long sigh. "Afraid."

Rhiannon cautiously shifted to her knees and crawled over to him, then wrapped herself around him from behind. "What do you need from me?" She stroked his arm with her nails.

Tristain angled his head to meet her eyes, his scruffy facial hair grazing her lips and cheek. "To be here."

"There's nowhere else I'd rather be." Rhiannon placed a gentle kiss at the edge of his lips.

He was still the man she loved, but she'd seen the strength the Volskruga held over him, and it'd rattled her. It wasn't fun to tease out that darkness anymore; it had become undeniably dangerous. For both of them. She wanted to curl into his warmth and lose herself to the feel of his lips on hers, but worry had latched itself deep within her, and she couldn't relax.

"Why were you trying to wake me?"

Tristain held her gaze a moment longer, seeming to sense her apprehension. "Oh, the journal—I looked inside." He picked up a piece of parchment from beside him and handed it to Rhiannon. "I think this is what we were looking for."

Rhiannon's eyes moved quickly over the carefully written text that completed the instructions for the spell.

—soil from the land where the entity derives its power, an item the tied soul holds precious, two candles one black and one white, twine, and a blade.

Rhiannon finally allowed the strangled breath to escape from her chest. The list was simple enough; these were all attainable.

"Where will we find soil to break your bond, though. We don't know where your magic originated. It could have been anywhere in Larindia," Tristain pointed out.

"Fuck." Rhiannon closed her eyes, racking her mind for any clues she might have come across.

They had no idea where her monster had come from—at least, not in the physical sense. Gathering the soil to break Tristain's bond to the Volskruga would require a trip to the Vrugian Woods.

Rhiannon shuddered at the thought. But at least they knew where to find it. In her case, it was another dead-end.

"Maybe Delphine or Morana will know something."

She wasn't optimistic, but she wasn't giving up and needed Tristain to remain positive, given his current state. She feared the day before had been the first in a pattern of him slipping away.

Rhiannon placed a kiss on top of his head, savoring his scent, as she reluctantly stood and went into the washroom to start her day.

By the time they'd joined the others at the main house, they were at the tail end of their meal. Tristain and Rhiannon filled their plates with the remaining helpings of seasoned potatoes, eggs, and toast.

"Are you feeling okay, Tristain?"

Samara's brow furrowed as her gaze roamed over him suspiciously.

"Just tired," he answered without making eye contact, focusing wholeheartedly on the orange spread he was putting on his bread.

He was the worst liar, and they all knew it.

Samara flicked her gaze to Rhiannon's, and she returned it with a nearly imperceptible shake of her head.

It wasn't the time to talk about it. Besides, her attention was focused on the animated expressions brightening Kyra's face as she leaned toward Jade, who sat across the table.

The two were swept up in a mock argument peppered with shy smiles and playful jabs in hushed tones that Rhiannon couldn't make out. She didn't need to know what they were saying to warrant her smirk. It was so obvious when her sister was enamored with someone. It was in the nervous way she ran her fingers through her inky-black hair, the way her cheeks darkened with undertones of pink. Then there was Kyra, who'd practically melted into the table to be closer to Jade's warmth. Her friend's fingers curled around the edge of the table, like it was the only thing keeping her from wrapping her hand around the back of her sister's neck and pressing their lips together.

Ever the observant one, Kyra shot her a warning glare from the corner of her eye when she caught Rhiannon staring, but the sparkle gracing her amber gaze hadn't dimmed.

The image of them together brought a lightness to Rhiannon's demeanor she hadn't felt in so long. She wanted to see them happy, and if that was together, she couldn't deny they would complement one another.

Kyra had said she wanted someone who was caring with a good soul, and there was no one who embodied those two things more than her sister.

But guilt quickly infected that sliver of joy that had wound its way through her. They were leaving, and when they did, they'd be facing a threat they didn't fully understand. She recalled what Kyra had told her on the ship, about her desire for love. Being part of what stood in the way of that soured her appetite before she'd even gotten a chance to eat.

Rhiannon cleared her throat. "We should get going soon."

Her eyes focused on her companions, pointedly ignoring her mother's and sister's hurt gazes burning into her cheek.

"You just got here," Jade argued.

Reluctantly, Rhiannon turned to face her. "I told you we weren't going to be able to stay more than a day or so."

"Well, I'm asking you to stick to the 'or so.'" Tears pooled along Jade's dark lashes. "I'm not ready for you to go just yet."

"Is one more day really too much to ask?" her mother chimed in, always taking her sister's side.

This time, Rhiannon couldn't begrudge her. They both clearly missed her, and she, them.

With a long sigh, Rhiannon turned back to her companions, searching their expressions for any objections, but there were none. "Fine. But we leave first thing tomorrow. It's urgent that we return to Wispombra."

Jade let out a squeal, pulling a laugh from deep within Rhiannon's chest.

Fuck, it feels good to be home. It feels good to be happy.

She clutched those feelings so tightly she feared she'd chase them away too soon. *Just for now*, she told herself. She could have this fleeting moment of joy. Just for today. Tomorrow, she'd be prepared to face her fate. Tomorrow, Rhiannon would step into her role as the prophesied *Daughter of Desire, born of Death and Blood*. Today, though, she was just Rhiannon. *Daughter. Sister. Friend. Lover.*

Chapter Twenty-Five

S weat coated Rhiannon's palms as she wiped them on the skirt of one of her favorite cream dresses she'd missed. She reached up tentatively and rapped her knuckles on the heavy oak door in front of her. If this had been before, she would have simply walked in, but things had changed, given her behavior the last time she'd seen him. The way she'd stormed away from him at the festival still haunted her. He had been a good friend, trying to find out what was going on with her, and she'd shoved him away. Nerves of excitement flipped in her stomach as the door swung open.

"You came back." Idris's soft brown eyes lit up like a night full of stars when his gaze roved over Rhiannon's shorter stature. She didn't have a chance to respond as he crushed her against him. "You're the fucking worst, but I missed you. Where have you been?"

"It's a long story." Rhiannon clung to her oldest friend, like he would disappear if she unknotted her fingers from his silky sage shirt that, of course, perfectly complemented his gorgeous onyx complexion.

As she searched his features, she realized not much had changed from his tightly coiled hair to his graceful yet muscled physique.

"I have time." Idris squeezed her.

He'd always understood what she needed.

Damn, she'd missed that comfort.

When he tried to pull away, she quickly wiped away tears. "I've missed you, too."

Tension she'd been carrying in her shoulders eased away as her friend stared down at her lovingly. She was basking in that comfort and relaxation that only being around those who truly cared for you could bring.

"I'm sorry I left things the way I did."

"Well, you always were one for the dramatics. I should be angry with you, but it's been dreadfully boring and lonely here without you." He tugged on her chin playfully. "Why don't you come inside? Maybe I can truly forgive you if you tell me all the trouble you've gotten into. Anything will be more interesting than my life these last few months."

"Actually"—Rhiannon laughed—"I was hoping we could go for a drink? For old times' sake? I have some important people I'd like you to meet." She looked over her shoulder at the carriage where her nosy friends peeked out the windows.

Always up for anything, Idris nodded. "Let me put on my boots, and I'll be right there."

Rhiannon got back into the carriage, leaving the door open for him.

"All your friends are so beautiful. Aren't you fortunate?" Samara smirked, and Rhiannon rolled her eyes.

"Are you blushing?" Tristain teased. "Do I need to be worried?"

"Are you jealous?" Rhiannon raised her brow.

"No," Tristain answered before pulling her forward and claiming her lips possessively.

"Oh, good, you kept him." Idris slid in next to Rhiannon and Jade, sharing a warm smile with the others who sat across from them. "I have to say, I'm impressed you've made it this long." He turned his attention to Tristain. "Idris, it's a pleasure to formally make your acquaintance."

"Tristain." He shook Idris's hand. "And you as well."

Despite his teasing, Tristain appeared at ease as he leaned back into the seat and conversed with the other man about his travels.

Rhiannon let her attention wander back to the window, where she watched a lifetime of memories flick through her mind among the backdrop of Oakhaven's plentiful trees. Summers spent picking flowers with Jade, late nights of sneaking around with the village boys, days at the market with her mother trying new oils and fragrances, and even that last time, she watched her father leave for a voyage.

Every couple of moments, they'd pass one of the beautiful stone homes that Oakhaven was known for. Some had large iron gates marking their entrance, since they were tucked away from the frequently traveled roads, while others were clustered off to the side. As the homes made their way for the outskirts of the village, the first signs of spring's approach were evident with hints of white-and-yellow flowers peeking out above the ground. It seemed like no time had passed when Tristain rested his hand on her knee, letting her know they'd arrived.

Rhiannon took a deep breath as they all unloaded from the small carriage. Her muscles tensed as she stepped out onto the smoothed dirt and gravel and made her way toward the tavern, lingering behind her friends. Uncertainty worked its way through her. Rhiannon's last memories here during the festival weren't good ones, but perhaps they could replace them with something fonder.

"What's wrong?" Jade linked their elbows as they walked inside the familiar tavern.

"Everything and nothing." Rhiannon leaned into her sister's shoulder. "Nothing that can be fixed tonight. It's just difficult being back here. It stirs up a lot of memories, many that aren't good."

Jade nodded. "Try to enjoy the moment. Your worries will be there tomorrow." She kissed the top of Rhiannon's head, then sat at the table where everyone gathered.

The afternoon sun gleamed through the open windows and door, and fresh air swept away the lingering scent of spilled ale. The tavern was mostly empty at this time, but it would become busier as the hours passed and the sun fell. She'd enjoy the quiet that allowed her friends' laughter to bounce around the atmosphere.

Tristain and Samara had gone to fetch them all drinks, but Rhiannon joined them when they realized four hands couldn't carry everything.

"What did you get me?" she asked Tristain as she set the glasses in front of their respective owners.

"The darkest ale I could find."

Tristain's dimple gave him away, and Rhiannon rolled her eyes as he handed her a light, sour beverage that was much more her taste.

"So, tell us, what's Wispombra like?" Idris asked Kyra.

"Cold this time of year. Covered in crisp white snow and bare trees. It's beautiful. I miss it." Kyra answered with a wistful look in her eyes.

"Rhiannon in the snow. That, I'd like to see." Idris laughed at her, his eyes gleaming with good-hearted mischief.

"You'd be surprised what I've come to tolerate. Like Kyra said, it's actually quite beautiful there. But it can be a bit brutal." She averted her gaze as the harsh half-truth left her lips.

"Oakhaven is peaceful." Samara changed the subject. "I've never seen a snowless winter. I think I'd miss it, but it is a nice change."

Their conversations were casual and carried from one subject of little importance to another, but it felt mundane. Better yet, her monster had been quiet since the incident with Tristain. Something she would enjoy while it lasted.

The drinks flowed, and the pitches of their laughter heightened. However, as night approached, more people filed in, including a few Rhiannon recognized. She ignored some of the double glances tossed her way. Gossip lasted a lifetime here, but it no longer mattered to Rhiannon. She'd dealt with so much more since she'd left her small village.

"Do you want something else?" Kyra asked as she stood from the bench across from her.

"No thanks. I think I'm done for the night. We have an early morning."

She didn't miss the tension in her sister's jaw.

Jade stood quickly, almost losing her balance, but Kyra's hands on her waist steadied her.

"I'll come with you. I want another."

Rhiannon pressed her lips together to keep herself from commenting.

"I'm having water. I'll get some for *everyone*," Kyra said as they walked away.

"They seem to be getting close."

Tristain's breath feathered across Rhiannon's cheek as he straddled the bench next to her.

"They do. It's too bad we're leaving tomorrow." She turned toward him.

Tristain reached out and rubbed up her thigh. "It is. But maybe Jade can come visit us once all of this is over."

"Maybe." Rhiannon sighed as she leaned into him, resting her chin on his shoulder. She'd barely relaxed in his embrace when her muscles tensed once again, and fury licked through her.

"Ouch, Rhi. What the hell?" Tristain yelped.

Rhiannon looked down at his back to see that her elongated nails had dug into it and drawn blood, but she couldn't move. She couldn't breathe. She couldn't hear anything else he said.

Everything fell into the background as she stared at Hugo Durant's unmistakable side profile. The councilman's thick mustache and combed back hair were unmissable in the warm light blanketing the tavern.

He appeared completely at ease as he sipped ale with other men who were heads of the most revered families in Oakhaven.

Rhiannon's fingers twitched with the need to break that glass across his face and use one of the jagged edges to slice his dismissive tongue.

Kill him. Kill him. Kill him.

Her monster was wide awake.

Tristain's grip on the back of her neck pulled her attention away from the snake of a man for a moment.

"What's going on?" he asked as his gaze traveled across the crowd before he backtracked to where Hugo stood. "Rhi, he's not worth it. Killing him won't change anything."

She reeled back from him, as if he'd slapped her. Sometimes, it confused her how she could be in love with someone so add odds with her nature. "It won't change anything? How can you say that to me? Who knows how many other women he and his council have shamed and dismissed. Do you have any idea how many they have silenced?" Rhiannon stood, unable to be in his presence any longer. "Neither do I. How could I? They're responsible for sweeping so many people's pain under the rug. They're responsible for so much of the greed and pain that's plagued this town. They've gotten away with all of it for too long. Who else can hold them accountable if not me? What's so wrong about using this magic that's been forced upon me to do some good while I still have it?"

The memory of her leaving the council chambers, feeling utterly defeated, echoed through her. It had been the defining moment that had propelled her down this path. And here, she found herself at a similar crossroads again: bury the betrayal and move on or get revenge.

"Rhiannon," Samara hissed, her eyes bulging pointedly at Rhiannon's hands. "We need to leave."

She was shaking, her composure failing as pure rage coursed through her.

"Think of your sister and your mother. What will happen to them when you're gone?" Tristain asked as his fingers latched around Rhiannon's wrist. "I thought we were trying to defy prophecy, not barrel toward becoming what you fear?'"

Her feet were frozen as her priorities battled for her attention. Her monster was restless beneath her skin, fighting to get out. The fear in her sister's eyes, however, doused some of the fire stoked within her.

She stood abruptly and tore her wrist from Tristain's grasp, the bench screeching across the dirty floor as she made for the exit. Ragged breaths billowed around Rhiannon as she made her way to the carriage awaiting them. At the last minute, she turned right onto the path. She needed to walk. She couldn't think, being trapped in that tiny cage with all their judgmental gazes. Her feet were moving quickly and then she tore off into a sprint.

"Rhi, wait."

Tristain's desperate voice was a distant call. She ignored it.

"Rhiannon," he said a moment later.

She stumbled at the closeness of his deepened voice. When Rhiannon turned, Tristain was only feet away from her. It wasn't his soft brown gaze that greeted her. Her pulse spiked, and her monster jumped into action, rising to the surface.

"Leave me alone. I don't want to talk."

She itched to leave, but she was hesitant to turn her back on him.

"I'm not giving you a choice." He continued walking in the direction toward her home.

Rhiannon noted the carriage following them in the distance as she turned and resumed her walk. "So be it." She took a deep breath, then summoned her magic.

When he turned to see what she was doing, she unleashed a large cloud of scarlet mist enveloping him and eased him into a sleep.

Guilt came and went quickly.

The others would see him when they passed by in just a few minutes.

With one last glance back, she sped through the remaining miles and closed herself behind the safety of her front door.

Alone at last, she thought she'd feel at peace, but her need for bloodshed only heightened as her mind was given free rein to race into the darkness of her past. Memories of that day in the council's chambers battered her. Their callousness toward her, their inability to see Silas for what he was, and their refusal to pursue her claims. But then she recalled another memory.

Silas had paid for their favor. They'd been accomplices to her trauma. Worse than not believing her, they knew, and they didn't care.

That fresh wave of betrayal was what chased away reason. That cold, hard truth was what unleashed her monster and sent her back into the night with one thing on her mind: vengeance.

CHAPTER TWENTY-SIX

S ilver moonlight guided Rhiannon through the trees as she stayed far away from the path most traveled, avoiding being spotted by her friends, who may still be on the way home. The scent of turned soil and brisk air coated her breaths as she covered the miles quickly.

I can smell him from here. That coward's flesh smells of sweat and misdeeds. Ripping screams from his throat will be most pleasurable. A man with that much to atone for will be desperate to evade his fate. He'll probably even beg before we tear out his treacherous tongue.

Her monster's glee was her own. Excitement mingled with her fury as the tavern came within view. Rhiannon slowed her steps.

A cacophony of voices traveled from the establishment. It was still full.

She'd have to lay in wait for him to leave. She wasn't going to completely disregard Tristain's warning. Rhiannon had no intention of leaving her mother and sister to deal with the consequences of her actions. They hadn't been seen together, and multiple people could vouch that she'd left much earlier than him.

Besides, nobody would assume that a woman could take out the councilman. Their small-mindedness would work in her favor. No one would know what happened to their precious council leader. He'd simply cease to exist. Missing without a trace. Erased without a care. Just like he'd let happen to too many women in that seat of undeserved power.

The moments ticked far too slowly as Rhiannon waited in the shadows. Her monster was growing impatient, but she was determined to take dear Hugo by surprise. She wanted to watch as he realized just how compromised his position was one suspenseful moment at a time.

Finally, he stumbled out of the tavern, calling his goodbyes through the open door.

Hugo Durant was drunk and alone, and unlike most of the women who resided in their village, completely unperturbed by that idea. He was about to learn just how dangerous that arrogance of his could be. It was about time.

"Hello, Hugo. It's been a while," Rhiannon taunted from the cloak of darkness the nearest shop provided.

The council leader's feet tangled with one another as he peered through the night to get a better view. He took several uneven steps forward, unwittingly walking into her trap. As soon as he was hidden between the two buildings, Rhiannon snatched the front of his cloak and shoved him against the wall. Confusion, followed by recognition, flashed across his tired eyes as he stared at Rhiannon.

"What do you think you're doing, young lady? Unhand me this minute."

His voice betrayed the confidence he was trying so hard to exude.

"Hugo, Hugo, Hugo, you're not the one in control here." She tossed her head back, a strangled laugh echoing in the quiet air.

Fuck, this was going to feel good.

His dull nails dug into her hand, and she used her free one to snap his wrist backward before it clapped over his mouth to dull his screams. "Does it hurt, Hugo? I hope so."

"What do you want?" he whimpered against her cupped hand as tears leaked from his eyes.

"I want you to fucking suffer." Rhiannon dropped her glamor, reveling in the way his eyes doubled in size. "I want you to beg me to grant you mercy. I want you to cry for help." She shifted her fingers from his cloak to his throat, then dug her claws into the skin, drawing blood.

His shivering frame and rapid heartbeat caused scarlet to coat his neck quicker than she anticipated.

"What I really want, my deepest desire, Hugo, is for you to admit what a cowardly, vile man you are. I want you to be honest for once in your life."

"I'll tell you anything," he sobbed between quivering lips.

Disgust and satisfaction mingled in Rhiannon's stomach as she watched him unravel. "Tell me, knowing that it's going to be what cost you your worthless life, was it worth the money, was it worth the status, to betray us all? You left us with our spirits bleeding out as you lined your pockets. I wonder how heavy they were as you took each step away from any honor you once had."

"Please, Ms. Savatia." He swallowed thickly, his eyes roving over the inhumane features that had taken over the woman he'd once known. "Surely, we can come to some kind of understanding. You wouldn't want to find yourself in trouble. You're already a whore. We wouldn't want to add murderer to that list, would we?"

A growl left her lips as she slid her blade from her holster beneath her dress. She unleashed sprawling webs of blood that crushed him to the wall. With both hands free, she used one to grip his foul, slippery tongue and the other to saw her blade through the thick, muscular organ. Blood flooded from his mouth and down his chest. Even the rain that had started to fall in heavy drops couldn't wash it away. It was a beautiful sight, him painted in the crimson consequences of his deeds. But she wasn't quite finished. His cries barely pierced the frenzy she and her monster had entered as they ran through the potential ways to end his life in the most painful manner possible.

Rhiannon's heart raced. Her blood was pounding through her, along with the intoxicating magic. Her head felt light with power as she watched the terror and misery dance in his eyes. She'd never felt more alive.

Her decision made, she stepped closer to him. But when his eyes widened at something behind her, she froze. Irritation tensed her shoulders as she turned to find who would dare interrupt.

She was met with something she couldn't have predicted. The forms of ten other women, their figures made up of ebbing and flowing red mist, fanned out behind her. They looked just like the ones she'd manifested that day in the woods, when she was still learning to wield her magic. She'd almost forgotten about it.

Rhiannon's breath caught in her throat as their feral, fanged smiles gleamed in the moonlight back at her. They were glorious. They were just like her, made from the same thing. Carved from the same tragedy. Come to life from the same all-consuming rage that had awakened them from a long sleep.

As her gaze traveled across the souls, she saw their truth play out behind the lids of her eyes. Flickering memories of pain, abuse, violence, and broken spirits. Her heart clenched; she could relate to them well. They were her kindred.

Upon her realization, one after another, they bowed their heads to her as their forms shifted and pulsed, in tune with her emotions. They were part of her, and she, part of them. It reinvigorated her to finish what she'd started.

With them at her back, Rhiannon wrapped her nails tighter around the councilman's bloodied throat. The pressure roused him back to consciousness. He flailed ineffectively with the little strength remaining.

"Hugo Durant, councilman, twisted, lying piece of shit, while we, the council"—she waved to the ravenous forms behind her—"empathize with an old man's pain and heartbreak, we feel that your choices have been unforgiveable." Rhiannon leaned closer to his ear as she twisted the words he'd once sealed her sentence with to suit her own needs. "We cannot grant your request to continue to live out your wicked life. You will be required to remit payment for our suffering and will be sentenced to death."

Hushed, gurgled whimpers were his only response.

Guilty. Guilty. Guilty. He must pay, her monster chanted excitedly within her.

Rhiannon agreed. It was time to carry out his sentence, but she didn't want to use her magic.

She would take him by her own hand. He wasn't her monster's to kill and maim. The fading councilman was all hers, and she wanted to feel the life drain from him. Rhiannon sank her knife into his stomach over and over, letting the warmth of his blood coating her hand settle something that had been restless for too long deep inside her. With one final twist of the blade, she tore it out and tossed him in front of the women lying in wait.

Seconds later, they'd descended upon him in a flurry of scarlet mist. They scratched and clawed and bit and ripped until he was nothing but a puddle of splattered blood on the muddied ground.

She watched, hypnotized, as the last of his blood seeped into the dirt, disappearing beneath the soil he'd helped weigh down through the damnation of the women who'd come to him and his fellow councilmen for help. And he wouldn't be the only one to pay.

"Find them. Make them suffer," Rhiannon whispered into the night as her kindred spirits spread out and darted out into the village.

She turned back toward the path that led home and started down it once again. The screams of the four remaining councilmen were a lullaby to her ears as she inhaled cool night air and breathed peacefully for the first time in months.

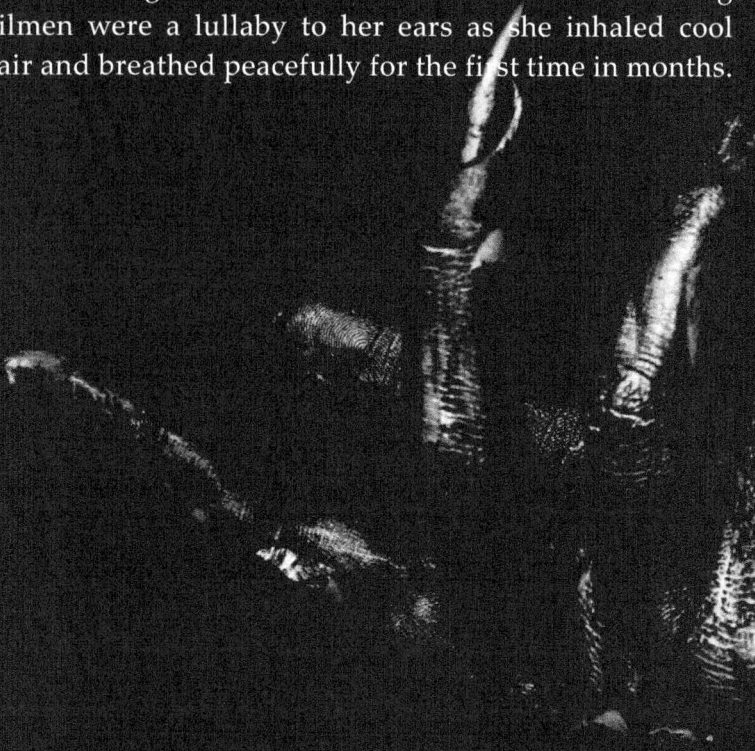

Chapter Twenty-Seven

With light footsteps, Rhiannon followed the stone path that led around the garden to her home. She faltered and froze, her feet weighed down by guilt, as Tristain's worried gaze met her own. She swallowed thickly. There was no denying what she'd done, covered in the councilman's blood like she was. Her monster had gone back to sleep long ago, sated by the violence.

"Is he dead?" Tristain asked.

"They all are." Rhiannon straightened her spine as she pushed past him and into her home. He followed. "The council got what they had coming."

"What about your mother and sister? Someone is going to find out what you've done."

Tristain's expression was hard, not shifting even a fraction away from her eyes as she pulled off her blood-drenched dress.

"Do you not think that I have any concern for them? Do you not think I'm capable of thinking rationally? Do you not think that I would take precautions to protect them?"

Her monster stirred awake as Rhiannon's irritation mounted to anger.

"When you're like this? I don't know." He averted his gaze from her naked form. "I don't like the way this magic influences you. It's dangerous. I'll be happy when you're rid of it."

A growl hummed low in Rhiannon's throat. Her monster paced just below the surface, ready to pounce at the perceived threat.

Maybe we won't keep him after all.

Rhiannon's fear and objection mingled with the monster's growing eagerness. Rhiannon's exhaustion and the taste for blood made the urges more difficult to control.

"You need to stop talking like that," she warned.

A tingle of suspense crept up her spine and across her scalp.

"I don't care if it's not what you want to hear. We're in this together. We agreed that this magic needs to be put to rest. It can only bring pain and destruction. Or have you changed your mind?" He took two steps closer, but Rhiannon held up her hand that sprouted claws at his approach. "You can't possibly think that this will end well. Look at what it's doing to you. It has to go."

He must go. Kill him. We can start with his tongue, just like we did the other one. Don't you remember how good that felt?

Rhiannon searched for her control, scrambling to grab the fraying ends of her restraint as her monster grew impatient. "You need to run."

"What?" Tristain stepped closer.

Rip and stab and maim and kill. Ending him will be such a thrill.

Her monster was insatiable now that the idea had crossed her mind.

"You need to run. *Now.*" Rhiannon buckled over with the pain flaring through her as she resisted the ancient power that stirred within her.

Tears of blood trickled out of her eyes, leaking down her face, and meeting the trails that had begun to spill from her nose as well. "Stop standing there and fucking run."

Tristain bumped against the door, but he wasn't listening to her.

She was going to be sick from all the contrasting emotions pounding through her. While her monster was excited and hungry, Rhiannon panicked. She would sooner tear herself apart than hurt Tristain, but that was if she could even help it. Resisting it was becoming less manageable by the second. Her ears rang with a fevered pitch as she kneeled and dug her claws into her scalp, trying to use the pain as an anchor to focus on staying in control of her body.

It's too late. There's no running. It'll be for the best when it's just you and me. You'll see.

Sickening images of Tristain struggling against her hold with her blade across his throat turned Rhiannon's stomach. In her mind, she could see the light fading from his eyes as blood poured down his front. And when he'd stopped breathing, she could see her heaving figure as she hacked his head off, his soft waves covered in his own blood as she clutched it in her hand. Burning vomit crawled up Rhiannon's throat, and when she opened her mouth to tell Tristain to run, it spewed across the floor. Her stomach clenched. Her nose and throat burned, but the worst was the devastating scene that replayed in her mind.

Stop being weak. Get up and end him. You don't have a choice anymore. We will not be threatened.

Uneven breaths choked Rhiannon, and her head swam as she tried to sift through her thoughts for a way to get out of this. Adrenaline and sickness racked her body with nauseating waves.

It was too much.

She was crumbling under the pressure. Her bones vibrated with tension plaguing her muscles as she held the monster at bay and fought against her own body.

"Rhiannon?"

An undercurrent of terror warped Tristain's voice in her ringing ears. He leaned down to touch her, and her arm flung out against her will, slashing through the thin tunic, cutting deep, jagged lines across his chest that immediately bloomed crimson.

Tristain staggered back, his hand pressing the wounds spanning far wider than his long fingers.

Rhiannon's eyes met his, and whatever he saw finally convinced him to run.

Instead of saving him, though, it piqued the interest of her predatory instincts. He was no sooner out the door when she scrambled to her feet in pursuit, sliding on his blood.

As they passed the garden and ran into the trees behind her family home, Tristain only remained a short distance ahead of her.

The need to slow pulsed through Rhiannon as she begged her body to cooperate with her, but the magic, her monster, pushed back harder, silencing her wishes and driving them toward the edge.

Desperation clawed at Rhiannon's lungs as her unsteady breathing and sobs fought for the little oxygen she was inhaling. Her head was light as confusion, fear, and despair whipped through her.

She couldn't live with herself if she harmed him, if she killed him. The possibility was unbearable, yet her legs didn't stop pressing forward after him.

His fear is delectable. I can't wait to lick it from his cold skin.

Her monster's taunts sent a chill through Rhiannon.

A dense thud and the sound of Tristain's breath knocking out of his chest caused an uninvited thrill to spark within Rhiannon.

Sorrow and panic pinched his expression as he looked up at her from beneath the dark curls that hung over his forehead.

Seeing his struggling form on the ground as he pulled at the root caught around his foot forced Rhiannon to act. This was her last chance to save him.

She dug her claws into her own abdomen, piercing deeply beneath the skin. The excruciating pain slowed her steps and buckled her knees. Just a few feet shy of where the man she loved lay, Rhiannon desperately fought to distract her monster by causing herself debilitating pain. She forced her fingers deeper and scratched back and forth, opening the wounds wider. A cold sweat broke out over her naked skin.

What are you doing? Stop that and get up. We can't let him get away.

Rhiannon ignored her monster and ripped her hand free, only to plunge the long nails into the top of her thigh. She cried out in pain, her own voice foreign to her ears.

Enough of that.

Her nails pulled out of her and planted themselves in the dirt as her arms pulled her forward, closing in on where Tristain watched in horror. He scrambled backward, finally pulling his foot free. But in the loose dirt, he couldn't find purchase before Rhiannon's hand snapped around his ankle and dragged him toward her.

"Rhiannon." Tristain said it like he wasn't sure if she was there anymore. "Rhi, stop this. You're in control. Fight it." He yelped as her fingers dug into his skin and grated the bone.

Panic was all she knew in that moment. She wanted to stop more than anything else. She needed to regain control. Yet, her fingers clenched harder.

The fear in his gaze struck a chord that disrupted the symphony of chaos booming within her. In that moment of clarity, she tore her other hand out of the dirt and wrapped it around her own throat, digging the dangerously sharp nails into her own skin on either side of her trachea.

"If you harm him, I will end this all."

And she would do it, too. If she were responsible for Tristain's death, she couldn't live with that. There was a lot she could bear, but the weight of that loss would break her into a thousand tiny shards that could never fit back together.

"Try me."

She threatened the rogue entity within. Her heart beat wildly against her rib cage as the seconds passed, with everything hanging in the balance.

Finally conceding to the threat, the magic receded, and her monster silenced.

Rhiannon didn't dare move, letting the blood trickle over her fingers as he waited for the ravenous hunger to flare once again. When the claws retracted on their own and Rhiannon's breathing finally evened to catch enough air to fill her lungs, she unwrapped one finger, then another, from Tristain's ankle and sat up to her knees.

Rhiannon pulled her gaze from his and looked down at herself. Caked dirt covered her breasts and stomach, where it had seeped into the deep cuts, and mingled with her blood. Her thighs quivered with the pain of the fresh wounds. The breath she'd finally caught sprinted away from her once again, and this time, it competed with sobs that rattled her chest and hollowed her stomach.

Hesitantly, Tristain sat forward and crawled toward her to pull her into his warm embrace. "Shh . . . Rhi, it's okay." He stroked her hair as she sat, frozen, too afraid to touch him back.

Rhiannon clutched her arms across her chest, scraping at the small patches of clean skin, as she shuddered and sobbed.

It was as if her mind had drifted far from her body, and she was above, watching them sit in shock beneath the trees, with moonlight scattered across their bodies between the branches.

She refused to believe that she had come so close to ending Tristain's life. She loved him. She would never hurt him. She never would have felt the thrill pulsing through her. It wasn't possible. It wasn't real. She must have been sleeping. The entire night had been a dream turned into a nightmare.

Tristain's lips against her forehead brought her consciousness back into her body. She searched his gaze for fear or disgust for what she'd just done, but there was nothing but worry—for her.

Tears flooded with the immense impact of that realization. He was worried about her. He feared for her safety, just as he had his a moment ago. Instead of running from her, he'd crawled toward her.

"Rhi, it's not your fault. Please don't cry. I know you'd have done everything in your power to fight for me to the very end." He gulped as his eyes searched hers. "You were ready to sacrifice yourself for me. You were so close to . . ." His hand left her to tangle in his hair. "I almost lost you again."

"There was no other way." Rhiannon's voice was as vacant as she felt. "She'd decided you were going to die. I saw it. I saw us kill you. There would be no living with myself after that. Anything else, and I could press on, but if I were the reason you no longer breathed, there would be no coming back from that loss. My guilt would have consumed me from the inside out. It was better to end it my way." She dared to look at him. "Can't you understand that?"

Tristain nodded, tucking her dirty hair behind her ear.

"I don't know when it happened, but at some point along the way, you became my reason to live and breathe. So, if it was you or me, it was really no choice at all."

The first drops of rain pattered her head, a cool relief from the pain burning through her.

"Again and again, you choose me. And I'll always choose you. Even when you think you've strayed too far away, I'll stand at the edge of everything and call you back until you find your way to me." He wiped the blood and grime from her cheeks with the rain dripping down her face.

Rhiannon closed her eyes, reveling in the gentle touch he bestowed on her, like she was just the woman he loved and not the monster who furiously hunted him minutes ago. She bit her wobbling lip, forcing it into submission.

Tristain's fingers moved upward, stroking through her hair as he brushed the soaked strands away from her face, giving her space to breathe. A calloused thumb tugged at the lip between her teeth and then his lips brushed across hers, asking for permission.

Rhiannon allowed a soft breath to pass through as she parted them, a tentative invitation.

Tristain dared to enter, his tongue exploring the seam of her lips and cautiously stroking her waiting tongue. So slowly, so softly, he moved his mouth in tandem with the gentle fingers that swept up the sensitive skin of her sides. When she leaned into his touch, he traced the undersides of her heavy breasts.

Rain was slick between their bodies as they touched ever so slightly at the points where her figure was fullest. The roundness of her lower stomach brushing his soft abdomen. The peaks of her taut nipples tickling his chest. The tops of her plush thighs seeking the warmth of his muscular legs.

Every touch was cautious, an unspoken request for forgiveness for all they'd put each other through the last few days. And when neither of them pulled away in revulsion, their bodies pressed together feverishly in a desperate apology.

They'd both crossed lines they'd never imagined and had lost themselves to the feral forces within them.

Individually, they'd overcome the urges forced upon them and threatened to make them forget themselves.

Together, they'd survived each other.

As Tristain bent his head and trailed his lips delicately over her torn throat, Rhiannon started to believe that maybe there truly was a chance that they could survive all of this together.

And when his strong hands cupped her breasts, knowingly teasing her nipples in a way that had her arching into him, she even ventured to imagine that they might be able to piece together the broken shards of their past.

His sure hands on her full hips guided her onto his lap and into the safety of accepting that possibility. As he eased back into the soil where they'd tried to take each other's lives and gave over all control to her, she dove headfirst into the pursuit of that happy ending that she'd never allowed herself to believe she'd have. And when she arched her back and slid down onto his thick cock that fit so perfectly within her as her cunt stretched around him, she clung to the belief that it could be hers, that it *would* be hers. That they would fight for it together.

With each thrust, their souls twined closer together, finding solitude in one another, perhaps for the first time. Knowing that they would be each other's last. That they were the only ones who could mold to each other's jagged edges. The only ones who could fill the emptiness in one another's hearts that had left them wide open to all the hurt for far too long.

Rhiannon's hips rolled against Tristain's in a relentless effort to get closer to him, to bury him within her and make them inseparable. His hungry fingers were insatiable as they ran over her skin, gripping the dimpled flesh of her thighs, anchoring Rhiannon to him yet careful not to dig into the wounds she made saving his life.

Rhiannon needed more of him. Her hand traveled up his abdomen and wrapped around his neck. An echo of where they'd found themselves the morning before. But this time, the touch wasn't to steal his last breaths like he had hers. Instead, it was a claim to keep those breaths for herself. To be their keeper, their protector, until the end of their days. Because the moment they'd plead for forgiveness and granted it to one another, they'd stopped being Rhiannon and Tristain.

They'd become an inseparable pair that would face off with their darkest demons for one another and come out the other side together. Hand in hand, they'd deny the curse thrust upon them.

As she clenched around him and he spilled into her, their names on one another's lips sealed their fate. They'd see this through the end, together. For better or worse, their paths crossing for more than the purpose of walking into a cruel end hand in hand was the only fate they'd accept.

CHAPTER TWENTY-EIGHT

Rhiannon's mind was clearer than it had been in quite some time, but her heart was heavy as she embraced her mother. This was a simple comfort she had taken for granted before and would deeply feel the absence of.

"I love you. Promise you'll come visit for longer next time. I miss having you at home. It's not the same without you." Her mother wiped the tears painting her cheeks.

Rhiannon fought against her own as more tiny fractures etched themselves across her heart. It was so much harder to leave them this time. Her outlook on the world and the reasons she had to keep fighting made her hypersensitive to the risks she was taking. She was having trouble reckoning with the full potential for loss this time around. It stole Rhiannon's breath as she stared blearily at her mother, memorizing the love in her eyes and the strength that straightened her spine and helped her let Rhiannon go. She would match that resilience.

"I will see you again as soon as I can. I love you, too." After another lingering embrace, she moved onto her sister.

The unconditional love and decades of sibling companionship enveloped her in a joyful bubble she didn't want to burst.

"I'm going to miss you. I know you already do but take care of Mother. I worry about her being lonely."

Jade sniffled. "She won't be. But I'm more worried about you. I didn't pry as to why you came back, and I won't now. I don't think my heart can bear it. But whatever it is that you're rushing back into, when it's all over, write to me. I'll come see you."

"You'll come see me or us." Rhiannon smirked as Jade shoved her shoulder.

"Don't be like that. Yes, to see you. And if I get to see your unforgettable, gorgeous friend again, well, that would be just lovely."

The darkening of Jade's cheeks gave away just how exciting that prospect was for her, and Rhiannon couldn't help but match her smile.

"We'd love for you to come visit." She wrapped her arms around her sister's lean frame. "I love you."

"I love you, too," Jade whispered against her hair.

Idris slid a firm arm around her shoulder, and Rhiannon tilted her head back to see him fully.

"You ran out on us last night. I barely got to see you," he complained.

"I know. I'm sorry about that. I"—she searched for an excuse—"wasn't feeling well. But I'll be back. And maybe you can come with Jade to visit in Wispombra?"

"I'll be seeing you one way or another. You can't get rid of me after all this time." Finally, he loosened his strong arms and let her out of his possessive hold, then turned his attention to Tristain. "Take care of our girl."

"Always," Tristain replied affectionately.

She loved seeing all of the people she cared about getting along so well, as if it had always been this way. But Rhiannon's attention particularly snagged on the unexpected pair who had come out of all this.

Kyra wove her fingers into Jade's hair intimately as they said their goodbyes. The ease of their touch and the light in their eyes as they gazed at one another held so much promise.

It was another rung on the ladder of hope that had drawn Rhiannon out of the pit of despair she was stuck in when this had all started. Whether she'd fully make it out depended on where things went from here.

As the carriage her mother had lent them set off, the weight of what they were walking into was heavier than the rain threatening to break through the gray clouds above. The lingering emotions of their goodbyes seemed to trail them, even as they traveled north.

Between the rocking carriage on the uneven path and the need for sleep that had been nipping at Rhiannon's heels after her late night, she was nodding off within the first few minutes. As they crossed the outskirts of Oakhaven, Rhiannon gave herself over to rest.

When her eyes fluttered open, the sun was low in the sky. She leaned toward the window and scanned the open green land. Small scattered hills interrupted the stretches of grass and flowers coming to life around them. In the distance, she was surprised to see the clustered trees that signaled hours had already passed, and they were quickly approaching Norhavalta.

Rhiannon was pleasantly surprised by how much faster the miles went by as they traveled across the familiar terrain.

It was still silent in the carriage, the rest of her companions taking the opportunity to catch up on sleep. Between stormy seas, their near constant movement from destination to destination, and the overwhelming stress of all they'd been tasked with, the last few weeks had been arduous to say the least. Exhaustion clung to Rhiannon's bones in a way that told her if she succumbed to it, it would be nearly impossible for her to become reinvigorated any time soon. At the thought, she straightened her back and rolled her shoulders, forcing her body to return to alertness.

It was tempting to take comfort in the shelter of the warm carriage and the lightness that had surrounded them for most of their visit back home. But it was not the time to lose focus or let her defenses fall by the wayside.

Rhiannon would use this short window of opportunity to fortify her determination and refine her plans. There was no way to predict how severing Tristain's bond to the Volskruga or hers with her monster would go, but Rhiannon wasn't naive enough with her newly adopted optimism to think it would be anything but challenging—and possibly even devastating.

Both she and Tristain had seen just how corrupt they'd become under the magic's influence. Rhiannon had no delusions it would give up that control over them easily. No. They were in for the fight of their lives.

It wasn't just the ownership of their minds and bodies they were fighting for. They would be facing off for the fate of Larindia and beyond. What happened next would determine whether all these unsuspecting people they'd passed in these last few weeks would find their lives overturned in the face of wrath and destruction or if they'd continue living peacefully, oblivious to the evil lingering between the trees and beneath their feet.

Warm, delicate fingers pressing into her thigh stirred her from her troubling thoughts. Gleaming blue eyes watched her carefully.

"You're not in this alone. Don't even think about retreating into yourself and pulling away from us again. We all agreed that we were doing this together, and we meant it. We're seeing this through to the very end." Samara gave her another firm squeeze before sitting back against the opposite side of the carriage.

Rhiannon nodded, but her words were stuck in her throat. That new flicker of hope was rekindled, causing repressed emotion to bubble up and steal her voice. The last time she'd faced the Volskruga, she'd marched into the Sangravian Woods with the surety that death waited for her there. And she'd accepted that, fully resigned to the belief that the only thing she could dare to hope for was the survival of her friends. But this time, Rhiannon wasn't walking into this face-off with death alone. She'd been emboldened by the unconditional acceptance she'd found. She had people who believed in her, who trusted her to overcome the evil that had rooted itself so deeply in their lives. The only question was whether she'd be strong enough to finally sever those ties and free them from the burden that had taken so much from them.

As the familiar inn that had marked the beginning of this journey so many months ago rolled into view, Rhiannon allowed her heart to open to the possibility that they could all make it out of this alive.

CHAPTER TWENTY-NINE

espite the resolve that had washed over her when
they entered Norhavalta, that was shattered by
the cries that pulled her from her sleep. The fear
that drove the pitch higher and higher sank claws of urgency
into Rhiannon as she dressed, pulling on a pair of pants, a
sweater, a cloak, all of the deepest black.

Another scream sent her rushing down the stairs two at a
time and into the brisk night air.

At this hour, the busy streets settled into an eerie, foreign
quiet. There were no carts laden with goods drawing the eyes
of onlookers or rowdy voices flowing through open windows
and swinging doors lining the path she walked. It was only
Rhiannon and the crush of dirt beneath her feet as she walked
in the direction of where she'd thought the scream came from.
When the fluffy trees marked the end of town and the trail
led to the cluster of homes in the distance, suspense tightened
painfully in Rhiannon's gut. There was something undeniably
unsettling about the silence that fell across Norhavalta that
night.

Halting, she scanned the vast emptiness around her. There
wasn't a single person roaming pointlessly like her. There
wasn't anyone stumbling home on uncoordinated feet. There
weren't even any animals searching for their next meal under

the moonlight. She stood still and let her senses detect the source of the sporadic sound. But she heard nothing.

When she'd almost written off the cries were a figment of her imagination, the bristle of fabric against trees drew her attention.

The hairs on Rhiannon's arms and neck stood at attention as her heartbeat doubled. Her magic sprang to alertness as Rhiannon prepared to defend herself and charged into the overgrown trees. She walked a few feet, then stopped again as she searched for any faint sound. Heavy, muffled breaths had her cutting a path right. The pounding of a set of thudding heartbeats grew closer with every step. And then she saw what she was looking for: a rogue lock of fiery hair peaking out in stark contrast against the blackness of night.

Rhiannon lunged around the trees behind which the two people hid.

One was a frail girl with freckled ivory skin and moss-green eyes. The second was a muscular man with sun-kissed skin and a hazel gaze. Their strong chins and high cheek bones were nearly identical, but the man didn't appear old enough to be her father. Their relation didn't matter, as understanding their anger lanced through her when she saw the restraints hanging from the girl's wrist. One shattered open, while the other weighed her arm down to her side. The man's hand slid away from the girl's mouth and around her neck as Rhiannon pressed them into the trees.

"You have three seconds to let her go."

She would rather have the girl out of harm's way before she tore this man apart.

Instead, his hand clenched tighter around the girl's slim neck. Rhiannon let out a heavy sigh. She didn't want to traumatize the young woman more than this man already had, so she released a small cloud of mist, and they lost consciousness. She dipped quickly to catch the girl before her body crumpled on the ground, but she let the man fall with a hard thud.

Carefully, she carried the young woman a safe distance away. As she looked over her youthful features, Rhiannon concluded she couldn't have been more than nineteen or twenty. She hated that the girl had endured such suffering so early in life.

Fierce protectiveness tightened her muscles and hardened her jaw as she walked back over the man and kicked him in the stomach repeatedly. He woke before she even landed the second blow, but she gave him four more for good measure. The man curled in on himself.

Rhiannon nudged him with her boot to roll him onto his back. "Get up."

The man closed his eyes against the horrifying sight of her. She would say she hoped that the image would haunt his nightmares, but Rhiannon didn't plan on letting him live. When the man didn't make any move to stand, she dug her elongated nails into the meat of his arm and forced him to his feet.

"What have you done to her?"

"Please, just let me go, and you can have her."

He had the audacity to plead for mercy when he'd shown the girl nothing but brutality.

"And why would I do that?" She tightened her grip, and blood oozed out of the punctures in his arm.

He cried out an answer as she dug her nails into the underlying muscle. "Because that's what you want, to save her, isn't it? What do you need with me? I promise I won't do it again. Just let me go. I have a wife."

"In that case, I'm happy to do her the favor or freeing her from that unfortunate union."

The man tried to flee, but she drove a hard knee into his groin and pinned him in place against the tree trunk. Before he could disgust her any further with his begging, she pulled her dagger from the holster and drove it into his frantically beating heart, then his gut for good measure.

As his breathing slowed, she made sure to twist and grind it into him to wrench every last bit of agony from him until the life finally faded from his eyes. Her mist ate up what was left of him, removing his foul presence from Norhavalta for good.

She recalled her glamor, the magic slipping away before she woke the girl.

Confusion pulled at her features as she searched frantically around her for her rogue relative and captor.

"Where is he?"

Her weak voice shook.

"He won't hurt you ever again. Where do you live? I'll make sure you get home."

"Just there." The young woman pointed down the path where a row of houses sat.

She'd barely gotten anywhere. Rhiannon's heart clenched at the realization.

"Okay. Go home, then. Don't tell anyone about this. Promise?"

The girl nodded. "Thank you." She took off before Rhiannon could respond.

She sat in the quiet, her mind reeling. The reprieve didn't last long when another presence at her back forced her to call on her lingering power.

Gathering around her were more of the spirits that had manifested the night before. There were easily twice as many, and if they'd been anything but an extension of her own magic, she would have been fearful. However, as she stood with them in silence, a wave of sadness swelled within her.

Moments later, she shook with the overwhelming energy radiating off them that matched her own pain so well.

"Why are you here?" she asked no one in particular.

"We have come to walk with you, to serve you."

VENGEANCE FREES HER

A chorus of voices flooded her mind. In unison, their heads bowed, and they continued.

"She will scorch the earth with her fury and those gone before her."

The mothers, siblings, and lovers who have been preyed upon, decade over decade.

Those who were stripped of their choices and were shown no mercy.

The ones whose lives were drained away by the rotting infection of their own pain.

Passed down from one generation to another.

From land to land, across seas, and into the depths of the soil.

A sapling seed of the restless spirit of their torment will be planted.

Year after year, it will be watered by the tears, blood, and bones of the ones who fell at the hands of their tormentors.

When those seeds of despair take root, they will grow strong and spring to the surface.

And finally, the one who can carry out their retribution will bloom.

A thorned flower that is alluring as it is lethal.

The perfect weapon.

From her devastation, she will bring destruction.

When the power of men that has trapped the world in its poisonous fangs is wounded from within, the spirit will be awakened.

And it will be born of flesh unto her, by a willing sacrifice at her own hand.

In death and rebirth, they will be bonded, spirit to soul.

Her magic will manifest in the form of the blood of those who have fallen before her, becoming hers to wield and exact their vengeance.

She will get retribution for the greed and violence that has caused unnecessary suffering.

The Daughter of Desire, born of Death and Blood will reset the scales of power and make them regret ever creating an imbalance."

Rhiannon was breathless when they finished.

They were the mothers, siblings, and lovers they spoke of. This explained why they kept coming to her. This hadn't been in the prophecy that she'd found, but they believed this to be true.

Tears tracked down her cheeks as the weight of it settled over her—their expectations and her impending failure of them.

But they weren't done, and everything they'd been forced to take to their graves surged into Rhiannon. After years of being ignored and then forgotten, they were rejoicing in being seen by her and clamoring for the validation they never received. The cacophony of need sent her to her knees.

One by one, haunting voices buzzed around her head like bees in a frenzy searching for their queen. Speaking over one another, they whispered the secrets they'd been forced to bear in shame. They spoke the truth of their misfortune, and they screamed the names of those who had abused them, ruined them, betrayed them.

Low voices still belittled by the shame they'd been made to feel.

Panicked voices living on an endless loop of the worst night of their lives.

Vicious voices that had nurtured the seeds of their anger all this time.

They were her kindred spirits, and their stories resonated with her to an excruciating degree. The brokenness that had humbled her. The fury that had rebuilt her. The vow of vengeance that had saved her and damned her in equal parts.

It was all amplified into a vibrational force threatening to shatter her bones under the pressure. And still, she kneeled on the cold ground, head bent, teeth gritted as she let them be heard like they'd always deserved.

"His grip was so tight on my thighs I bore the marks of his greed for weeks . . ."

"They found me on the path, and I never finished the walk home . . ."

"The sharp scent of ale-soured breath lingered on my skin, no matter how much I bathed . . ."

"His hand swallowed my screams as he watched the light leave my eyes . . ."

"He stole the most vital pieces of me . . ."

The horrific recounting of their suffering seemed unending, and by the time Rhiannon's voice was the only one in her head, her joints had gone stiff, and the moon had moved in the sky above.

She forced her eyes open against the skull-shattering ache of her ravaged mind. She looked at them in understanding, and even though their features weren't well defined, she could see agony so clearly painted on their naked scarlet bodies and their rage evidenced in the unwieldy movements of the red mist suspended around them.

Finally, she stood on unsteady feet. "What now?" she whispered to herself.

They will help you end our suffering once and for all. They go where you go. They are part of you. They will help you fulfill your purpose, her monster answered back.

Unease rippled through Rhiannon. They might be part of her, but she was under no delusion that she had full control of them. It was undeniable they could be of use to her, especially if the Volskruga returned to full power before they could break the bond. But she wondered, would they be loyal to her, Rhiannon, or were they only aligned with the ancient power that had made her their revered Daughter of Desire, born of Death and Blood?

She feared that distinction would matter when they came to blows. She would need to prepare for that unfortunate likelihood, but for the time being, she would take comfort in their presence.

And perhaps she could give them something as well. She let her voice carry over them.

"Go forth and take your vengeance. If your tormentors still walk among us, make them regret ever laying a hand on you. If they found peace without payment for their transgressions, take it out on the next man you see who would dare perpetuate the cycle of harm. The scales could use a bit of balancing, after all."

Their vibrating forms combined into a swirling red blur and then they were off into the night, taking the stifling energy that had settled among the trees with them. As blue hues broke through the cloak of night, Rhiannon turned toward the village and started her walk back to the inn. So many things now made sense. And while the version of Rhiannon, who hadn't yet bore the burden of this power, would have eagerly carried the torch of destruction against those who had wronged her and the women before her, this Rhiannon, the one who knew the true risk of wielding such power, couldn't fulfill the fate of death and blood that had been forced upon her. No matter what she had to do, she would find a way to defy that path, and this only assured her of it further.

Relief coursed through her when her head finally hit the pillow, and she circled into Tristain's steady warmth. The events of the night had left her depleted, and she was grateful her body didn't fight sleep.

Not long enough later, she woke to Tristain's lips on her forehead. Rhiannon leaned into the softness of him while she lingered in the quiet world between sleep and wakefulness. She wasn't ready to return to reality, yet his persistent gaze heavy on her skin pulled her out of slumber. His eyes were more orange than brown that day as sunrays fell across them.

"We should be going soon," Tristain whispered as she buried her face against him.

"How long do I have?"

"Not long. Samara should be back soon and then we'll leave." He stroked her back.

"Did she go see her family?" Rhiannon tilted her head back to look at him.

"Yes. She wanted to make sure they were making do on their own."

"I told her she should stay with them. She'd be safer. They'd be grateful to have her." Rhiannon sighed. "But I understand why she feels the need to see this through to the end. I just hope it doesn't end up being her last regret."

"Don't say things like that." He smiled, satisfaction curving his lips against hers.

The thing about hope, Rhiannon had found, was that it was contagious.

While she was tempted to lose herself to the simple comfort of his embrace and reassurance of each loving kiss, it would have to wait. The sooner they left, the sooner this would be over, one way or another. She was ready to move on. She wanted there to be mornings where she could wake up and choose to never leave the safety of her covers. She needed to spend days lying beneath the trees and getting lost in her books. She was eager to sleep at night, wrapped in Tristain's arms, without the weight of the world crushing them.

That possibility was what drove her as she readied for another day of travel. They were so close to the end. She could almost taste the freedom.

CHAPTER THIRTY

As they continued their journey north, Rhiannon was grateful that the frozen air and deep snow had started to thaw, making room for warmth and new life to grow with spring upon them.

The trees were still mostly bare of leaves, and their roots were hidden beneath the expanse of white, but the stirrings of something new could be felt along their upward-reaching branches.

Once everyone had time to fully awaken, Rhiannon decided it was time to share what she had learned about the spirits attached to her.

"I've learned something new about my magic."

Their gazes rested on her expectantly.

"I have kindred spirits. Those that have fallen at the hands of men before me. They are bound to the source of my power."

Silence.

"What does that mean?" Kyra asked cautiously.

"Their souls, they were drawn to me. Several of them came to me in Oakhaven and then again last night, but there were far more of them." Rhiannon chewed the side of her thumb. "More will come, and these ones will follow me. I think they could be of use if we find ourselves unfairly matched. But they're vengeful spirits. They crave unrest. They seek justice.

I don't know how much control I'll be able to wield over them if we are in opposition."

"Are they dangerous?" Samara's eyes were wide with curiosity and fear.

"Yes. They've killed, and I don't think they have any reservations about doing it again. My hope is that they will be loyal to me. That they can be laid to rest when I break the bond that has tethered me to the old magic. I don't want to exact decades or centuries of revenge or lay destruction to the land that too many have already died on. I want peace. I want to be free of this burden once and for all. I've faced the loss and devastation it brings once. I don't intend to allow it to happen again. But I did give them permission to exact their personal vengeance in the meantime."

"You did what?"

"Of course you did."

Samara and Kyra spoke at the same time.

"What's done is done." Rhiannon shrugged.

She wasn't going to apologize, and it was too late to change anything.

Tristain ignored them and leaned toward her, resting his hands on either side of her knee. "Would they hurt you?"

"I want to think they wouldn't, but if anyone understands how all-consuming the need for vengeance can be, it's me. I don't know if I could begrudge them their resistance. I just hope the time I gave them is enough to let them get the closure they need. But for those who don't succeed, I don't know, we'll see. It's not that I don't think that pursuing justice for all those wrong in the world is not a worthy cause anymore, but the weight of this power is too much. The risks, the costs I would be forced to pay, are far too high."

"Hopefully, when we break the bond and lie the magic to rest for good, they'll find peace," Kyra added.

Rhiannon nodded, although she wasn't sure what would happen to them when all was said and done. Part of her was saddened that she would disappoint them, the spirits of women who were just like her, but the extent of suffering and loss of innocents, that would result in her magic being fully unleashed wasn't a compromise she was willing to make. Perhaps it was selfish of her. She'd gotten her vengeance. But it'd also required a hefty sacrifice, and she wasn't giving any more of herself. Even for them.

She was done. She was reclaiming her life. She'd done what she could for them, and she'd find peace in that.

Inner turmoil and doubt had kept her preoccupied for hours, but Samara forced her to part from her thoughts.

"Please tell me we're not sleeping in the Vrugian Woods again?"

The blond's knee bounced up and down.

"The horses need to rest, and the woods span too far for us to make it out tonight."

Tristain had the decency to at least sound regretful.

"We can just stop long enough to sleep a bit. Once the sun is up, we can leave." He turned his gaze purposely toward the window.

Tristain's tone was reassuring, but his posture was stiff.

Rhiannon examined his clenched fingers in his hair. Her eyes traced the tension in his jaw and the furrow of his brow. The tension transferred to her without her permission. Rhiannon hated the uncertainty and dread that worked its way through her system. Her legs suddenly felt trapped by the thick fabric of her pants. The carriage was too small. Her fingers flexed, needing to see action. Yet, she sat absolutely still, not wanting to spread this contagious anxiety to the others.

Despite her best efforts, tension ratcheted with the gradual descent of the sun. When they finally rolled to a stop, Rhiannon burst through the door and gulped in air.

As if disturbed by her presence, the wind howled through the trees, yanked at her hair, and whipped it across her face.

A deep chill settled into her bones and burned her exposed skin. The elements hadn't affected her in some time, but the frigid air wasn't solely due to snow surrounding them. It was the culmination of restless spirits making themselves known.

Rhiannon didn't wrap her arms around herself or bury her face. She stood her ground, acknowledging and accepting their displeasure.

Their existence was complicated, she understood. Bound to something they didn't ask for, held tightly within its grasp, forced to act on its behalf.

Rhiannon stood in the same cage, rattled at the same bars. She, too often, felt unheard.

The energy shifted, and slowly, the wind died down, dulling to soft rustling. At the concession, Rhiannon continued into the trees and relieved herself after far too long on the move. It was one of the few times she was thankful for her monster when she managed to navigate the dark without fire.

When she emerged into the small clearing where they'd stopped for the night, the first embers crackled to life, casting an orange glow across her companions' faces. All looked pleased to find themselves here again.

"Where are we sleeping?" Rhiannon asked.

"The carriage."

Tristain didn't take his eyes off the bread and cheese he was dividing into five servings.

"That sounds fucking horrid." Rhiannon let out a long sigh.

What she wouldn't give to enjoy the comforts of a normal bed for more than a few days at a time.

"Unfortunately, none of us had the forethought to prepare for a night in the woods."

His tone wasn't bitter, but there was an uncharacteristic bite to the words.

Rhiannon accepted her food as he passed it around.

She let out a long sigh. Last time, she'd been on edge, terrified of what lurked in the darkness between the trees. Since then, she'd come face-to-face with the Volskruga so many times. While she was still wary of its power, their familiarity had dissipated the fear she once held for this place. Knowing they'd be sleeping here still caused her unease for other reasons, though. The souls of all those who had fallen to the Volskruga over the centuries were stuck here in perpetuity. It wasn't hard to understand the bitterness and unrest it bred.

They ate in silence, suspense and the wary eyes of their carriage driver sealing their mouths shut and chasing away their usual easy conversation.

Rhiannon offered to take first watch. While she was as tired, it made most sense. If any threats were to arise, she was best suited to face them. She didn't mind the time alone, either. It was her and the soothing crackle of the burning wood.

The moment of peace in such an unexpected place washed over her. She was completely alone with her thoughts, and for once, they weren't wrapped up in the tangled mess of her emotions. Rhiannon let her mind wander, appreciating the glowing moonlight cascading through the tall trees to light slivers of the forest. With concentration, she could hear the faint trickle of water traveling down the distant river. She'd let her head fall back to gaze at the twinkling stars that shone twice as bright here, but their shimmering shapes became hazy when pressure was suddenly applied around her throat.

Rhiannon threw her weight back, unseating herself from the log and restoring her air flow. She quickly rolled back to her feet and turned to her attacker.

Tristain stood before her, one of his belts in hand, his blacked-out eyes unseeing. His full lips were flattened in an angry line as the thick, dark veins pulsed rapidly.

Rhiannon searched desperately for a glimpse of the man she loved. His arms hung at his sides, his head was cocked at an awkward angle, and his demeanor was shrouded in disdain for her.

Tristain wasn't here.

Rhiannon was too slow to react once the Volskruga caught wind of her recognition. She flew back against the solid base of a nearby tree. Darkness swallowed moonlight. Her eyes searched frantically in the pitch black, but even her predator's eyes couldn't decipher her surroundings.

A gritty laugh vibrated in the air right in front of her. Rhiannon responded with a slash of claws as soon as she felt the warm blood slip over her. She was thrust back by an invisible force. A loud crack rang in her ears. It could have been her head or the bark, she couldn't be sure. Her thoughts were disoriented as the pain radiated within her skull and sent them scattering.

Her monster let out a shriek of rage only Rhiannon could hear.

"Are you still fighting what you are, Rhiannon?" Amusement laced the Volskruga's tone. "So stubborn. So ungrateful. So"—it searched for another insult—"unwise."

Irritation drove her next action as she sliced through the air again. A flicker of moonlight broke through.

It responded with another surge of power that threw her back. Heat bloomed in her shoulder as something pierced her skin. She thrust herself forward, but this time, she fell to her knees. Rhiannon pounded her fist into the ground with a grunt of frustration. Cautiously, she rose to her knees, moving her head back and forth uselessly. She was only met with an unfathomable blackness. It was as if the world had swallowed her whole, and she was in the deepest pit of its gut.

"What are you going to do? Suppress your magic until you wither away to a sad shell of a thing? Will you be demure and gentle just to keep the hunger at bay? Would you lock that beautifully ferocious spark within you and let it burn out by keeping it locked away in a box? Can you throw away the key?" The Volskruga whispered the taunts into her ear, its breath so frigid it made the snow beneath her palms seem warm.

"What the fuck does it matter to you? You won't be around to see what becomes of me."

Rhiannon's uneven breaths tore at the quiet around them. She was grateful for the confirmation that she was still alive, that she hadn't been cast away into an eternity of torment.

Get up, her monster hissed.

Rhiannon closed her eyes, frantically seeking answers. She needed a plan. She wasn't foolish enough to believe herself stronger than the Volskruga. They were on its soil.

On its soil. They were on its soil.

Rhiannon dug her fist into the ground, gathering as much dirt as she could and shoving it in her pocket. She repeated the motion, filling the other. It wouldn't help her now, but she'd need it to break Tristain's bond.

Tristain.

She needed to find a way to escape the Volskruga without hurting him. That was proving to be harder and harder, as its hold over him strengthened.

"You think that you and this little dagger can keep me at bay? You're nothing without this magic. Wasted potential. Too afraid. Too weak. Too human."

Her face met the ground with a sting that made her jaw throb. She was sure the skin had split from the impact as a burning spread from her eye to her cheek. Rhiannon twisted quickly onto her back and sent out webs of blood. Shadows scattered momentarily as bright moonlight peeked through once again.

She let out a frustrated growl as she scrambled to her feet. There was no way to tell whether this was having any effect on the Volskruga, but she hoped it would at least let her find a way out of the dark. When it didn't retaliate, she pressed forward, sending out a cloud of red mist, rippling the blackness around her and clear. Rhiannon caught a glimpse of the carriage in the distance.

She pressed forward, red mist breaking through dense obsidian. She only had several more feet to go, but the touch of metal at her throat stilled her.

"Tristain, please don't do this."

She hadn't feared the bite of a blade in a long while, but with the Volskruga's power driving it into her, she couldn't be sure what the outcome would be.

"Begging doesn't become you, Rhiannon." The Volskruga's angry voice rumbled against her ear. "Tell me, is it truly worth your life to fight this? Would you not rather succumb to the magic that thrives within your veins? Give me one good reason why we shouldn't let terror and destruction reign. Humans aren't worthy of our forgiveness or peace. At the first sign of personal gain, look at what they do. You have seen the true face of man's greed, yet you would protect them. You would sacrifice yourself for them?"

The dagger dug into her skin, punctuating its last word. And despite herself, Rhiannon flinched against the too-cold body pressed against her from behind.

Just give in. Let us be free. Stop fighting. You will see how good it can be. We can do anything we want. We can make the world as we see fit. We can become the ultimate predator. They will fear us instead of the other way around. Isn't that what you wanted?

Reassurance washed over Rhiannon as she addressed the Volskruga.

"You want my reason?" She turned her head, hoping it could see the defiant spark in her eye. "Because I don't fucking want to."

She whipped her head back, bashing it into the solid mass behind her to create distance between them. She slid down in the little space she'd made and turned toward him, letting her magic thrust forward. Red mist broke through the darkness and descended upon the Volskruga. As the shadows opened, a cluster of crimson spirits waited for her. Their attention was focused on the Volskruga, sharp teeth shining hungrily.

"Wait." Rhiannon sprinted forward, putting herself between them and the Volskruga still inhabiting Tristain's body. "Stand down. Nothing can be done to it right now. You have to wait."

Red mist around them pulsed with impatience. Rhiannon stood there, breathing heavily, waiting for them to disobey her. Instead, the mist swelled and carried away with the wind. Her heartbeat thundered in her ears as she turned back to the Volskruga. It stood still, but Rhiannon could see the flicker of Tristain trying to surface, evident in the furrow of his brow and the distant light in his eye. She reached out, cupping his face, trying to pull him out of the depths of his mind.

Instead, the light was snuffed out, and a firm hand gripped her throat, lifting her off the ground. The other rested over her chest.

Rhiannon froze in fear. She'd been here before all those months ago. The face had changed but struggling here, with the pain starting to emanate within her chest, she could see the resemblances they shared. It was in the shape of their mother's eyes, the square of their jaw, and the way they peered hatefully up at her beneath thick dark brows.

Rhiannon's mind went blank as her heart further fragmented. Her worst fears were coming true before her very eyes. There would be no fight left in her if she'd lost Tristain to this. Her fingers shredding the skin of his knuckles stilled. Her feet stopped pedaling air. She quit, gasping for the breath that wouldn't come.

A high whistle came from behind her, piercing the too-still air. Something sliced through the side of her arm before she was jerked forward sharply. Tristain fell back, his head smacking the ground in a concerning thump as Rhiannon landed on top of him. When she looked down, the air in her lungs was sucked back out. Scarlet pumped out of his body and down his shoulder and chest.

She shook her head, blinked the terrifying image away, but nothing happened. Tristain lay bleeding beneath her, and it wasn't at her hand. Slowly, she looked over her shoulder to see Samara, with her bow pointed in their direction a second arrow nocked. That's when Rhiannon registered the long shaft sticking out of Tristain.

Snow crunched under hurried footsteps, but Rhiannon couldn't tear her eyes from the blood pouring out of the man who had become the only thing worth living for.

Samara pulled Rhiannon's shoulder back, trying to force her off of him, but she only gave a few inches. She wasn't leaving him.

"Rhiannon, move. I need to get the arrow out."

Samara's voice wobbled.

Fury tore through the fog, and Rhiannon scrambled to her feet. "What the fuck were you thinking? Why would you shoot him?"

Kyra stumbled out of the carriage, her sword pointed outward. Her eyes flicked between, slowed by sleep and shock.

"That wasn't Tristain. You know it. That's why you didn't do anything to stop him."

Samara's bow had fallen to her side, and her other hand was raised, an accusing finger pointed at Rhiannon.

"Correct, I didn't do anything. So, what fucking gives you the right?"

Everything felt out of control as her world fell apart.

"I wasn't going to sit there and watch him—it—kill you. Because that's what it was. The Volskruga, wasn't it?" Samara took Rhiannon's silence as an answer. "You can pretend that you wouldn't have done the same if the roles were reversed, but I know better."

Kyra leaning over Tristain's unconscious body caught Rhiannon's attention.

"What are you doing? Don't—"

Rhiannon watched as Kyra snapped the shaft and pulled it from his shoulder, then lifted him and removed the other end. Quickly, Kyra wrapped thick fabric around the wounded area. Immediately, it reddened.

"Whatever it is you two are doing will need to wait. We need to leave now. He needs to be tended to before an infection festers."

White clouded around Rhiannon as she took several steadying breaths before shooting a glare at Samara. The blond held her gaze unapologetically despite the tears clinging to her lashes.

Shaking her head, Rhiannon helped Kyra lift Tristain to his feet. Once they reached the carriage, they struggled to get him inside, laying him across one of the seats.

"Where the hell is the driver?" Kyra asked as she peeked her head through the open door.

Rhiannon stood to help her search, but when she looked out the window on her side, their questions were answered. His bloodied body lay in the snow.

"One of you is going to have to take over. I'm not leaving him." She gently lifted Tristain's head and placed it in her lap.

Their gazes followed hers, noting the scarlet lump on the ground.

"I'll do it." Samara huffed as she exited the carriage once more.

After another minute, the carriage jolted forward, and they resumed their journey to Wispombra.

CHAPTER THIRTY-ONE

T ristain had drifted in and out of wakefulness as the carriage jostled him. Each time his weary eyes met hers, Rhiannon's heart clenched, and her throat burned with the reluctant flood of tears she was holding back. She wouldn't let the dam break. She would be strong for both of them.

Every turn of the wheel, every drawn-out second, every wince of discomfort made the distance to Wispombra excruciatingly long. She wasn't the one bleeding out, but she might as well have been.

Agony was watching him suffer.

Despair was wondering if he'd live.

Devastation was facing one single minute without him.

She'd come so far from thinking she could lead an existence without him. When he'd been just a means to an end. When she thought that her need for vengeance was a higher calling than loving him. Rhiannon couldn't recall when Tristain had become the anchor tethering her to her world turned upside down. But even as it had tilted on its axis over and over until she didn't know which way was up, he'd been there. He'd thread his strong fingers through hers and walked into the unknown fate awaiting them.

Had she done the same for him? She wanted to think that she'd grown, that she'd learned to make choices for them, ones that assured their future. But looking back, she remembered the moments when she'd let him down over and over. She'd dragged him along into the thickets of danger, and he'd been scratched and starved and wounded in the process. Rhiannon wanted to blame her monster. There were some things that were out of her control. But she'd seen this outcome clear as day. She'd told him that, she'd begged him to stay away. Yet, he'd followed her. He refused to let her go.

Could their love story have ever ended any differently?

A calloused finger brushed her cheek, erasing the evidence of that rogue tear.

"I wouldn't change anything. Not one single second." His voice was ragged, his eyes watery. "In this life and the next, I will love you. When the wind tousles your hair, know it's me touching you in the only way I can. When the sun beams down on that beautiful, soft skin, know it's me sharing that moment of peace with you. And when darkness presses in around you when you lay down for sleep, know it's me holding you in safety while you rest. You'll never be without me, Rhi. I know you say you can't bear it, but you're the strongest woman I've ever met. You can do anything, and you never needed me to tell you that. But I'm telling you now. Don't die out on me. Promise me you'll keep the spark alive, Rhi."

His hand dropped to his chest as his eyelids struggled to remain open. The smallest sliver of warm brown watched her carefully as she nodded her agreement she couldn't possibly hold herself to.

With that concession, they finally closed and didn't open again as his breathing slowed. Rhiannon forced herself to stare as she watched for the rise and fall of his chest. The movement was so slow it was nearly imperceptible, but she was grateful for the persistence of his heart and lungs.

There was no holding back the evidence of her heart breaking. Hot tears cascaded her cheeks, over her lips, and spattered across his face in quick succession. She moved one hand to his chest, needing to feel the melody of his pumping heart. The other clamped over her quivering lips as sobs slipped through and her restraint failed.

So absorbed in Tristain, she'd forgotten that Kyra sat on the other side of the carriage. Sucking in harsh sips of air, she found her voice.

"How much longer?"

"It's not far. I told Samara to take us directly to the doctor. He has a chance."

"A chance," Rhiannon bit out angrily. "He will live, or else."

"Or else what?"

"Or there won't be a world for me to exist in without him."

Kyra opened her mouth to say something, but the words died on her tongue as her gaze roamed over them. She must have seen the fracturing facade of control Rhiannon was holding together.

When the carriage settled to a stop, Samara opened the door, and Rhiannon and Kyra carried Tristain out. He groaned and gasped with the uncoordinated movements that jostled him and pulled at his injury.

Rhiannon looked anywhere but at the miserable expression on his face as they burst through the heavy door, not even bothering to knock.

"We need help. It's urgent." Samara rushed to the doctor, who sat at a table with papers strewn in front of him.

He jumped up and rounded the long wooden examination table Rhiannon and Kyra had laid Tristain on.

As soon as her hands moved from under his arms, she clutched his cool hand. "Stay here. Don't you fucking go anywhere. Do you hear me?"

If she could have opened her veins and bled her life into him, she would have. Instead, she sat there helplessly as his life hung in the balance, with his fate left in the hands of someone she didn't know and couldn't trust.

A swell of frustration rose within her, pushing back the sorrow, as the doctor looked over him far too slowly, given the amount of blood he'd lost.

"Well?" Rhiannon asked.

She hated being so helpless. Relying on others was not something she did well. Especially not when it came to Tristain. He was hers to care for. Hers to fight for. And she would make sure she did everything she could to bring him out on the other side of this.

"What caused this wound?"

"An arrow."

Samara's voice was small. *Good.*

"It appears to have gone straight through, and it was removed properly. He's lost quite a bit of blood but nothing that can't be restored."

The doctor placed his fingers on either side of the wound, but Rhiannon snatched his wrist, using all her willpower not to crush it. *They needed those hands,* she reminded herself. "I didn't see you clean your hands."

Her jaw tensed, but she eased her fingers. She cast a pointed glance toward the trough used as a sanitation area.

When the doctor returned from thoroughly cleansing his hands, he examined the wound. "As long as infection doesn't set in, he should survive this. It's good that you came straight here."

"Should?" Rhiannon asked through gritted teeth.

"I can't make any promises. Human life is a fragile thing," the doctor responded wearily.

"And so are bodies. Fix this, or I will rip your fucking spine out of you and wear it as armor while I burn this village to the ground around your worthless corpse. If he dies, I will unleash a terror you can't possibly imagine."

The doctor grabbed his instruments with shaking hands and proceeded with care under Rhiannon's watchful eye. It didn't take long for him to clean and close it up. When it was properly dressed, he gave them instructions on how to avoid an infection.

Rhiannon paid him as the others helped a now-conscious Tristain back to the carriage. "If he dies, I will be back. Let's hope you did your job right."

The man's eyes doubled in size, but he was smart enough not to say anything.

Satisfied with his trepidation, Rhiannon followed them out.

"Is he still breathing?" Kyra asked.

"For now," Rhiannon answered in all seriousness.

Samara resumed her spot at the front of the carriage as they headed toward the outskirts of town and into the Sangravian Woods.

Surprisingly, Rhiannon was relieved when the cottage came into view, and she felt a brief peace wash over her when she saw Morana waiting for her outside.

"I've missed you," she spoke into the wolf's mind.

In response, Morana let out a long howl.

Kyra helped her get Tristain into the bed, and after they'd said their goodbyes, Rhiannon crawled in beside him. It took a while of watching his steady breaths before she allowed sleep to take her. What she found waiting there for her was anything but pleasant. Instead of rest, she was faced with an onslaught of nightmares that ranged from Tristain bleeding out beside her to the Volskruga slicing her throat with that blade. Each time, she woke up to find everything as it should be, but she knew that she'd never truly find peace until she ended this once and for all.

CHAPTER THIRTY-TWO

O ne of the only good things about Tristain's bond with the Volskruga was that it helped him heal faster. After several days of Rhiannon fussing over him, he was up and about on his own. No one would know he'd suffered a potentially mortal wound. Rhiannon was worried, but she couldn't deny the relief at the quick improvement.

Kyra and Samara had promised to return with the twine and black-and-white candles so that Rhiannon could perform the spell to break the bond for Tristain. She was no closer to severing her own, but he was her primary concern. As long as he was safe, she could bear the burden of her monster just a bit longer.

Warm arms wrapped around her from behind, and she sank into them as she pressed her ear against Tristain's chest and took solace in the steady beat of his heart. It was a song she would never grow tired of. He tucked his chin atop her head and held her there, in tune with her need to feel him.

"I hope you're not worrying yourself sick over me. I'm fine, Rhi." His lips pressed into her hair, and she reveled in his breath against her scalp. "Everything will be okay."

Rhiannon turned in his arms, needing to see the conviction in his gaze. "Say it again."

"Everything is going to be okay." He tucked a wave of hair behind her ear. "I'm not leaving you. Nothing can pry me away, not even magic."

An unsteady breath escaped her, but she nodded. It had to be true. She'd questioned Delphine about the spell, and the witch had reassured her—multiple times—that it would work. It was standard, she'd insisted.

"It is," Delphine intruded.

While Rhiannon had often struggled with Delphine's presence in her mind, she'd been a source of comfort and reassurance over the last few days.

Rising on her toes, she brushed her lips against Tristain's, greedy for each reminder that he was still with her. "Aren't you nervous?"

"No. I trust you," Tristain answered easily.

Before Rhiannon could respond, Samara and Kyra walked in. Samara rushed over to the table and dropped the bag she'd been carrying atop it. It looked ready to burst at the seams. A small black candle rolled out and onto the floor, and Rhiannon scrambled after it, terrified something might happen to it and interfere with the spell.

Kyra waved her off. "It's fine. We have about a dozen." She laughed. "Samara cleared out their stock."

Rhiannon laughed, but truthfully, she was relieved her friends were as invested in this as she was. She hadn't doubted that, but it was still comforting to see it so plainly.

"Are we ready?" Kyra asked.

"Yes," Tristain answered as he twisted his ring—the one he'd be finally giving up—around his finger.

After walking into the kitchen, Rhiannon collected the jar of soil from the Vrugian Woods. She'd been relieved to find that most of it had made it back with them. Samara had cleared off the table, and Kyra was tying the twine around one of each colored candle. With steady hands, Rhiannon poured soil onto two plates and wedged the candles into the dirt until they were held steady.

They took a collective deep breath.

"You'll need to light the wicks. It will burn down the candle and through the twine. When it breaks apart, it will sever their bond. Have Tristain put the ring in the soil with the black candle on the left, the one that represents the Volskruga. He'll need to cut his hand and drip blood in a circular motion around the white candle on the right before you light them," Delphine instructed.

Rhiannon nodded and grabbed Tristain's forearm to get his attention. "You need to put the ring here." She pointed to the candle on the left.

He pulled it off his finger, hesitating only a moment as his gaze lingered on the engraving inside the band. Once he placed it in the soil, he stepped away to grab the dagger that had started this all.

Rhiannon followed him and whispered, "Are you sure you're going to be okay with parting with that?"

"Yes." He turned to her and stroked her hair. "It's time to let go. I'll never forget Leylah, but I'm ready to move on from this chapter of my life, and she needs to stay in the past. We both deserve to move forward."

She nodded, letting go of the guilt gripping her. But unease crept through her once again when Tristain stood before the candles and held the dagger over his palm. It was so similar to the night she'd found him standing in this very spot, and she watched him sacrifice a vital part of the man he used to be. He'd been robbed of his consent, so it was important that he was ready for this. That he was choosing it.

Tristain winced and inhaled sharply as he dragged the dagger across his open palm. They were a captive audience as he made a fist and dripped blood around the white candle. It absorbed into the dirt.

"It's time," Delphine encouraged.

Rhiannon stepped up to the table and struck the match, then brought it up to each wick. They caught quickly, the flame bursting to life. Relief sparked within her.

Before they melted the wax, blood gushed from Tristain's nose, and his eyes rolled back as his limbs cracked and moved unnaturally.

"Tristain?" she whispered.

"Blow out the candles."

The voice that answered carried the force of ten lifetimes with it as it echoed in the small space.

Fear trapped her words behind her lips, but she shook her head vigorously. Samara leaned against Rhiannon. Kyra drew her swords and slipped one into Samara's hand.

"I will not ask again," it bellowed. "Blow out the candles, or I will make good on my threat."

Rhiannon racked her brain for the memory. She found it. An image of the Volskruga tearing out Tristain's heart with his own hand appeared in sharp clarity at the forefront of her mind.

"Don't," she pleaded.

Bile rose in her throat at the sound of her own desperation.

"Three."

Her muscles were frozen.

"Two."

Her vision blurred, and her words failed her.

"One."

Before anyone could act, a flame jutted up violently between them, and the two candles fell on their sides as the twine broke apart. Everything happened so quickly as fire spread across the wooden table and engulfed the floor. Samara and Kyra's hands were on her, tugging her toward the door as it climbed the walls.

Rhiannon squinted against the heat that sprung endless tears to her eyes. Her gaze swept the area in front of her eagerly, but she couldn't see past the flames roaring before her. She fought against their hold, but her terror caused her strength to fail.

Fresh air speared through her lungs as she breathed deeply between a scream. Her friends collapsed in the thin layer of snow on the ground, pulling Rhiannon down with them. As soon as their hands left her body, she scrambled toward the cottage consumed by flames. There was so much fire. She could feel the heat of the knob when she ripped the door off its hinges, but there was no burn. She was numb to any real sensation other than the sheer terror and desperation pushing her body forward.

"Rhiannon."

Morana's voice rang loudly in her mind.

She ignored it, looking for a gap in the flames so she could go inside and search for Tristain.

A low growl came from behind her, causing her to jump. She flicked an angry gaze over her shoulder, but her rage melted when she saw Morana dragging a choking Tristain. Disbelief warred with what she was seeing before her eyes. She crouched in front of them and ran her hands through his hair, confirming the relief in his gaze. Only then did she release her breath.

"Thank you." She used her other hand to stroke the cool smoke that ebbed and flowed around the wolf. "Thank you." Rhiannon whimpered with relief as she dropped her head against Tristain's chest.

"You're okay." She shifted him between her legs and allowed him to lean against her as he choked on ragged breaths.

Tristain pulled in deep lungfuls of air. His eyes darted around with worry. It took her a moment to realize he was searching for the Volskruga.

"It's not in me anymore. Where is it?" He struggled to sit up.

"When we broke the bond, it was forced to return to the Vrugian Woods." She pulled him back against her and stroked a calming hand through his unruly curls. "It can't harm you anymore. You're free."

Even though she knew it was true and could feel it in the air, she, too, was struggling to accept it. They'd done it, and they were all still here to see another day. Rhiannon pulled him tighter against her. He was safe.

Tristain covered his mouth with a bloody hand as tears spilled down his smoke-streaked face. His body shivered against her, and all she wanted to do was pull him into her and hold him until he felt safe once again. But she didn't know if he ever would truly feel that again. How could he? After everything they'd been through, how could either of them really put this all in their past? Once again, guilt wormed its way through her and sat heavy on her chest.

They all sat in silence as they watched the cottage fall in on itself as the fire raged. Cracking beams and ruptured floorboards made them jump on occasion, but for the most part, watching a small symbol of all they'd been through destroy itself was comforting. It felt like the beginning of the end. It was hard to tear her eyes away from it, even though the smoke had made them tired and sensitive.

"What now?" Kyra finally asked.

"We're going to stay at the inn, I suppose." Rhiannon let out a long sigh.

It was a mix of relief and exhaustion. They were one step closer to a new life.

"I meant what about your bond?" Kyra clarified.

That brought her crashing down to reality. They still had so far to go.

"I don't know." Rhiannon dragged a dirty hand through her hair. "We're no closer to an answer. I have no idea where my monster—the entity—originated. Wherever her power lies, that's where I'll have to go."

Samara let out a laugh that had them all whipping their heads in her direction. "How did we not think of this?" she said between laughter. "We're already there. Rhiannon, she came to you *here*. You tried to sacrifice yourself *here*. You spilled your blood *here*. You originated the bond *here*."

They marveled at her in silence.

"I think she might be right," Delphine supplied.

Her voice was light for perhaps the first time in their entire fucked-up relationship.

CHAPTER THIRTY-THREE

T he inn was warm, and the bed was comfortable, but dread stirred in Rhiannon's gut. Kyra hadn't been joking about Samara buying out all the black-and-white candles from the shop they'd visited. By the time they'd checked, the only other shop that had them had already closed, so they'd have to wait until the next day to perform the spell.

Her monster hadn't stirred, not even during the fire.

Rhiannon couldn't help but worry about what that meant. It's what caused her to shift relentlessly beside Tristain. It was as if hundreds of tiny bugs prickled against her skin. There wasn't enough air in her lungs, each breath too short. Her mind buzzed endlessly with what-ifs. She couldn't even take comfort in Morana or Delphine's reassurances. They'd taken to the woods for the night.

Instead of sleeping, Rhiannon resigned herself to count over and over until the sun finally pierced the dark.

She rolled out of bed and disappeared into the washroom to ready for the day. She didn't care if the shop wasn't open yet. She'd wait outside and be the first one in. Rhiannon couldn't wait any longer. Tristain didn't even stir as she watched him through the door and closed it gently.

When Rhiannon rounded the front of the shop, she was surprised to find Kyra standing there already.

"Couldn't sleep?" her friend asked, her voice low with exhaustion.

"Not a single second," Rhiannon responded, handing her the warm beverage she held.

Kyra took a grateful sip before giving it back to her. They sat in silence, passing the brown drink back and forth, as it slowly worked through their systems and made them more alert. Just as they'd finished it, the shopkeeper approached the door. The thin, pale woman shook off her hood and indicated with a tilt of her head that they should follow them inside.

They got to their feet eagerly and entered the shop. They quickly found what they needed and gave the woman extra for opening so punctually.

"Where are we doing this?" Kyra asked.

"The inn?" Rhiannon answered.

"Is that such a good idea?"

"What other option do we have?" Rhiannon's gaze swept across the line of shops and taverns surrounding them.

"My home?"

Hesitation was clear in Kyra's voice.

"I won't put your family in danger." Rhiannon grabbed her friend's hand.

"Do you really think you can contain such an entity in such a tiny room? And what if someone hears? Surely, it won't go quietly. I mean, look at what happened with Tristain."

Kyra was right.

"Fine. In the woods, behind the tavern, then. We'll set ourselves back far enough that there will be little risk of anyone discovering us."

Kyra considered the suggestion. "Okay, we'll meet you there, then."

"You don't need to be here for this. We can do it."

Nerves raced through Rhiannon.

"I don't think so. I'm not leaving you now. What if your monster fights back? We don't know what to expect."

Rhiannon searched her friend's face for any apprehension, but her words rang true. She sighed. "I suppose you're right. Meet us back at the inn. Room number eight, second floor."

Kyra nodded her confirmation, then set off in the opposite direction.

When Rhiannon returned to the inn, she went behind the building instead of inside. She wanted to observe the area before they put their plan into action. A glimpse of black fur and shadow shifted at the corner of her eye as Morana followed her. They walked together deeper into the expanse of trees.

"Are you ready?" Morana asked.

"Do I have any other choice?"

"No. It's time to end this." Morana was silent for a moment. *"We will see this through to the end with you. You are not alone."*

"You will make it out the other side of this."

Delphine's voice joined in her mind.

"Why does this feel like a goodbye?" Rhiannon's throat tightened with apprehension.

"It's likely that, when the spell is done, we won't be with you any longer," Delphine answered, her voice shaking with barely contained emotion.

"What? Why?"

"We're tied to the magic that you possess. Morana is the only reason I'm still here with you, and when you sever the bond, she will not cease to exist," Delphine explained solemnly.

"And if I'm not ready to let you go?"

Tears trailed down Rhiannon's cheeks, but she didn't try to hide them. They'd been through so much together. They'd come to her at her lowest moments. They'd found her on the brink of death. They'd *saved* her.

"You are, Rhiannon. You were always going to be meant for more than this." Morana pressed their foreheads together.

"More than being a foretold harbinger of destruction?" Rhiannon laughed through her tears.

"You were always meant to live, Rhiannon. The spark within you is far too bright to be dimmed by even the darkest parts of this world."

Delphine's words broke Rhiannon's last sliver of composure. She wrapped her arms around the wolf, not quite holding her, but the caress of her smoky fur was comforting all the same.

"Thank you," she sobbed, *"for everything. You've given me so much. I could never tell you how grateful I am."*

"We know," Delphine assured her as Morana nuzzled against her. *"It's time. Go get the supplies. We'll wait here."*

Rhiannon nodded as she tried to process this information.

"And, Rhiannon." Delphine's voice followed her. *"When this is all over, live. That's how you can show us how much it's meant. Honor our memories by grabbing hold of everything you've fought so hard for."*

Rhiannon forced herself to reign in her sobs as she stood, holding the wolf's gaze before she forced her feet to turn back toward the inn. Her legs were stiff as her mind remained stuck on the harsh reality that she would be losing them, too.

Would it ever end?

As she ascended the stairs and approached the open door of their room, she took a moment to observe her friends, and Tristain gathered there, ready to take this on with her. Again and again, they faced uncertain odds, just as committed to overcoming this as she was. She was lucky.

Rhiannon allowed her gaze to flick toward the mirror in the hall before entering the room. Her eyes were red and rimmed with tears. Her nose and cheeks were flushed, too. She wiped her face and took a few centering breaths before continuing.

"What happened?" Samara covered her hand gently.

"They won't be here once the spell is complete." She saw her friends exchange confused glances behind her. "Morana, Delphine, they're tied to the magic. Once it's gone, so are they." Her voice shook as control slipped its short leash.

Tristain approached her and pulled her into his arms. "I'm so sorry, Rhi. I know you went through so much together."

Rhiannon was tired of losing. She was tired of having things taken from her. Everything she'd found comfort in had been stripped from her. It had cost her humanity once. She hoped she could hold on to it. But today, she was going toe-to-toe with her monster, and she would do whatever she needed to come out the other side victorious.

Rhiannon shifted out of Tristain's arms and put on her harness, both daggers in their designated holsters once again. As she tightened it, she felt more like herself than she had in a while. She took a steadying breath, centering herself, then grabbed the bag of supplies from the dresser. Resolve washed over her as she turned to her friends.

"It's time to get my life back."

Her friends exchanged wary looks, but they followed her outside and through the trees to where Morana waited.

Rhiannon kneeled, pouring soil she'd collected from around the cottage onto the two plates she'd set atop a tree stump. She was doing her best to maintain a composed facade, but her heart thundered in her chest. The hair raised on her arms, and her fingers twitched. It took her several tries to tie the twine around the candles. On unsteady legs, she stood and stepped back. Her eyes roved over the setup frantically, searching for anything that might interfere with its effectiveness.

"What will you sacrifice?" Tristain asked, his voice quiet over her shoulder.

Rhiannon pulled out Silas's dagger and stabbed the mound of dirt so it sat beside the candle.

His brow furrowed. "Will that work?"

"I don't see why not. It's mine. I reclaimed it." Rhiannon stroked the end of the handle, remembering all the comfort it'd brought her when she'd held it in her hand and drawn it across the skin of those who would've harmed her without it. "It'll work."

Rhiannon pulled out her other dagger, the one holding the Volskruga. She admired the gleam of the emeralds that had been restored to their green glory now that the dark magic had been eradicated.

Forcing her muscles into motion, she dragged it across her palm and gritted her teeth against the sting as she let it drip into the soil around the candle. She wiped the remaining blood on her black pants and returned the blade to the holster.

"Are you all ready?" She cast a glance around, taking in the brave group that still stood beside her despite everything.

No one objected as Kyra held a lit match out to her. "You should do it."

The wind whistled ominously as Rhiannon grabbed the match with her uninjured hand and brought it to the candles. The flames caught and started their slow journey down the wick. Her heart took off at a sprint, adrenaline racing through her.

A chorus of movement sounded behind her as Kyra pulled her swords, Samara nocked her bow, and Morana howled.

Tristain came to her side, sword in hand. He watched her closely, eyes wide, as they waited for her monster to come forward.

Seconds passed, and the flame grew. The sweat of wax tumbled down the candle. The knot in Rhiannon's stomach started to unravel. She and Tristain exchanged glances, the tension in his jaw loosening. As she turned to look at Kyra and Samara over her shoulder, a sharp gust of wind lifted her hair into the air and stole her breath along with it. She whipped her head toward the candles. Flames extinguished, only faint wisps of white smoke floating above their barely blackened wicks.

None of them moved, shock rooting them in place.

At the first pulse of magic awakening within her, Rhiannon ran forward, hand outstretched toward the matches on the stump. She didn't make it. Instead, her thighs locked in place.

"I don't think so," her monster growled. *"If you can't be obedient, then I will have to force you. You said you wanted to have a choice. I tried to give you one, but you couldn't see that. You had to have things your way. Didn't you? Selfish, stubborn girl. Think of all the others you're letting down. But you don't truly care, do you? As long as you get what you want. You never should have been trusted with this power. You aren't worthy."*

"I never asked to be," Rhiannon grunted out.

Her limbs contorted as she wrestled internally for control of her muscles.

Kyra rounded on her, standing between Rhiannon and the candles. "Don't come any closer." She held her swords crossed in front of her, sharp tips threateningly pointed in Rhiannon's direction.

A booming voice that was not Rhiannon's came out of her mouth as her monster lunged forward. Her chest pressed into the blades carving through her skin, but her monster didn't care.

"Are you foolish enough to think those will have any effect on me? I don't think your friend would appreciate it, but we'll be fine. But you? I don't think you'll survive my claws ripping out your guts."

Kyra's hands shook, but she didn't give any ground. "Tristain, light the candles. Samara, keep that bow on her. It might not kill her, but I think a few holes in her organs will slow her down a bit. Give those candles the time they need to burn down. Then this bitch will be gone for good." A determined smirk curled her lips.

Rhiannon's monster let out a guttural laugh. "Light them, and I will tear her apart from the inside. You do away with me, and I'll make sure there's nothing left of her to save."

Morana snarled beside her, teeth exposed in a promise of violence. Her monster growled back, and Rhiannon watched from within herself as undiluted terror widened Tristain's eyes.

Weightlessness overcame her, and a scream left her throat as her feet lifted off the ground. The warmth of calloused fingers slipped over her skin. The distant call of her name on the wind rang in her ears.

But she couldn't move. She couldn't respond. She couldn't even think clearly as her world shrank down to the slivers between her rapidly fluttering lashes. The tops of trees were the last things she saw before her mind was lost to that of her monster. Her wolf snapped and snarled from below her.

Rhiannon was granted a moment of calm darkness before a barrage of horror battered her exhausted mind.

Visions of her with scarlet eyes and a malicious smile came to mind as she watched a version of herself using her magic to bend and break people who cried out for mercy they wouldn't find. Villages she'd never seen before were ravaged and bloodied in her wake. Her friends lay limp with lifeless eyes, impaled on their own weapons. There was no trace of the woman she knew herself to be. Only her monster who'd been set free. This was what the prophecy had warned them of. This was the price of Rhiannon's failure. And it was far too steep. The spell had to work.

The heartbreaking scenes paused as tugging from everywhere at once sent a roll of nausea through Rhiannon. Prickling discomfort sparked every inch of her, as if she was being pulled in all directions at once. The ghost of fingertips of at least a dozen cold hands dug into her as they grabbed onto her with all their might. She shuddered and shrieked as the mounting pressure became too much. Surely, she was going to burst at the seams.

"Rhiannon," Delphine's familiar voice whispered just out of reach. *"Don't let her push you out. Come back to us."* Her voice grew louder with each word as the monster's hold on her weakened.

"There will be no separating us. If you will not usher in a new era with me, then you will not carry on at all," her monster hissed.

One of Rhiannon's clawed hands tore across her own face and down her chest, stopping over her heart. Sharp talons with a mind of their own dug into her skin. Desperation pierced Rhiannon as she realized the intent. Meanwhile, the tugging on her limbs intensified. She groaned and cried out, but the all-over pain didn't stop. Panic seized her as her breaths came in rapid pants. It needed to stop. She couldn't take it anymore. Her endurance was failing under the stress. And then, she was falling.

Rhiannon hit the ground, the wind knocking out of her in a harsh gust. An echo of that impact radiated through her bones as she lay motionless.

If she hadn't possessed the power that had been imbued in her against her will, she likely wouldn't be alive. It felt like she was wading through thick mud as she slowly, so slowly, regained control of her body. Her eyelids twitched as she forced them to open. A slash of the surrounding woods peeked through. Her limbs felt like they were tethered to boulders, but she regained movement in her fingers, then her wrists. Up and up, she urged the muscles into action until she could move her arms. Rough dirt and rocks dug into her palms as she pressed her full weight into them and pushed up onto her hands and knees.

A cool tongue swiped up her face, and Morana whined beside her with urgency. She slid her arms beneath her and forced herself to her knees. Her back bowed in pain.

"Rhiannon, get up." Morana licked her again.

"What happened?" she asked, her voice hoarse.

"Your monster won't stay dormant for long. Get up." The wolf tugged at her clothing.

When Rhiannon stood, her knees threatened to buckle, but she grabbed a nearby tree. Her eyes traveled across the scene. Kyra and Samara stood in front of the candles that were lit once again and had nearly burned down to where the twine rested, awaiting its fiery death. Tristain was running toward her. They all appeared to be fine. The monster had been preoccupied with torturing her.

Good.

When he pulled her into his arms, whispering something against her hair she couldn't quite make out, she noticed them. Dozens of spirits of swarming scarlet mist surrounded them. The tugging, the cold hands . . . they'd helped her. They'd chosen to save Rhiannon. They were loyal to her, not her monster. Their comradery reinvigorated her to finish this. She didn't have to do this alone. She would use every weapon at her disposal, including her kindred spirits, who pressed in around them. She shifted away from Tristain instinctually. They gathered closer and closer, then stopped just shy of touching her. With a coordinated bow of their heads, their mist-born forms blurred together into a swirling cloud of power that whipped around her. The sheer force of it blew her hair into the air and forced her to close her eyes against the burn. The speed of it tore at her clothes, and she cried out, unsure she could withstand it. And between her open lips, the gust burst through, filling her until her head spun, and her lungs begged for a reprieve from the stretch of it.

Her monster reared its head at the threat. *"No. No. No. You were supposed to be loyal to me. You serve me. We were supposed to do this together,"* it hissed.

Another roll of nausea overcame her, and she swayed on her feet. Rhiannon shook from within. It was as if her body was being shredded layer by layer as her monster thrashed and whipped into a frenzy beneath her skin. Her bones vibrated. The landscape around her tilted, and sweat poured over Rhiannon. A war was being waged within her, and it threatened to tear her apart. Sticky wetness trailed down from her eyes, ears, and nose as the pressure mounted. She stumbled and staggered as she tried to remain upright.

Tristain reached out to steady her, but Rhiannon put her hand out.

"Don't."

The bite in her voice was a chilling blend of her monster and herself. Sharp heat lanced Rhiannon's arm as a shadowed crimson limb struck out of her body, followed by another. The mind-numbing burn intensified as the rest of its form struggled to separate from her. A featureless head with a wide, gnashing maw turned on her with a ferocious growl. Rhiannon tried to scramble back, but the shadow remained attached to her as her back hit the tree behind her.

"Rhiannon, don't move," Delphine commanded.

She froze. Morana's jaw latched around the squirming shadow, and everything stood still. A shrill screech erupted from her as something snapped in agonizing finality within her, and the shadow was ripped out into the open. Its billowing form vibrated with fury.

Rhiannon folded at her waist with the impact. The duality of feeling so full and empty left her unsteady.

Growling and shrieking from the figure of dense red mist that was her monster drew her attention. Determination fortified her body, and she found the strength to stand upright. Putting one foot in front of the other, she was driven by pent-up rage and loathing as she closed in on where Morana held the struggling form. If it weren't for the spirits anchoring the remnants of the magic within her, she wouldn't have been able to lift a finger. But with their combined source of power and her sweltering fury, she had enough strength to exact this last act of vengeance.

"I'm going to end you, you greedy fucking cunt." Rhiannon latched a hand around the entity's writhing figure and pulled their faces close together. "You will rot forgotten as you suffocate on your own misery beneath that lonely, deadened soil. No one will come for you. The prophecy will be kept safe, a long-lost memory for generations to come. I will make sure of it. I hope you find no peace. I hope you're tormented by your failure for eternity. And I hope you remember who put you there."

The monster roared in Rhiannon's face, but she ignored it and instead focused within to communicate with whatever consciousness remained with the spirits.

It's almost time for you to finally find rest. But I have one favor to ask, go to Sangravian Woods. Make it so that no one will be able to travel through there again. It's best if she's left to toil alone for eternity.

A brief pause froze where the throbbing power within her stilled, then her head whipped back, and plumes of crimson billowed from her open jaw. When the last wisp of mist left her, she fell to her knees. Minutes felt like hours as Morana struggled to keep the monster within her grasp. But then the flame went out, and everything happened at once. Morana's form faded, and with one last sharp wail, the monster slipped away into the wind. An eerie, unfamiliar stillness settled over Rhiannon.

"You did it."

A caress whispered across her mind with Morana and Delphine's final goodbye.

Tristain kneeled in front of her, shaking her shoulders. "Rhiannon, it's over. The bond is broken."

His voice grew faint as Rhiannon's eyes fell closed. Her body was sore and tired. Cold seeped into her bones. She was shivering. All she wanted was to rest. She'd earned it. Yes, that sounded nice. His voice fell away, and she drew into the quiet of her mind. It had been so long since she'd known solitude, so she gratefully let it take her.

It was done.

It was over.

She was free.

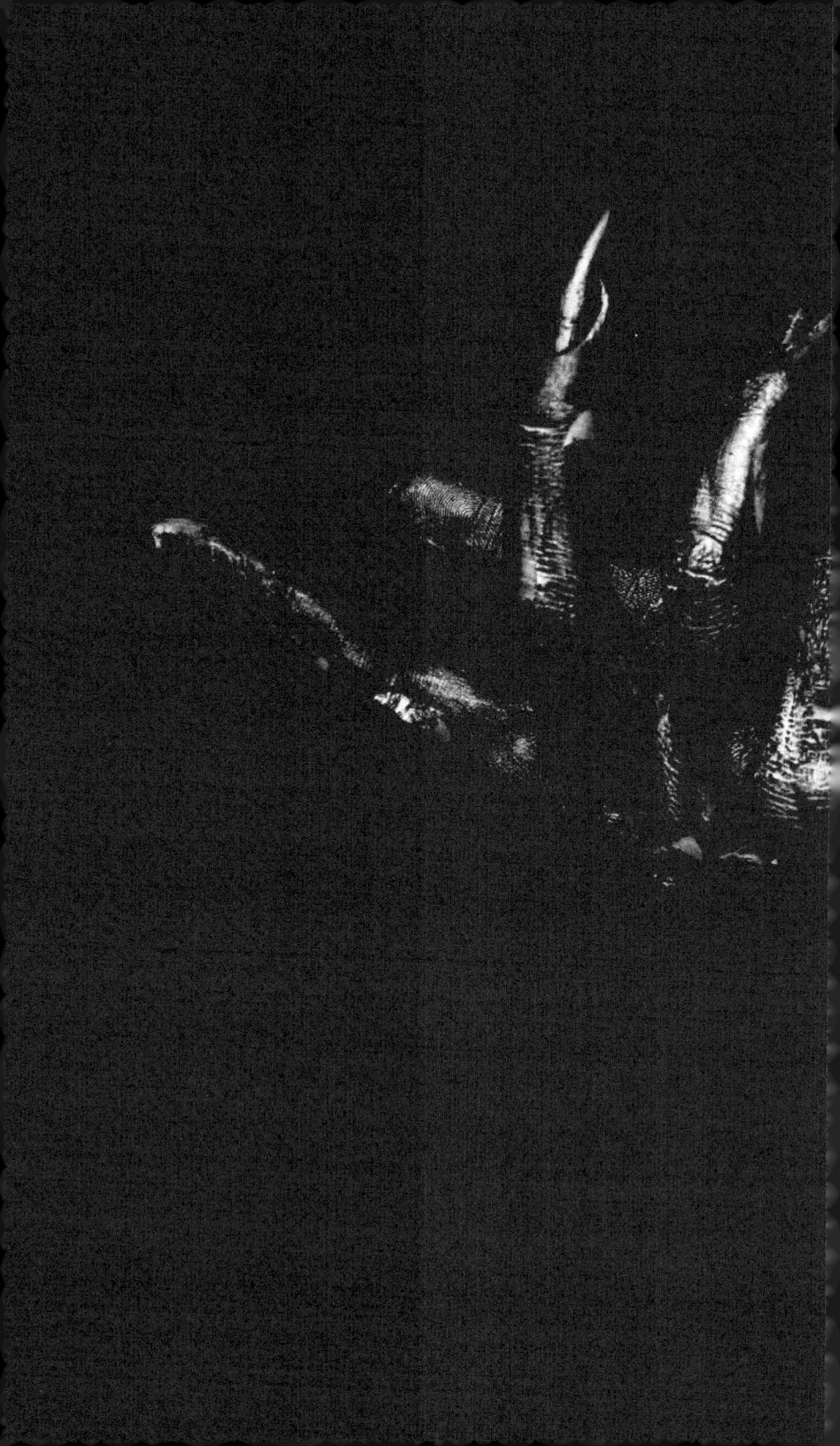

CHAPTER THIRTY-FOUR

T he energy around her was soft and calm, a foreign feeling after all this time. Rhiannon wanted to sink into it forever, but the sting of her dry throat pulled her from the brief comfort she'd found. Concentrating, she blinked her eyes open. A crack in the curtains revealed the hazy indigo of early morning. The glistening water sitting on the table beside her motivated her to lift her fingers. She inched a heavy arm toward it, trying to be careful not to knock it over as her shaking fingers clasped around the cool glass.

The refreshing liquid quieted her need, and she allowed her gaze to wander the room. With the shelves of medicinal books and the white linens on the bed, the realization dawned on her that she was not in their room at the inn.

Panic spiked through her and attempted to spring into action, but a lash of heat down her spine kept her in bed. Rhiannon whimpered as her back throbbed, but she stilled the sound in her throat at the sight of a sleeping Tristain. His width barely fit in the seat, the arms digging into his sides, yet his relaxed expression said he was content to wait for her.

Rhiannon's eyes blurred with emotion. Fuck, she loved this man. And then something far more surprising crossed her mind. If she'd been forced to choose to do this all over again just to end up with him by her side, she would. The truth of it stilled her breath. All of the suffering, all of the uncertainty, all of the long nights of begging for relief from her grief and loneliness was all bearable because she'd found him.

A genuine smile curved her lips as she remembered how vehemently she'd wanted to be rid of him when he'd shown up at her home, uninvited, with those disarming dimples. But while she'd been busily distracted with finding ways to push him out, he'd snuck into one of those cracks Silas had left in her heart and gradually filled it with his unconditional love and enduring affection, giving her time to adjust to his presence. Always so patient. And she was glad of it, the way he'd tended to her so carefully. His very own rose with thorns. He didn't love her despite them. He appreciated her nature, threatening barbed edges, ability to draw blood and all.

Rhiannon's eyes traced his handsome face appreciatively. Those plush lips that spoke words of affirmation and devotion, the gentle sweep of his lashes hiding the pools of fire that lit up only for her, and that strong nose that pressed into her air and breathed her in like she was the essence of life. For the first time in a while, she genuinely felt lucky.

Over and over again, he'd told her they would make it. And still, she'd doubted him. No. She hadn't been brave enough to believe him. But he'd been right. She should have known he wouldn't make a promise he couldn't keep. He'd followed her into the darkness, intent on being each other's guiding light, and they'd come out on the other side alive.

Alive. She was alive. Despite all the times she'd wished she wasn't. In spite of those who tried to keep her down. Silas. The council. The Volskruga. Her monster. *Herself.* She'd overcome it all.

A delirious laugh escaped her, the uncharacteristically light sound finally rousing Tristain. As his tired eyes fluttered open, Rhiannon's throat dried once again. They simply stared at one another, equally in awe of each other and the impossibility of their perseverance.

"Rhi." Her name was a whispered reverence as a shuddering breath of relief forced its way out of him. "How do you feel?" The mattress sank beneath him as he moved to her side.

Rhiannon's lips parted and closed several times before she found the words. "We did it. I'm free." Her voice shook as emotion whipped through her.

"We did." Tristain watched her carefully as he stroked her hair.

The mirror above the worktable across from the bed caught her attention. She gritted through the pain as she leaned up to peer at herself. The first thing she noticed was the stark white of her hair had returned without the magic coursing through her system. The sight of it used to spark sadness, but now, it felt like a gift, a restoration of the life she had before. She decided she wouldn't resume dying it.

Continuing her self-exploration, Rhiannon swept her hands over her cheeks and strained to study her expression. She traced over the bandaging over her deep gashes that dragged across her forehead, nose, and cheek. Similar bandaging pressed against her chest where her monster had tried to claw her heart out. She held her hand over where she'd drawn Silas's blade so long ago, the echo of cold metal a distant memory. But after everything, that battered organ still beat defiantly.

Rhiannon smiled at her reflection, where glimmers of her true self shone beneath her bruised and exhausted exterior. She would wear these scars proudly, a reminder of all that she'd survived.

The longer she studied herself, the more obvious it was that the weight of the power no longer bore down upon her shoulders. She clenched her eyes shut and searched for the magic that had once thrummed within her. Nothing answered.

She was alone. She was whole. She was Rhiannon.

The truth of it settled over her soul. A soft blanket draping over old wounds that needed to heal. She wasn't quite ready to relax into that promise of peace and let her guard down. She might never be able to. Perhaps her hand would always ache for the reassuring comfort of her dagger. The whistle of wind through naked trees may always strike a chord of paranoia as she listened for whispered threats. Her overworked muscles might always be coiled springs ready to strike. Or, with time, she could relearn how to move through the world with ease as she once did. Only time would tell.

Tristain's hand stilled as he placed a kiss on her forehead. "Do you want to rest more, or is it okay if I tell the others you're awake?"

"They can come in." She was eager to see with her own eyes that her friends were okay. Her chest clenched, the reminder of Delphine and Morana's departure sending a fresh throb of loss through her. *Most of her friends were still here.* She could be grateful for that.

There wasn't much time for her to sit with her grief as a welcome surprise flooded her when her sister entered the room.

"Jade?" Disbelief stilled her until she was pulled into a hug. "What are you doing here?"

"I told you I was going to come. I just didn't wait for you to invite me." Jade laughed against her. "I'm glad I came when I did. It must have been my sisterly intuition."

"I'm glad you're here, too." Rhiannon allowed herself to sink into Jade's embrace, not missing the warm wetness soaking into her bare shoulder. Too many emotions flooded through her to process.

"And I'm sure it had nothing to do with your undeniable infatuation with a certain sword-wielding woman," Rhiannon teased, lightening the mood to catch her breath.

"That may have a bit to do with it." Jade rolled her eyes. "Thankfully, Kyra retrieved me from the inn a few days ago when she heard about me inquiring around the village for you." Jade squeezed Rhiannon's hand as her gaze roamed over Rhiannon's battered body. "What happened?"

Tristain opened his mouth, but Rhiannon cut him off. "Would it suffice to tell you that the only thing you need to know is I made it out okay, and I'm just glad you arrived when you did?"

"For now." Jade arched a severe dark brow at her. "I will get the truth out of you. But I suppose I'll let you recover first."

Rhiannon agreed that her sister deserved to know the truth of what she'd been through . . . one day. The creaking of the heavy wooden door drew her attention away from her sister and to her two friends, who were peeking through the small crack.

She laughed at their antics. "You can come in."

Samara shoved the door open and loped up to her bedside, placing a small hand on top of Rhiannon's cold fingers. "You did it."

"*We* did it," Rhiannon corrected. She swept her gaze over her friends as Kyra joined Samara at her bedside. "Thank you both. I couldn't have done it without you."

"We know," Kyra responded with a wink. "But when I say that is the last evil entity I'm dealing with, I mean it. I'm ready to settle into a life of peace. And I hope you will, too." She emphasized the sentiment with a tender squeeze of Rhiannon's leg.

The love surrounding her was overwhelming, and she squirmed under their affectionate attention. When had she gotten so sappy? It was unsettling.

"Well, it's been fun catching up, but I'm hungry, so can we get out of here? And where *is* that exactly?"

Tristain laughed and shook his head. "No, we can't leave. You're under medical supervision for the next few days. You did almost die . . . like twenty times in the last year." He stood and stretched beside her. "But I will bring you food."

"Twenty times?" Jade's eyes swelled before shrinking into accusatory slits. "Don't think I'll forget your promise."

"He's being dramatic." Rhiannon glowered menacingly at Tristain but softened.

Kyra stroked Jade's fist with her thumb at her side until their fingers laced together. "Come on, she needs to rest. But don't worry, I'll make sure she gives you the truth of it." With a final threatening glare, Jade followed Kyra out the door.

"We'll be just outside if you need anything." Samara closed the door gently behind them.

Rhiannon wanted to protest, but exhaustion stole the snark from her lips and forced her to return to that peaceful slumber she'd pulled from too early.

The bitter but wise doctor who'd begrudgingly cared for her and Tristain had finally deemed her well enough to move to the inn until she regained enough strength to travel. She may have whispered a tiny threat in his ear when he'd come to check on her the last time, but she really was feeling much better, at least well enough to be free of his suffocating presence. Apparently, she'd worn off on her love because the doctor confessed in a huff that Tristain had issued threats of his own. Rhiannon knew they were empty warnings of worry more than anything, but still, it warmed her heart. So, when he insisted they walk at a snail's pace after she'd rejected the carriage he'd arranged for the short trip to the inn, she didn't huff her displeasure like she wanted to. She simply leaned into him and let him fuss over her the whole way there. She could admit, perhaps, it wasn't so bad letting herself entertain his need to care for her. She might even consider embracing it in her current condition.

The scent of warm bread wafting from the open entrance of the inn was enough to ignore the ache that radiated up her back as she hastened their pace. Tristain shook his head but matched her step for step.

Kyra, Jade, and Samara were seated at a table by the fire, five glasses of fireale sitting in front of them. They all looked like hell, but they were alive. They'd made it. They'd done it together.

Rhiannon smiled easily as she slipped her legs beneath the tabletop and as Tristain took the spot next to her. Surrounded by people he loved and who loved her, she felt an echo of the woman she used to be stirring back to life. The one who lived freely and danced boisterously. Fuck, it felt good.

Her companions held their glasses raised and Rhiannon brought hers into the center as they clinked them together. Was this what happiness felt like? She'd nearly forgotten.

"You're not sad you don't have the magic anymore?" Samara asked cautiously as she grimaced against the burn of the fireale.

"Sad? No. I never chose to take on that power. It was thrust upon me without my consent. It took things from me that I can never get back." She ran a hand through her hair. "I never wanted that responsibility. All I ever wanted was the freedom to choose my fate."

"I'm proud of you," Tristain murmured against her ear, and she preened under his affirming words.

"What will you do now?" Samara asked.

Rhiannon exchanged a glance with Tristain. She hadn't thought that far ahead, hadn't allowed herself to.

"I think Rhiannon would like to take up a life at sea," he teased, that dimple charming her enough to dissuade her from retaliating against such a heinous suggestion.

"Will you two stay here?" Kyra asked through a laugh.

Rhiannon didn't miss how her friend leaned into her sister. Their pairing was easy and well-matched. She was happy they would have each other.

"No, I want to go to Saldova. I want to bask under the sun, like nothing could ever go wrong. I want to smell the flowers carry on the salted air as they bloom. I want to fall asleep to the distant crash of the waves. And most importantly, I want some fucking peace."

Tristain's smile was blinding. They knew he belonged there, and she believed she did, too.

"You two are nauseating." Samara shook her head, but her blue eyes shone with approval. "I'm going home. I love you all, but I miss it desperately. I'm ready to be with my family. I want to watch my sisters grow up."

Rhiannon nodded.

Samara had seen so much of their world, more than she had probably wanted.

"And you two?" Rhiannon turned her attention to Kyra and Jade.

"I'm staying here," Jade answered, her lips turning upward as she shifted closer to Kyra. "Will you come visit?"

A sigh of resignation left Rhiannon. "I hope that, one day, I'll be able to set foot here and remember the good over all the bad. I think it'll be awhile, though." She reached across the table, taking her sister's hand. "Would you come to Saldova?"

Jade nodded. "I'll bring Mother, too. She's always wanted to go. It's been a long time since Father was lost. I think she'll be open to it after all these years."

With a long pull of her drink and a squeeze of Tristain's deliciously thick thigh that sat reassuringly against her own, Rhiannon allowed lightness to flow through her freely. She didn't shut it down with any pessimistic thoughts. She didn't try to scare it away with worries of looming danger. She didn't fight it.

She'd earned this.

Her vengeance had freed her.

Acknowledgments

To the readers who loved book one,
Thank you so much for being invested in this series enough to finish it. Taking on a series as a still-new author is such an intimidating feat, I truly appreciate you being here. Setting out to write the second book in the duology started with me at a very difficult crossroads. In the end, I decided to honor all that Rhiannon meant to me and the readers who resonated with her backstory most and make his a true survivor's story. I hope you enjoyed reading it as much as I loved writing it.

Amberlee,
Thank you for being one of the very first people who believed in this story. And then to have you bring Rhiannon to life both on the cover and in the illustrations inside, I can't tell you how much that's meant to me. You've been such a huge supporter of my author career and encouraged me so much, I don't think I'd be here without you. I'm so grateful for you in every way.

Emily,
Thank you so much for alpha reading VFH! Your questions, commentary, and suggestions were so helpful to fleshing out this book and building up those big moments. I appreciate your honesty when things weren't working and when they could be better. Thank you for pushing me! And more importantly, thank you for loving these characters with me.

Angie,

My lovely, smart dev editor, thank you so much for all of your input and help with perfecting Rhiannon's journey. Your belief in this story and excitement for making it better means so much to me.

Sam,

Thank you for helping me polish this book up, your expertise is so appreciated! I love how beautiful the interior for this series has turned out, thank you for helping me bring my vision to life!

To my beta readers,

Thank you so much for reading the beta version of this book on such a tight deadline and all of your valuable feedback, you helped make this story what it was.

Alexia,

Thank you for your thoughtful feedback and sensitivity reading services. I always appreciate your thoughts and love working together!

BookTok,

I don't even know what to say other than that I wouldn't be here without you. Your friendship, community, and encouragement has been everything. Special shout out to Eva Moore and the Late Night Writer's Club who kept me accountable and helped me build a writing routine that was actually manageable.

Elle,

The one, the only, the marvelous Elle M. Drew, I don't think you realize how much of an impact you've had on me. You were so kind and supportive when I came to you with so many questions and literal tears while writing book one.

Your Patreon (and now blog) have been A LIFELINE for me even now as a high-anxiety, neurospicy writer. Thank you for friendship and generosity.

About The Author

Alexis C. Maness is a mood author who is fully committed to writing books that center "Big Babes & Badassery". In her books, you can look forward to reading about plus-size characters having their main character moment.

Another important facet of Alexis's books is exploring aspects of her identity that her readers can connect with. As a member of the LGBTQIA+ community and as a neurodivergent person who struggles with anxiety and depression, she believes representing these experiences is a crucial part of writing meaningful stories.

When she isn't glued to her keyboard weaving words into something worth reading, you'll most likely find her with a glass of sparkling wine in hand, reading her latest dark romance obsession.

She lives in San Diego with her bossy yet adorable cat, Satine, whose dedication to sitting in one spot for a long time is the main reason these stories have finally made it to you.

Keep up with Alexis's latest releases on her socials:

https://www.tiktok.com/@authoralexiscmaness

https://www.instagram.com/authoralexiscmaness/

Sign up for her newsletter to get sneak peeks and updates first!

Printed in Great Britain
by Amazon

23288501R00193